W9-AAT-829

A FAMILY CONCERN

A FAMILY CONCERN

Anthea Fraser

This first world edition published in Great Britain 2006 by
SEVERN HOUSE PUBLISHERS LTD of
9–15 High Street, Sutton, Surrey SM1 1DF.
This first world edition published in the USA 2006 by
SEVERN HOUSE PUBLISHERS INC of
595 Madison Avenue, New York, N.Y. 10022.

British Library Cataloguing in Publication Data

Fraser,   Anthea
    A family concern
    1.   Parish, Rona (Fictitious character) - Fiction
    2.   Women authors - England - Fiction
    3.   Murder investigation - Fiction
    4.   Detective and mystery stories
    I.   Title
    823.9'14 [F]

    ISBN-10: 0-7278-6351-7 (cased)
                    0-7278-9164-2 (paper)

Typeset by Palimpsest Book Production Ltd.,
Polmont, Stirlingshire, Scotland.
Printed and bound in Great Britain by
MPG Books Ltd., Bodmin, Cornwall.

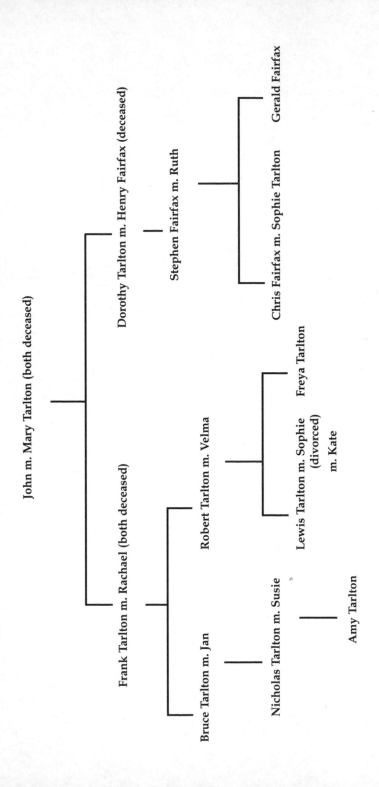

John m. Mary Tarlton (both deceased)

Dorothy Tarlton m. Henry Fairfax (deceased)

Stephen Fairfax m. Ruth

Gerald Fairfax

Chris Fairfax m. Sophie Tarlton

Frank Tarlton m. Rachael (both deceased)

Robert Tarlton m. Velma

Freya Tarlton

Lewis Tarlton m. Sophie (divorced) m. Kate

Bruce Tarlton m. Jan

Nicholas Tarlton m. Susie

Amy Tarlton

Prologue

A tune was circling in her head, a senseless jingle that was somehow full of menace. Then she was falling, falling . . . *Suppose he hadn't gone after all, but was waiting, just out of sight, to catch her?*

A scream clogged her throat as she scrabbled frantically for a finger-hold – but too late! Her arm was seized in a tight grip and shaken, gently at first, then with increasing urgency.

'Freya! *Freya!* Wake up – it's all right, honey, it's all right!'

Slowly, fearfully, she opened her eyes to see, in the dim light from the uncurtained window, Matthew's concerned face looking down at her.

'Thank God!' she said shakily, feeling the sweat coursing over her body. 'Oh, thank God!'

'Welcome back. You frightened me to death with that blood-curdling shriek.' He smoothed the damp hair off her face. 'The dream again?'

She shuddered, gripping his hand. 'It was – annihilating. I was falling . . .'

'Well, you're not falling now, you're safe in bed with me. So turn over, there's a good girl, and I'll rub your back for you, then we can both get some more sleep.'

But she was sitting up, swinging her feet to the floor. 'You go to sleep, Matthew,' she told him, reaching for her dressing gown. 'I daren't – not yet; I might drop straight back into the dream. I'm going to make myself a drink.'

He sighed resignedly. 'All right – I'll come with you.'

'There's no need,' she protested, though not, he thought, convincingly. He shrugged into his own robe, taking her arm

1

as they went down the narrow staircase. These nightmares were becoming a pain; this was the third she'd had in a week, and he couldn't imagine what had kicked them off.

The little kitchen looked alien at this hour, Freya thought, as though they were somehow trespassing. Or perhaps her vision was still distorted by the dream. She shivered, watching as Matthew filled the kettle and switched it on. 'I'm sorry to keep waking you,' she said contritely. 'If you like, I'll sleep on the sofa for a while.'

'Then I'd have even further to dash to your rescue!' But the disturbed sleep of the last week was starting to tell, clouding his concentration during the day. He spooned chocolate powder into two mugs, filled them with the boiling water, and brought them to the table.

'What exactly do you dream?' he asked as he sat down. 'Might it help to talk about it?'

She was silent for a while, staring down into her mug. Then she lifted it and sipped gingerly at the hot liquid. 'It's always the same,' she said at last. 'I'm falling – I'm not sure where from, and—'

'That's one of the most common nightmares,' he interrupted, in an attempt to reassure her. 'Everyone has it at some time or other. No doubt Freud would have an explanation for it.'

Freya shook her head. 'It's more than that. There's this tune going round and round in my brain.'

'What tune?'

'I can never remember it afterwards. And someone else is nearby, someone who mustn't know I'm there.'

'A man?'

She considered. 'I think so.'

'Anything else?'

'Not really.' She gave an embarrassed little laugh. 'It sounds pathetic, I know, but at the time it's terrifying, believe me.'

'Worth seeing the quack, d'you think? For something to help you sleep through, just till you break the pattern?'

'I'm not taking sleeping pills,' she said positively. Then she smiled, putting her hand on his. 'Poor Matthew! You

2

didn't expect this when you asked me to move in with you.'

He smiled back. 'I'm prepared to take the rough with the smooth,' he said.

One

For the first time that she could remember, Rona Parish was not looking forward to Christmas. Nothing would be the same, she thought miserably. Her parents' marriage had recently broken down and her father was in the process of finding himself a flat while the divorce went through. Furthermore, the split had resulted in tension between herself and her twin sister, Lindsey, since they tended to side with different parents.

Admittedly, her mother had invited her and Max for Christmas lunch as usual, but Rona had still not committed them, fearful she might appear to be letting her father down. Nor had she felt able to ask him if he'd be spending the holiday with Catherine, the woman he proposed eventually to marry, though it was more than likely she'd be with her son and his wife in Cricklehurst.

'You can't keep putting it off,' Max remarked one evening. 'At this rate, we'll end up in solitary splendour. What's Lindsey doing?'

'We haven't spoken for nearly two weeks,' Rona said expressionlessly. 'She's as prickly as a hedgehog at the moment.'

'She might opt out and spend it with Hugh.'

Hugh Cavendish was Lindsey's ex-husband; now, to the concern of her family, back in Marsborough.

'No, I'm almost sure she'll go to Mum. She's still blaming Pops for all this.'

'Well, technically speaking, he is the guilty party.'

'Would you have put up with all he has over the last few years?' Rona demanded hotly, adding after a moment, 'On second thoughts, don't answer that.'

Max grinned. 'Come on, love, lighten up. Find out what he's doing and we can take it from there.'

Rona was mulling over this conversation the next day as she walked along Guild Street, now festooned with decorations and coloured lights. The shop windows glittered with tinsel, fake Christmas trees were draped with scarves, belts and sequinned evening bags, and in Netherby's Department Store, children queued to see Father Christmas. And they were only halfway through November, Rona thought impatiently. But concerns about Christmas could wait: a more pressing worry was that it was only ten days to Pops' retirement, and since no one outside the family knew of the split, Mum would be expected at all the festivities. Rona was quite sure she wouldn't attend.

Max was right, she decided suddenly; she needed to know her father's plans, both for next week and for Christmas, and it was no use pussyfooting around waiting for him to volunteer them. A glance at her watch showed it had stopped again, and she swore under her breath, shaking her wrist and lifting it hopefully to her ear. Silence. Admittedly it had been a twenty-first birthday present, she conceded ruefully; perhaps it was unreasonable to expect a watch to last indefinitely.

Above the noise of traffic and the chattering crowds, the Town Hall clock helpfully relayed the three-quarter chime. Two forty-five, Rona thought; with luck, she'd catch him at the bank.

But luck was not with her. She was informed that Mr Parish would be in on only alternate days this week. 'Winding down, as you might say,' Mavis Banister, his secretary, told her. 'He'll have a full schedule next week, though: on Monday there's a reception for key clients and their wives – some sixty-odd people; on Wednesday it's the presentation at Head Office, followed by dinner with the General Manager and *his* wife; and then on Friday, as you know, we have the farewell party here. A good excuse for your mother to indulge in some retail therapy!'

Rona smiled dutifully. 'Don't worry,' she said. 'No doubt I'll run him to earth.'

*   *   *

6

At the other end of town, unaware of his daughter's frustration, Tom Parish stood in the middle of the room and looked about him. It wasn't, he told himself, as though this was a long-term project; he could manage very comfortably here for the two years or so it would take for the divorce to come through. The furniture and fittings, though not what he'd have chosen, were comfortable enough, and with his books and personal belongings, he could soon make it look like home. And though Guild Street was a fifteen to twenty minute walk away, Catherine's house in Willow Crescent was just round the corner. In fact he'd noted, with a lift of the heart, that the roof of her bungalow was visible from the kitchen window.

The room in which he stood was at the front of the building, overlooking Talbot Road. There were, in all, three blocks of flats along the length of it, one at either end and one, the building in which he stood, roughly in the middle. Each was distinctive in style and replaced a rambling old house that had been demolished in the 1960s. There'd been an outcry at the time, Tom remembered, about the insensitivity of placing these stark, modern blocks in such a setting, but lack of interest in aesthetics was as rife in Marsborough in the sixties as it was in the rest of the country, and protesters could only be thankful that at least they weren't built of concrete. Now, forty years on, they had melded into their background, and only newcomers to the area professed astonishment that such sacrilege should have been countenanced.

His sole reservation, Tom reflected, was that Hugh, his ex-son-in-law, had a flat in one of the other blocks. Still, it was a long and winding road, and they were more likely to run into each other in Guild Street than here.

From Hugh, Tom's mind slid automatically to his daughter Lindsey, and he sighed. She'd been deeply hurt by his, Tom's, behaviour, heaping on him all the blame for the breakdown of the marriage. Bless her, he thought fondly; she'd even coerced Avril – who for years had taken no interest in her appearance – into buying a couple of new outfits and some make-up. His heart contracted as he recalled his wife

7

standing in their sitting room in her new finery, awaiting his reaction. The tragedy was that it had all been too late.

He turned back and studied the room again, planning how he'd rearrange the furniture. It would be a relief to move in here; they'd decided not to cause waves during his last days at work, and to keep up appearances till after his retirement – at that stage, five weeks away. In the interim he would remain at home; there was always the chance of emergency calls from the bank, and the neighbours would notice if he weren't there.

Strangely, since her initial tears, Avril had shown no emotion, and once his possessions had been moved into the guest room, things had in fact been easier than for some time. They met only at breakfast, when they treated each other with punctilious politeness. He knew she'd be as glad to see the back of him as he would be to go. Well, next week was D-Day. His last day at the bank would be Friday, his sixty-third birthday, and then he'd move in here and the next stage of his life could begin.

He walked slowly out on to the landing, where the estate agent was tactfully waiting.

'I'll take it,' he said.

Avril Parish stood at the window of her guest room, lost in thought. That morning, over breakfast, Tom had broached the subject of his various leaving engagements. 'Everyone's expecting you to attend,' he'd said gently.

'And you know that I can't,' she'd replied. 'We agreed not to go public and I've honoured that, but playing happy families before all your colleagues is just not on. I've given it some thought, and decided the best solution is a diplomatic dose of flu.'

He hadn't met her eyes. 'There'll be gifts for you, too, in recognition of your support all these years,' he'd said, adding quickly over her choked laugh, 'and you *were* supportive, Avril, for most of the time.'

Beneath the table, her fingernails had dug into her palms. *She would not cry.*

'Whatever,' she'd said after a minute, 'but I'm not going

8

to play the proud little wife, Tom, and that's final. Take the girls with you.'

Well, she'd brought it on herself, she reflected now, though she'd been too pig-headed to see it at the time. Over the last two or three years she'd gradually let herself go, slouching round the house in old clothes, not bothering with her hair or make-up. And she'd begun – she couldn't remember why – to needle him constantly, in an attempt to evoke some response. She should have known Tom wasn't confrontational, that he'd patiently deflect her complaints and criticisms, and in the process add to her resentment.

Pops is still an attractive man, Lindsey had warned her, and he meets attractive women every day in the course of his work.

Indeed. Well, no use crying over spilt milk. Though too late to save her marriage, she had finally taken herself in hand. In the last six weeks she'd had her hair restyled, bought some much-needed new clothes and taken a job at the local library. And when Tom finally moved out at the end of next week, she'd take her plans one stage further. That was why she'd come into this room which, since he'd been using it, she had entered only once a week in order to clean it.

She turned from the window and surveyed it critically. It was a good size, she thought with satisfaction, the fitted wardrobe giving extra floor space and adding to the air of spaciousness, while the button-back chair that had been her mother's, into which she had loved to snuggle as a child, afforded comfortable seating. Since Mother had died, though, the room had been little used; its wardrobe was the repository of summer clothes in winter, winter clothes in summer, while the bed's sole purpose had been to provide a surface for laying out things to take on holiday. All that would be needed, she concluded, was a fresh lick of paint and some new curtains.

She returned to the landing and regarded its closed doors, picturing what lay behind them. Until a month ago, she had shared the other front bedroom with Tom, and the two back rooms she still thought of as belonging to the girls. In between the master bedroom and what had been Rona's was the door leading to the small box-room. Avril opened it and looked inside. Piled higgledy-piggledy were suitcases, carrier bags crammed with the girls' university papers, old picnic hampers and a dusty violin case, memento of a passing interest of Lindsey's. It would need a good sorting out and, by the look of it, several journeys to the tip and the charity shops.

Pushing open her own bedroom door, she studied the wall adjoining the box room, and nodded slowly to herself. It shouldn't present any problems.

Rona reached her father on his mobile as he got into his car outside the flats.

'Hello, sweetie, how are you?'

'Fine. I just called at the bank, and discovered you were playing hooky.'

'To good effect. I've found myself a flat.'

'Well done. Where is it?'

'In Talbot Road. "Mulberry Lodge", if you please. Sounds grandiose, doesn't it? It must be the name of the original house.'

Rona hesitated. 'That's not where Hugh—?'

'Same road, different block. I've arranged to move in at the end of next week. Now, what can I do for you?'

'Actually, it was next week I was wondering about.'

'Ah yes. All this business put it out of my head, but you, Max and Lindsey are, of course, invited to my leaving party. Sorry for the short notice; I hope you can make it?'

'I can't answer for Linz, but we'll certainly be there.'

'That's great.'

'And Mum?' Rona asked after a minute.

'Intends to go down with flu,' Tom said drily, 'so I'll be solo at the first two bashes.'

'And then there's Christmas,' Rona went on tentatively. 'Will you be spending it with Catherine?'

'No, she's going to Cricklehurst, as usual.' He paused. 'You'll all be at Maple Drive, I take it?'

'I don't know,' Rona said miserably.

'Of course you will, your mother will expect it. Don't

10

worry about me, sweetheart, I'll be fine. Sorry, but I'll have to go now – I'm supposed to be following the estate agent back to his office to sign papers. I'll be in touch about the arrangements for the twenty-fifth.'

'It's also your birthday, Pops,' Rona put in quickly. 'What about after the reception? Would you—?'

'I've arranged a quiet dinner with Catherine. It seemed best, under the circumstances.'

'Fine,' she said. And wished she meant it. They exchanged goodbyes and she switched off her mobile, stepping out of the doorway she'd made use of as a cheerful voice behind her said, 'Rona Parish, as I live and breathe!'

'Kate!' The two women hugged each other. 'I've not seen you for ages.'

'Just what I was thinking. Have you time for a cuppa at the Gallery?'

'Indeed I have,' Rona replied. It was just the antidote she needed to shake her out of her misgivings; she'd known Kate Tarlton – or Kate Halliday, as she'd then been – since her schooldays.

'Where's that hound of yours?' Kate enquired, as they went up the iron staircase leading to the walkway above the shops.

'At home, recovering from an injured paw. He got a thorn in it at the park and it turned septic. He's over the worst, but he has to wear one of those wide plastic collars to stop him pulling the bandage off. He hates it, poor love.'

The café was crowded on this cold afternoon. The coveted window tables were all taken, so they settled at a corner one and, after a brief consultation, ordered tea for two and toasted teacakes.

'Now,' Kate invited, 'tell me what you've been doing since I last saw you. What are you working on at the moment?'

Here we go! Rona thought. 'Helping people find their birth parents,' she replied, and resignedly watched her friend make the connection.

'Of course – that case that hit the headlines.'

'That started it, yes, but the two I've done since have been

11

decidedly less spectacular, thank God, and ended much more happily. Reunions and hugs all round.'

'Don't tell me you've located *two* sets of parents in a matter of weeks? Superwoman, or what?'

Rona shook her head. 'I didn't do the locating this time; I advertised for people willing to tell me their stories, and had a surprising number of replies. Barnie Trent, who's features editor at *Chiltern Life*, is quite keen on the idea – striking while the iron's hot, he calls it. He's commissioned an article per month, with a minimum of four.'

'Well, you certainly handed him a scoop with the first one,' Kate commented. 'The inside story, and all that. And your Buckford articles are still running, I see. You'll be taking over the magazine at this rate!'

Rona smiled. 'There are a couple more, but I finished writing them months ago. You're right – normally the new series would wait till they ended, but as I said, Barnie's taking advantage of public interest.'

The waitress approached and unloaded her tray on to the table.

'How's the jewellery business?' Rona asked as she poured the tea. 'Besieged by Christmas shoppers?'

Kate had married into the Tarlton family, whose prestigious shop was further along Guild Street.

'So-so, but it doesn't really get going till December. If you're thinking of buying anything, I'd advise an early visit.'

'Now that you mention it, I could do with a new watch,' Rona said reflectively. 'This one's been playing up for weeks, and it's so old, it's probably past repairing.'

Kate eyed Rona's wrist. 'The style's a bit dated, too,' she observed with professional detachment. 'We've a lovely selection at the moment, well worth a look.'

'I'll see if I can talk Max into it.'

Kate gave an embarrassed laugh. 'Sorry, I didn't mean to subject you to a sales pitch. We're not the only jewellers in town.'

'Relax – we always come to you, it's family tradition. This watch came from Tarlton's, as did my engagement ring, not to mention Lindsey's *and* my mother's.'

'I'm preaching to the converted, then.' Kate took a bite of her teacake. 'Your links go back a lot further than mine.'

'How long have you been there?'

'Six years, three as a member of the family.' She smiled. 'Funny to think of it now, but the first year I could hardly bring myself to speak to Lewis, he was so disagreeable. Mind you, I was prickly myself at the time. If you remember, I'd just extricated myself from a sticky relationship.'

Rona nodded. A married man, who, contrary to protestations, had never even contemplated divorce.

'Lewis, of course, was married at the time,' Kate continued, 'and later, when I realized how unhappy he'd been, I forgave him his bad temper. Then we started to come together, and it seemed I was destined to go through life as the Other Woman. Fortunately, it didn't work out that way.'

'Did it create any embarrassment,' Rona asked curiously, 'your continuing to work there while all that was going on?'

'Did they blame me for the break-up, you mean? No, I don't think so. The family hadn't expected the marriage to last; it was a flash-in-the-pan thing – mutual attraction and little else. Once the first flush had worn off, he found Sophie too sweet and docile. Lewis needs someone like me. I give as good as I get, and strike sparks off him. That's what keeps our marriage alive and exciting. Also, he's fanatical about the business, and apart from the end product, she wasn't interested. Hotel work was her scene, and she continued to work at the Clarendon, which Lewis resented. After the divorce, she married Chris Fairfax, the son of the owners. Any embarrassment – or awkwardness, rather – came from the family connection.'

Rona looked up enquiringly.

'The Tarltons and Fairfaxes are related,' Kate explained. 'Didn't you know?'

'No, I didn't.'

'Not all that closely – second cousins or something. We don't see much of them. Anyway, enough about me. How's life with you? You and Max still living in different establishments?'

'For three nights a week, yes.'

'Unusual for a married couple, isn't it? How did that come about?'

'Basically because we both work from home, Max painting, me writing. And he can only work with music blaring, while I need complete silence.'

'Jack Spratt and his wife?'

'Exactly. So he invested in Farthings, a cottage twenty minutes' walk away, where he can happily break all the sound barriers and leave me in peace.'

'I can see the sense in that – but nights too?'

'Well, that evolved because he gives classes three evenings a week, and by the time the students have gone and everything's tidied away, it's after ten o'clock. It seemed hardly worth coming home just to go to bed, then straight back to Farthings the next morning, especially since I'm often working to deadlines and not free to socialize anyway. So on Wednesdays, when he only has afternoon classes, he comes home, and, of course, on Fridays for the weekend. It works very well, gives us both space, and we appreciate each other all the more. And we speak on the phone at least once a day.'

Kate leaned forward to refill their cups. 'It's odd, isn't it? Lewis and I work together all day, every day, with no problems. I'd hate what you call "space" away from him.'

'I suppose it's different with family businesses. Do the other wives work in the shop? I see people behind the counters, but I've never known who they were.'

'Well, some of them are part-time staff. Freya, Lewis's sister, works there, but the only other wife in our age group is Susie, who's married to Lewis's cousin Nicholas. And Nick's mother, Jan, organizes the displays.'

'So the older generation's still involved?'

'Very much so. Bruce and Robert, the joint managing directors, are in every day. It was their father, incidentally, who was Dorothy Fairfax's brother. He's long dead, but she, as you probably know, is still very much alive. And as I said, Jan, who's Bruce's wife, designs the layout of the windows and showcases.'

'And Robert's wife?'

14

'Left him when the children were young, and he never remarried.'

'It's quite a dynasty.'

'We're the fourth generation, yes. What about your family? Are they all well?'

'Fine, thanks,' Rona said with a brittle smile. *Except that my parents are splitting up, my father has a girlfriend, and my sister is barely speaking to me.*

'I used to envy you being a twin,' Kate said reminiscently. 'It was always you two against the world, wasn't it?'

'We're pretty close,' Rona acknowledged with difficulty.

'And I had a crush on your father! Did you know? He was so tall and good-looking and had such a lovely smile, and I loved the way he always came to collect you both from parties.'

Some comment was clearly called for, but all Rona could think of to say was, 'He's retiring from the bank next week.'

'They'll be sorry to see him go, after so long.' Kate glanced at her watch. 'I should be making a move, I've a dental appointment at four. With the shop closed on Mondays, I rush round like a scalded cat trying to fit in as many things as possible. Anyway, it's been great to catch up with you, Rona.' She opened her purse and took out some money. 'Would you mind settling up? I'm cutting it a bit fine.'

'Of course. And I'll twist Max's arm about the watch.'

Her eyes followed Kate as she walked quickly towards the door, slim and straight, her chestnut hair caught up in a knot behind her head. Even as a child, she'd known what she wanted and gone for it, Rona reflected, and was not above stepping on toes to achieve it. Well, she seemed to have found her niche now, and would be highly efficient at her job. Can't hurt, either, to marry the boss's son. She thought for a moment of Lewis Tarlton, with his narrow face and deep-set eyes. Though she knew him only by sight, she wasn't surprised to hear his temper was volatile.

She signalled the waitress for the bill and picked up her bag, automatically looking under the table for Gus, until she remembered he was recuperating at home. Still, she was taking him to the vet tomorrow, and with luck both bandage and collar would be removed.

You two against the world, Kate had said – and it was true. Oh, Linz, I miss you!

Rona reached a sudden decision. She'd drive over to Lindsey's flat this evening, and see if they couldn't patch things up. Nor would she give advance notice; too bad if lover-boy from the office was there or even – perish the thought – Hugh. The ramifications of her sister's love life frequently left Rona bemused.

Feeling happier now she'd decided on action, she took the bill the waitress handed her, left a tip under her saucer, and made her way to the cash desk.

Max Allerdyce sat in his studio, staring moodily at the canvas in front of him. He needed to be in a peaceful frame of mind to paint, and, despite the soothing strains of Offenbach's 'Barcarolle', he felt anything but peaceful. On the contrary, problems seemed to be crowding in on him on all sides. As if the business with Tom and Avril weren't bad enough, tearing the family apart as it undoubtedly was, a phone call from his sister in Northumberland had added to his worries: his eighty-year-old father was unwell, and refusing to acknowledge the fact. Which figured, Max reflected. The awkward old devil regarded it as a sign of weakness even to have a cold.

'He's lost a lot of weight,' Cynthia had said anxiously, 'and I know he's not eating properly. Mrs Pemberton tries her hardest to tempt him, but he seems to be existing on just the odd mouthful. Could you come up and have a word with him, Max? He might listen to you.'

'That would be a first,' he'd commented, 'but I'll give him a ring, if you like.'

'That's not the same at all,' Cynthia had said sharply. 'Surely you can spare the time to come up? When did you last see him?'

To his discomfort, Max hadn't been able to remember. 'He doesn't exactly put the red carpet out for me,' he'd defended himself.

Cynthia had made a scoffing sound. 'You're too alike,

16

that's the trouble. You think the world of each other – no, don't argue with me – but you'd both rather die than admit it. He's very proud of you, you know; he has all your exhibition catalogues, not to mention every critique that's ever been written.'

That had surprised him, yet perhaps it shouldn't have. Roland Allerdyce, RA, was still a big name in the art world, and no doubt took pride in the fact that he'd passed his talent on to his son. The phone call had ended with Max promising to pay a literally flying visit within the next fortnight. That had been at the end of last week, and he still hadn't mentioned it to Rona, feeling she had enough worries with her own family.

And family problems, hers and his own, weren't the only things disturbing him. There was also Adele.

Max stood up abruptly and, abandoning all pretence of work, ran down the stairs to make himself some tea.

Adele Yarborough was a member of the first of his Wednesday classes, catering mainly for retired people and those at home. She'd joined last summer, soon after moving into the neighbourhood with her husband, and Max had been immediately impressed with the delicacy of her watercolours. But during an early class, as she'd pinned her paper to the easel, her sleeves had fallen back to disclose livid bruising on her arms. Acutely aware of his gaze, she had flushed scarlet and immediately covered them again.

Max, though, had been unable to get those bruises out of his mind, and when he learned the Yarboroughs had moved into the cul-de-sac where Lindsey lived, he'd inveigled her and Rona into inviting Adele to tea, in order to form their own conclusions. It had proved of little help; the sisters decided any bruising must have been the result of furniture shifting during the removal, and refused to consider other possibilities. It was apparent, too, that neither of them had taken to Adele.

'But she always wears long sleeves,' he had argued, unconvinced by their findings, 'even during the heatwave. Why would she do that?'

'Because she's aware of your concern and deliberately

prolonging it?' Rona had suggested uncharitably.

In the end, he had given up discussing the matter. Adele, meanwhile, had to his anxious eyes become increasingly pale and fragile-looking. She had cancelled a couple of classes at short notice, sounding decidedly stressed, and once she'd 'fallen' downstairs. It was a wonder, Max thought grimly, that she hadn't broken her neck.

So he continued to worry about her, convinced her husband was knocking her about, but since any mention of her now led to friction between himself and Rona, he'd learned to keep more recent suspicions to himself. God, though, he wished there was something he could do.

The shrill whistling of the kettle interrupted his brooding, and, mentally shrugging off his problems, he turned instead to his cup of tea.

Two

Rona pressed the button of the new intercom Lindsey had had installed, and as her sister's voice crackled down at her, said into it, 'It's me, Linz. Can I come up?'

There was a minute's stretching silence. Then the door buzzed and opened to her push, and as she closed it behind her, she saw Lindsey at the top of the stairs looking down at her.

Rona said, 'I come bearing an olive branch, disguised as a bottle of Chianti.'

'If you'd thought it through, you'd have made it olive oil,' Lindsey remarked, as Rona joined her. They hugged each other and moved together into the sitting room.

'Not that I wouldn't rather have the wine,' Lindsey continued, 'but why did you feel in need of a peace offering?'

'You didn't return my last two calls.'

'Ah.'

'Yes, "ah"! It's this blasted parent thing, isn't it? We mustn't get caught in the flak ourselves.'

Lindsey left the room without replying, returning a minute later with two glasses and a corkscrew. 'It's impossible to remain neutral,' she said. 'I can't forgive Pops for what he's done.'

'Linz, he's had the patience of Job for donkey's years. It's just bad luck for Mum that Catherine came along when she did.'

'She'd no right to "come along", as you euphemistically put it. He was a married man, damn it.'

Rona burst out laughing. 'Lindsey, just *listen* to yourself!'

Her sister had the grace to flush. Jonathan Hurst, with whom she was at present involved, was a married man. 'It's different at her age,' she said defensively.

19

'No, it isn't. In fact, your case is worse, because Jonathan's poor wife thinks everything in the garden's lovely. Mum could never have believed that, not for the last year or two anyway.' She took the glass Lindsey handed her, raised it in a silent toast, and they both drank. 'Have you seen Pops since he told us?'

Lindsey stared into her glass. 'Remember that colouring book we had, when we were about five? There was a picture of a little Royalist boy being interviewed by the Roundheads, during the Civil War. I've never forgotten it. It was called *And when did you last see your father?* and it always made me cry.'

'Oh, Linz,' Rona said softly.

'You've seen him, of course?'

'Not for a week or so, but I spoke to him today, and he told me he's found a flat.'

Lindsey frowned. 'Is it worth it? When Hugh and I divorced, it went through in a matter of months.'

'I already asked him about that; it seems that unless you're prepared for accusations – adultery, and such like – you go for two-year separation with consent. After that, everything goes through smoothly with no recriminations.'

Rona flicked a glance at her sister. 'The flat's in Talbot Road, but thankfully not the same block as Hugh.'

'I can't see why he doesn't save himself the money, and move in with madam.'

'He doesn't want her subjected to gossip. Hence the two-year arrangement.'

'And he fondly imagines there won't be any?'

'There needn't be – or at least, not the scurrilous kind. Plenty of people divorce, Lindsey.' She bit back the addendum, *as you should know*. 'Oh, and he asked me to tell you we're all invited to his leaving party. It's a week on Friday.'

'Well, he needn't think *I'm* going,' Lindsey said at once.

'Oh, please Linz! It's his birthday as well, remember.'

'Let him celebrate it with his fancy woman.'

This was too near the mark, and Rona said quickly, 'Mum's going to plead a dose of flu, but it would look very odd if you weren't there.'

'But by then, there'll be no need to keep up appearances; it'll be his last day at the bank, for God's sake.'

'Think it over,' Rona said placatingly. She paused, then asked diffidently, 'How's Mum?'

'Surprisingly upbeat. Have you heard what she's planning?'

'No?'

'To take in lodgers, no less.'

Rona stared at her. 'You're not serious? She doesn't need to, surely?'

'Not financially, no, of course not. It's for company. She's going to turn the box room into an en suite shower room, and let them have the bathroom. It'll add to the property value, if nothing else. When those houses were built, no one even contemplated two bathrooms; you were probably lucky to have indoor sanitation.'

'But – what kind of lodger? It could be tricky, surely?'

'Oh, she's got it all worked out. Originally she'd thought of a school teacher, but since the guest room has a double bed, she's now leaning towards a married couple – saving up to buy their own place, perhaps. As soon as Pops moves out next week, she'll have the plans drawn up. She's already begun to clear out the box-room.'

'Talking of plans,' Rona said quietly, 'what about Christmas?'

Lindsey pushed back her hair. 'God, it's going to be hell, isn't it? She's expecting us to turn up as usual, but we can't just pretend nothing's changed.'

Rona felt a wave of relief: at least Lindsey was in her corner over this. 'You could both come to us,' she suggested. 'Unless you have other plans?'

'Such as what?' Lindsey asked derisively. 'Jonathan will be playing happy families and Hugh's going to Lucy's.'

Lucy Partridge was Hugh's sister, who lived in Guildford.

'How do you know that?' Rona demanded suspiciously. 'You're not still in touch, surely?'

Again Lindsey flushed, twisting a strand of hair round her finger. 'It was Hugh who told us about Pops, don't forget. If it hadn't been for him, we might still be in the dark.'

Which, Rona thought despondently, might have been better all round. At least Pops could have got through his retirement without all this subterfuge, though she'd had her own suspicions for some months.

'But you're not still – seeing him?' she pursued anxiously.

'From time to time.'

'Does Jonathan know?'

'He could hardly object, if he did,' Lindsey said coldly. 'I'm not married to him. In fact, as you didn't hesitate to point out, he's married to someone else. With all that that entails. And since Hugh and I are divorced, *he* has no rights over me, either.'

Rona looked at her despairingly. Personally, she didn't care for either man or his sensitivities – and as Lindsey said, neither had any valid claim on her – but she did care deeply for her sister's happiness, and it looked as though once more it might explode in her face.

'Don't play with fire, Linz,' she pleaded. 'You've been hurt too many times before.'

Lindsey leaned forward to top up their glasses. 'Don't you worry about me, sister dear,' she said lightly. 'I can take care of myself.'

Rona doubted it, but there was no point in pursuing the matter. Returning to a safer topic, she said, 'So you'll fall in with whatever we decide about Christmas?'

'Hang on, I didn't say that. Will Pops be with Catherine?'

'As it happens, no.'

Lindsey stared at her. 'You haven't got some wild idea about us all spending it together? Have you gone out of your *mind*?'

'I've not thought it through yet, but provided we're not at Maple Drive, where we've always been before—'

'You really imagine we could get Mum and Pops round the same table? If we had to choose between them, you know you'd go for Pops and I'd go for Mum. It's dream stuff, Ro.'

'So much for peace and goodwill,' Rona said flatly.

An hour later, as she drove back to Marsborough, she reflected that although she and Lindsey were back on an

22

even keel, neither of the points she'd hoped to settle – the retirement party and Christmas – had been resolved.

'Describe it to me,' Catherine said.

Tom leaned back in the chair he already privately considered his, and took another sip of his drink. 'Well, it's on the first floor – nothing very fancy, but quite adequate, I'd say. There's a lift, though I suppose with my history I ought to use the stairs.'

'I said *describe* it, Tom!' Catherine protested, laughing. '"Nothing very fancy" conveys not a thing. Talk me through it, from the minute you go through the front door. Is there a hallway?'

'A small one, yes. Immediately to the right is the door to the bedroom – there's only one: did I say? – and opposite it, on the left, is the bathroom. Next to that, as far as I remember, is a walk-in cupboard with hooks and things for hanging coats. The living room's straight ahead and, as I said, pleasant enough. Sofa, two armchairs, small dining table, bookcase, TV.' He smiled. 'Is that enough description for you?'

'Kitchen?'

'Ah, that leads off the living room. And – *pièce de résistance* – from its window I can see your roof and a couple of the trees in your back garden!'

'That must put thousands on the price! Will we be able to semaphore each other?'

'Seriously, take a look tomorrow, in daylight.'

There was a moment's silence. Then she said, 'Well, I'm glad that's settled so satisfactorily. And it's lovely that you'll be so near.'

He looked across at her, marvelling at the good fortune that had come his way when he most needed it, when Avril had almost succeeded in persuading him he was fit only for the scrapheap. Compared with his wife, who'd become so sharp and critical, Catherine was a joy to be with, calm and comfortable in her skin. Her husband had died tragically young, but she'd built a life for herself as headmistress of a primary school in Buckford, until forced to retire four years ago and come to Marsborough to look after her mother. When she'd died, Catherine, deciding against returning to Buckford, had bought this bungalow, which Tom now loved almost as much as she did.

She had suggested, matter-of-factly, that he move in with her once he'd retired, but he'd firmly vetoed the proposal. Though he knew he'd be thought old-fashioned, he had no intention of compromising her in any way, and until they were married they would sleep under separate roofs. Which, he thought now with an inward smile, did not prevent them going to bed together during the day.

In the meantime, though, there were hurdles to overcome – his retirement week and having to field questions about Avril, and Christmas, which he was privately dreading. He wished uselessly that he could fast forward the next two years to a time when Catherine would be his wife, Avril comfortably settled, and the girls accepting of the status quo.

Catherine, watching his face, saw the muscles of his jaw tighten, and slipped on to the rug in front of him, taking hold of his hands. 'It'll be all right, my love,' she said, 'I promise.'

For the first time since he'd hurt his paw, Gus was waiting in the hall to greet Rona on her return from Lindsey's, proof that the basement stairs were less of a problem. She bent to hug him under the stiff collar.

'Good boy!' she said softly. 'With luck, Bob will take this nasty thing off tomorrow.' Used to his accompanying her everywhere, she'd missed his company during the last week or two.

He lopped down the stairs ahead of her, still favouring the injured paw, though perhaps now from habit. The answer-phone was blinking and Rona switched it on as she made a mug of coffee; the wine at Lindsey's had left her with a thirst.

'Hello,' said a voice she didn't recognize. 'You don't know me, but my name's Coralie Davis, and I've just seen your bit about birth parents in the *Gazette*. If I'm not too late, my story might interest you.' She gave a number which

Rona automatically jotted down. This series, she thought, could run and run, until either Barnie or the readership of *Chiltern Life* grew tired of it.

Well, she'd give this Ms Davis a call tomorrow. Though she now had several case histories, she hadn't decided which she'd finally use, and if a later one proved more interesting, or noticeably different from the others, it would take precedence.

She picked up her mug of coffee, switched off the light, and went up to bed.

When Tom reached the kitchen the next morning, an aroma of grilling bacon greeted him. Avril, an apron tied over what was surely a new skirt, stood at the cooker and didn't turn as he came in.

'That smells good,' he said, trying to remember when she had last made him a cooked breakfast. Whenever it was, he was pretty sure the bacon had been fried: was the grilling out of consideration for his heart scare? He felt a sudden warmth for her, and said spontaneously, 'You're looking very smart.'

The retort, *For a change, you mean?* came automatically to Avril's lips, but she bit it back, saying instead, 'Thank you.'

She put the plate on the table in front of him; the bacon was accompanied by a couple of sausages and a tomato, and there was fresh toast in the rack. She poured them both a cup of coffee and sat down opposite him.

Tom eyed her apprehensively. Was the breakfast after all only an attempt to soften him up before making some demand? Yet he'd begged her for weeks to discuss their situation, and until now she had steadfastly refused. Perhaps she was at last ready to do so.

'I wanted to ask about the house,' Avril began, confirming his suspicions.

'I'll be making it over to you,' he said at once. 'I thought you knew that.'

'It – won't be sold then, and the proceeds divided between us?' This possibility, unconsidered before, had come to her

25

in the early hours, filling her with cold panic. There she was, planning alterations, and for all she knew she might have to move out.

'Oh, Avril, of course not. Have you been worrying about it? You should have asked before – I could have set your mind at rest.'

'It's only just occurred to me,' she admitted. 'But the point is, I've been thinking of making a few alterations. Improvements, you might say.'

'Oh?'

'I'd like to turn the box room into an en suite shower room.'

If he was surprised that, alone in the house for the first time, she suddenly felt in need of a second bathroom, he did not say so.

'Can't see why not,' he replied cautiously.

'And the reason, in case you're wondering, is that I'm thinking of taking in paying guests.'

He put down his knife and fork and stared at her. 'Avril, you don't have to do that! God, you know I'd never—'

'I *want* to, Tom. It will be nice to have people coming and going, and to get to know them, and everything.'

He could think of nothing to say.

'And before you issue dire warnings,' she went on – how well she could read him, after all their years together! – 'I shall vet them very carefully. I'd thought at first of someone from the primary school – they're always wanting rooms for staff – but then I decided I'd prefer a young couple, perhaps help them out while they're saving for their own home.'

He gave her a wry grin, and she remembered, painfully, what it was she had loved about him. 'So as soon as you've got rid of me, you'll revamp the guest room?'

She smiled back. 'Something like that.' She took a sip of coffee. 'You've no objections, then?'

'What right have I to make objections? If you're sure that's what you want, I think it's an excellent idea.'

'That's settled, then,' she said with satisfaction.

*   *   *

Springfield Veterinary Centre was in Dean's Crescent North, only a couple of doors up from Max's cottage, Farthings. Normally, Rona walked there, but out of deference to the invalid she took the car, parking it alongside Farthings in the narrow alleyway leading to Max's garage.

Bob Standing, one of the partners and a fan of Gus, removed the bandage and examined the wound.

'Healing nicely,' he observed. 'I don't think the odd lick will do any damage now – might even help – so we can remove this protrusion. There,' he continued, putting action to his words, 'that's better, isn't it, old man?'

Gus replied by shaking himself vigorously, then giving his neck a good scratch.

'Relief all round,' Rona said. 'I've hated having to leave him at home all the time; he's just not used to it. Is there anything I should do?'

'It wouldn't hurt to bathe the area at night with a weak solution of salt and water, just till the end of the week, say. It would help ward off anything he might have picked up during the day. And if you have any worries, bring him back and we'll have another look at him. He's finished the antibiotics, I presume?'

'Last night, yes. I don't know which of us was more delighted.'

Bob Standing laughed. 'Right, we'll sign you both off, then. Give my regards to Max.'

Surprisingly, Rona found Max in the living room of the cottage, frowning at his laptop. Normally when she called, he was up in the studio surrounded by blaring music from the stereo. She wasn't used to silence at Farthings.

'Hello,' she said from the doorway. 'What are you up to?'

He turned quickly. 'Oh, hi.' His glance fell to Gus, who came trotting forward to greet him. 'Hello, fellow! Minus that awful collar, I see.'

'Bob says he's healing nicely.' Rona had come into the room, and now saw that the laptop screen was displaying the web page of a bargain airline.

'Thinking of leaving me?' she asked lightly.

27

Max followed her gaze. 'Oh, that. It's something I've been meaning to tell you. No,' he added with a grin, 'not that I'm leaving you. It's Father.'

'What about him?' Rona asked quickly. 'Is he all right?'

'Not really, according to Cyn. She wants me to go up and persuade him to see the quack.'

Rona frowned. 'When was this? That she spoke to you, I mean?'

'End of last week. I thought you'd enough worries without lumbering you with mine. Anyway, it's probably all a storm in a teacup. You know how she fusses over him.'

'It's as well someone does,' Rona returned. It was a bone of contention between them that Max didn't keep in closer contact with his father. They were, she'd decided, as stubborn as each other.

'So you're going up there? When?'

'I thought Friday, since it's my only free day and I shouldn't have to cancel anything. I'll spend the night there and fly back Saturday morning. You don't mind, do you?'

'Of course I don't mind. Would you like me to come with you?'

He hesitated. 'It might be easier, love, if I'm by myself. You know what he's like – if you come, he'll ignore me and spend his time being gallant to you. There's some hard talking to be done, and I don't want to give him any loopholes.'

'OK, fine.'

'Sorry to miss one of my "home" evenings.'

'I'll forgive you, on one condition.'

'Which is?'

'That when you get back, we can go into Tarlton's and choose my Christmas present.'

'Tarlton's, indeed? What are you after, a diamond tiara?'

'No, a new watch. This one has just about had it and it's driving me frantic. I had tea with Kate yesterday – I told you on the phone – and she said they've a good selection.'

'You didn't tell me that bit! OK, we can go and have a look. Now, just let me book my ticket, and we'll have some lunch.'

'Not painting today?'

'I'm not particularly inspired, no.'

'What's that you tell me about inspiration and perspiration?'

'OK, OK, but I needed to get this flight booked. Now stop nagging and let me concentrate on what I'm doing. Friday will be the eighteenth, won't it?'

Leaving him to it, she wandered through to the kitchen.

That evening, Rona phoned Coralie Davis. It was, she noted, an out-of-town number.

'Oh, hi! Thanks for ringing back. It's just that my story's a bit different: I wasn't abandoned as a baby, like most people; I was four years old.'

A new angle, certainly. 'Then you must have known your parents?'

'Yes and no. It'd be easier to explain in person, if you're interested.'

'I am, but I can't promise to use your story. I've received a lot of replies, and I'm not sure yet how long the series will run.'

'No problem, either way. I live out at Shellswick, but my job's in town and I could meet you after work, if that's more convenient?'

'It would be, thanks.'

'Where would you suggest?'

'How about the lounge of the Clarendon? We could talk over a cup of tea.'

An amused chuckle reached her, but all Ms Davis said was, 'Fine. I work in Windsor Way, but provided the bus queues aren't too long, I could be there about five fifteen.'

It was arranged that they'd meet the following afternoon. As Rona replaced the phone, she wondered what had amused Coralie about the Clarendon. It was, surely, the obvious choice; she'd often used it to interview people for her articles or, on occasion, take them to lunch. In fact, the hotel had run like a skein through her life: childhood parties; post-pantomime teas; family dinners on special occasions. It had been the venue for her first formal dance, she and Max's first date had been dinner in the Grill Room, and they'd chosen it for their wedding reception. The last time she'd been there, equally memorably, was when her father had summoned Lindsey and herself to tell them of his marriage breakdown.

Still, there were unlikely to be any bombshells tomorrow, and Coralie Davis's story at least promised to be different.

Dorothy Fairfax paused at the bend in the stairs, as was her custom, to take stock of the foyer below. The flowers on the reception desk were beginning to wilt; she must tell Cicely to have a word with the florist. That group of men going into the bar would be the eight thirty booking in the restaurant, their bill to go on the Palmer & Faraday account. There were, she'd noted earlier, only three tables available for casual droppers-in; very good for a Tuesday in November.

As she watched, Sophie emerged from the office and paused to speak to old Mr Tilbury, who'd just come through the swing doors with his wife. Merely looking at her grand-daughter-in-law gave Dorothy a lift. In her opinion, Sophie was one of the hotel's chief assets; there was a warmth about her, a natural empathy that was invaluable in her job, added to which she always looked so elegant. This evening, she was wearing an oyster silk trouser suit that complemented her dark colouring.

Thank God that ill-starred marriage to Lewis hadn't lasted. Christopher had always been besotted with her, and had gone off the rails when she dropped him, though to be fair there'd been nothing definite between them. Dorothy permitted herself a grim smile; Lewis hadn't liked it when Sophie continued to work here, rather than joining him in the shop. Perhaps he'd realized Christopher posed a threat.

Well, Dorothy thought philosophically, continuing her descent of the staircase, all's well that ends well. And, as she was recognized, she advanced smiling, hand outstretched to greet some of their regular guests.

*   *   *

The tune still filled her head, but now it was the background to different, more angry sounds, and she was becoming more and more frightened. Please make them stop! Make them stop!

Then, terrifyingly, she needed to sneeze. What if they heard her? Once, when she'd kept sneezing in church, Nanny had told her to pinch her nose, and the sneezes had stopped. Gingerly she freed one hand to repeat the cure, and immediately felt herself slither an inch or two. Panic washed over her. She couldn't hold on any longer – she was going to fall . . .

Three

Wednesday afternoon, and Max awaited Adele with some anxiety, aware of relief as her voice reached him from the hall below; late arrivals called up to check if they should put the catch on the door. He went to the head of the stairs.

'OK, Adele, everyone's here; you can lock it.'

'Sorry I'm late,' she said breathlessly, as she came up towards him. 'Daisy was ill in the night, but she was better by lunchtime, so I dropped her at school on the way.'

She was pale, Max noted, and there were violet shadows under her eyes which, as usual, shied away from his concerned gaze. Long sleeves, also as usual. What did they hide?

He cleared his throat, and turned to the rest of the class. 'Right, everyone; the still life's set out. Let's see what you make of it.'

Coralie Davis was an attractive young woman whose almond eyes, golden skin and blue-black hair spoke of the Orient.

'I didn't realize you were the one who found that girl's father,' she said chattily, seating herself opposite Rona. 'I don't read *Chiltern Life*, but when I showed my friend the bit in the *Gazette*, she told me about it.'

'That was what started the series,' Rona said.

'I'm glad *my* search didn't turn out like that, though it was tricky enough.'

A waitress appeared at Rona's elbow, and she ordered afternoon tea for two.

'It ended satisfactorily, then?'

'Well, it's not completely finished, but I've probably gone as far as I can.'

Rona felt a twinge of alarm, hoping her help wasn't about to be elicited. She was determined her own involvement would, from now on, be limited to reporting on other people's searches. However, it appeared that Coralie, who was looking round the room appraisingly, was in no hurry to get started.

'They've changed the colour scheme,' she observed. 'It used to be blue and beige in here.'

'So it did,' Rona acknowledged. 'You've a good memory.'

'I should have; I worked here for six months.'

'Really? In what capacity?'

'As a waitress. I was attending night school at the time, and it helped pay the fees.'

'Did you enjoy it?'

'It was all right. Some of the senior staff were a bit snooty, but Sophie was a poppet, and tried to make me feel at home.'

Sophie: she'd heard the name recently. Of course – Kate Tarlton had spoken of her: Lewis's first wife, who'd later married the hotel owner's son. But she hadn't come here to discuss the Fairfaxes.

'You said you weren't adopted until you were four?' she prompted.

'I said I wasn't *abandoned*,' Coralie corrected her.

'But you do remember your parents?'

'It's not as simple as that.' Coralie sat back in her chair, crossing one long leg over the other. 'I lived with a couple called Lena and Jim Chan, who I called Mummy and Daddy.'

She was silent, gazing into a past Rona couldn't see. After a minute she recrossed her legs and went on: 'But they weren't my parents. I didn't realize that until much later.'

'So what happened?' Rona asked gently.

Coralie caught her lower lip between her teeth. It seemed the memory still brought pain. 'One night I woke up to hear them shouting and Lena crying. In the morning her eyes were red and she wouldn't look at me. She said I wasn't going to playschool that day, we were going for a drive instead. Then she packed up all my things and put the case in the car. I asked if we were going on holiday, and she just nodded. She didn't say much during the drive, either, and she put on a tape of nursery rhymes to stop me asking questions.'

The waitress appeared and laid the table, setting out plates of triangular sandwiches, buttered scones with jam, assorted cakes. They waited in silence until she moved away, then Coralie said, 'It's funny – I remember that day so clearly. Much more clearly than what came after. I suppose it's because I went over and over it, trying to think what I'd done wrong.'

She reached for a paper napkin and began absent-mindedly to shred it, watching in silence as Rona poured the tea, and shaking her head at the offer of both milk and sugar.

'After a while we came to a town with a park in the middle of it. Opposite the park was a row of big houses, and we drew up outside one of them. Lena'd started crying again, and all of a sudden I was frightened, without knowing why. She took my case out of the boot and we went up the path and rang the bell. A woman opened it and just stood staring at us. It was all so strange that I started to cry too, so I didn't hear what they said to each other. Then Lena bent down and hugged me and said, "You're going to live here now, Corrie," and before I could take it in, she ran back down the path, got into the car and drove away. I never saw her again.'

Rona said softly, 'That was cruel.'

'Yes – no, not really. I don't know.' Coralie lifted her cup and drank the hot tea. Her eyes were full of tears. 'We went inside,' she continued after a minute, 'and there was a little girl there, younger than me, and a baby in a high chair who stared at me. Neither they nor the woman were Chinese. Nor was the man who came in, and then it was just like it'd been with Lena and Jim – raised voices, and the woman crying and pleading. The man went into the hall, and the woman ran after him, holding on to his arm and trying to stop him. But he shook her off, opened my case and took out an envelope that was lying on top. Then he closed it again, caught hold of my hand and led me straight out to his car. We drove in silence to the town centre, stopped outside a large building and went up some steps into it. Once inside, I thought he'd take off his sunglasses, but he didn't. He just handed my case to a woman behind a desk, said something about having to move his car, and went out again. He never came back.

34

So you see,' she finished rapidly, 'I was abandoned twice in one day.'

Despite herself, Rona wondered how, if presented with this scenario, she would have set about her search. It was certainly a challenge; the couple couldn't both be her parents, since neither was Chinese.

'The woman was your mother?' she guessed, passing Coralie the plate of sandwiches.

'That was the million-dollar question. When I started looking last year, I'd literally nothing to go on. Eventually I discovered Jim and Lena had emigrated, but that was as far as I got, and I didn't even know the name of the other couple. But yes, to cut a long story short, the woman – Judith Craig – was my mother. My father turned out to be Lena's brother, Samuel, who'd had an affair with her when she was working in Hong Kong.'

'What was the place he took you to, this Mr Craig?'

Coralie shrugged. 'Social Services? That's where things get hazy; I probably blotted it out. I do remember I was a difficult child – tantrums, disobedience, bed-wetting, the lot, so I was with a succession of foster parents before I was finally adopted. And everywhere I went, I kept asking for Mummy and Daddy. It didn't get me anywhere, because no one knew who they were.'

'Were you happy once you were adopted?'

'After I'd settled down, yes; I stopped looking back and started to live in the present. Then, last year, I saw a programme on TV about people searching for their birth parents, and began wondering again. Mum and Dad understood; they didn't try to dissuade me, just warned me I mightn't like what I found. But my goodness, it wasn't easy. All I knew was that I'd been Coralie Chan and my date of birth was the third of April 1981; but they couldn't trace me because I'd been registered under my natural mother's name. It must have been my birth certificate Craig took out my case, so I couldn't be traced back to them. As far as officialdom went, I didn't exist before I turned up in that building.'

'The Chans hadn't legally adopted you, then?'

35

Coralie shook her head, helped herself to another sandwich, and met Rona's eyes challengingly.

'Well, are you interested?'

'Yes, I am.' The inference was that nothing more would be forthcoming without a formal agreement, which was fair enough. Certainly it had aroused Rona's curiosity: why hadn't the Chans adopted the child? Why had they suddenly returned her to her mother? What happened to them later? Did Judith Craig try to find Coralie? Did she manage to trace her father?

'So what's the next step?'

Rona said tentatively, 'You do realize we can't offer you a fee?'

Coralie's face fell. 'But I thought—'

'So do a lot of people, I'm afraid, but we'd soon go out of business if we had to pay for every story.' She paused. 'Does that alter things?'

There was a brief silence while Coralie, looking sulky, bit on her lower lip. 'So what do I get out of it?' she asked with a touch of defiance.

Rona smiled. 'Seeing your name in print seems enough for most people. We'd include any photos you could give us, and it would be a kind of official record you could in time pass on to your children – a family history, if you like. And if, as you say, there are still some things outstanding, the publicity might lead to someone coming forward.'

When Coralie still did not speak, she added, 'Anyway, think about it. If you decide to go ahead, I'll call on you with a tape recorder and go through all the documents you've managed to unearth – photographs, and so on – while you tell me how you set about the search, and what success you had.'

At last Coralie nodded. 'I'll talk it over with my boyfriend, and let you know.'

'Fine. You have my phone number.'

The main purpose of the meeting having been achieved, they finished their tea, Rona paid the bill, and they made their way into the foyer. As they were approaching the swing doors, a man's voice behind them said incredulously, 'Coralie?'

They both turned. Since the speaker's eyes were riveted

36

on her companion, Rona was able to examine him at leisure. Probably in his late thirties, he was slightly above middle height, had mid-brown hair that fell over his brow, a long, straight nose and intent grey eyes. He was carrying a sheaf of papers.

She felt Coralie tense, but her voice was steady enough as she replied, 'Hello, Chris.'

'What are you . . . ? I mean . . .'

'We've just had tea in the lounge,' Rona put in smoothly, and his eyes switched to her.

'Rona Parish,' she introduced herself, since Coralie gave no sign of doing so.

He held out his free hand. 'Chris Fairfax. Good afternoon. I'm sorry, I must have sounded abrupt. It's just that I was – taken by surprise.'

'Oh, I'm still around,' Coralie said, with a brilliant smile. 'Nice to see you,' she added carelessly, and pushed her way through the swing doors, leaving Rona to smile a farewell and follow her.

Outside, Coralie allowed no time for questions. 'I'll be in touch,' she said quickly. 'Thanks for the tea.' And she set off briskly along the pavement in the direction of Alban Road, her high heels clicking on the pavement.

Rona turned and started to walk thoughtfully in the opposite direction. That had been a curious exchange between an ex-waitress and the son of the owner. There was obviously a story there, too, but Rona doubted that she would ever hear it.

Gerald Fairfax, Chris's younger brother, had also seen the exchange, and been disturbed by it. He hoped to God that Coralie wasn't going to stage a reappearance. Though nothing had been said, he knew her dismissal had been softened by a generous sum in lieu of notice – surely on the understanding that she'd stay away from the hotel? Yet what could they do if she chose to visit it? She could hardly be barred. And that young woman with her: her name had sounded familiar. Wasn't she the journalist who was making a name for herself settling old scores? If so, there was even more cause for worry.

And Gerald was used to worry. Slight of build and looking considerably less than his thirty-four years, he was a reserved young man who'd never been able to discuss his problems, and had years ago resigned himself to sleepless nights as a consequence. Principal among those worries was the ever-present fear that he'd lose his position as head chef, that his ideas would dry up and his father would lose patience with him – something, Gerald reflected ruefully, that in any case happened fairly regularly. Cooking was his one passion, his *raison d'être*, and life wouldn't be worth living without it. Consequently he spent all his free time pouring over recipe books and biographies of past *cuisiniers* from Escoffier onwards, and when not on duty, closeted himself in his little kitchen at home, experimenting with new dishes.

But Coralie, along with his other anxieties, would have to be put on hold. Shrugging on his white coat and hat, he made his way to the kitchens to begin his evening shift.

'Do you know anything about the people at the Clarendon?' Rona asked Max that evening as he prepared their meal.

'The owners, you mean? I met Stephen, that time I held an exhibition there. He's known as an awkward customer but I got on with him all right.'

'Is he the boss?'

'Officially, but I hear his mother still has an input, even though she's well into her eighties. Why the sudden interest?'

'I had tea there today, with that girl I told you about. She used to work there as a waitress, and as we were leaving we met Chris, one of the sons, and there was quite an atmosphere between them. I was curious, that's all.'

Max gave a short laugh. 'Nose twitching, my love?'

'Well, I wondered how it fitted in. Kate Tarlton said Lewis's first wife is married to Chris Fairfax. By the way, did you know the Tarltons and Fairfaxes are related?'

'Can't say I did, but it's not surprising. They're both old Marsborough families.'

Rona sipped her drink reflectively. 'Actually, I was getting quite nostalgic, thinking over the part the Clarendon's played in my life: childhood parties, our first date, our wedding reception. Come to think of it, the same applies to Tarlton's, which the family's been going to for years. Even Netherby's has hardly changed since we were taken to the grotto each year. In this day and age, when so many towns are clones of each other, Marsborough's lucky to have so many long-established firms.'

'Why don't you write about them?' Max suggested carelessly. 'Those that have been here since, say, the 1920s or longer? It might be quite interesting.'

'It might indeed,' Rona agreed, ideas beginning to form. 'Offhand, how many can you think of that would qualify?'

'Well, the Clarendon and Tarlton's for starters, and, of course, Netherby's. This was their original store, though they've now spread throughout the county. And Willows' Furniture on the corner has been going for years.'

He stirred the pan and tasted the contents on a wooden spoon. 'Then there's that speciality grocers at the far end of Guild Street – what's it called? Anyway, they have a framed display of their shopfronts going back to the early 1900s.'

'It would really be as much about the families who own them as the shops themselves,' Rona put in, her interest quickening. 'I don't know if it's true, but I heard that John Willow started as a barrow boy, and worked his way up.'

'There you are, then,' Max said enigmatically. 'A complete series, ready and waiting for you.'

'If they all agree.'

'You're joking! Refuse free publicity? Not on your life!'

'If Barnie would, then.'

'Well, he's pleased with the way the Buckford articles are going. You could have a pull-out section of these too, and a binder to put them in. A different slant on what you did for Buckford.'

'It's certainly worth thinking about,' Rona agreed, and, at his signal, moved to the kitchen table for supper.

'Tom?'

'Hello, my love.'

'I've a favour to ask.'

'Ask away.'

'Would you mind very much if we postponed our plans for the weekend?'

His heart sank. They'd arranged to drive into the country for a pub lunch, followed by a walk if the weather was good enough, before going on to the early evening showing at the cinema. He'd been looking forward to it.

'Of course not, if something else has come up,' he lied.

'Actually, it has. I've just had Daniel on the phone. As you know, they've been busy most weekends, then he was away on a couple of courses, so I still haven't had a chance to tell them our news.' She gave an apologetic little laugh. 'It's not something you can come out with on the phone.'

'He wants to see you?'

'Yes; they've invited me over for the weekend. It seems the ideal opportunity to put them in the picture; to be honest, I've been getting a little panicky about how far things were progressing without them knowing anything about it.'

'As you say, the perfect opportunity.'

'You don't mind?'

'My darling, we'll soon have every weekend together. Of course you must go.'

'I knew you'd understand,' Catherine said gratefully.

Max settled back in his seat, glanced out of the window at the rain-swept runway, and opened his newspaper. He was not looking forward to the next twenty-four hours. Deep down, he admitted he was fond enough of his family; it was just that he preferred them at a distance. His mother had died when he was thirteen, and Cynthia, five years his senior, had acted as stand-in till he left for art college. She had been, then as now, well intentioned but bossy, and he knew he'd not made things easy for her. And Father had always been an awkward so-and-so. Rona, with her own close-knit family, could never understand his keeping them at arm's length.

Suppose the old man really was ill, though? In the manner of most offspring, Max had subconsciously expected him to go on for ever. That there might come a time – sooner rather than later – when he wouldn't be there, to contact or not as

40

Max chose, was unsettling. Cynthia and Rona were right: he should make an effort to establish more regular contact. Though how his father would react to such an approach was, he acknowledged wryly, anyone's guess.

Cynthia was waiting at the airport, and as Max caught sight of her short, rounded figure, he felt a surge of affection for her. He put an arm round her and pulled her against him.

'Good to see you, Cyn.'

'You too, you old reprobate.' As always her tone was brisk, but he felt the tightening of her arm as she returned his hug.

'How's the old fella?' Max asked, as he followed her to the car park.

'A bit wheezy, and still not eating enough to keep a sparrow alive.'

'He knows I'm coming?'

'Oh yes. He might have had a heart attack if you'd walked in unannounced.'

Max grinned. 'OK, don't rub it in. So when are we seeing him?'

'I'll drive you over after lunch.' Cynthia stopped at a small Peugeot, opened the boot, and Max tossed his overnight bag inside.

'It's not a question of "we", though,' she continued as they got into the car. 'I'll drop you off, but I'm not coming in. You two need time alone together.'

Max was alarmed. 'Oh, come on now, sis, that's not fair!'

'What's not fair,' she retorted, 'is your cutting yourself off for so long. It's no use arguing, Max, it's all settled. I'll drop you off, as I said, then at five I'll collect you both and bring Father back for dinner with us all.'

'Does "all" include the boys?'

Cynthia and her husband had two strapping sons, Michael and David, who, in their teens, had rechristened themselves Mike and Dave.

'They sound like a comic double act,' Cynthia had complained.

'Yes, they're both living at home at the moment. Paul says we make things too comfortable for them; there's no incentive to find a place of their own, especially since they're both working in Tynecastle.'

'No sign of wedding bells?'

Cynthia's derisive snort was answer enough.

Lindsey pushed her way through the swing doors of the Clarendon, grateful for its warmth on her wind-chilled face, and made her way down the broad, carpeted stairs to the Grill Room, where François, the maître d', met her with a small bow.

'Mr Cavendish is already here, madame. If you would come this way?'

Obediently following in his wake, she caught sight of Hugh's red head bent over the menu at a corner table. He stood at their approach, giving her a quick kiss on the cheek as François pulled out her chair for her and took her jacket. For a moment longer she busied herself, taking off her gloves and dropping her bag to the floor, in order to cover the racing pulse that accompanied any meeting with her ex-husband.

'You're looking gorgeous, as always,' Hugh said quietly.

'Thank you, kind sir.'

'Would you like to stick to the grill menu, or go for one of the chef's specials?'

'I think steak and a salad would be fine.'

'A starter?'

She shook her head. 'I've under an hour and a half, Hugh; I'm seeing a client at two thirty.'

'It would be good to meet without always having an eye on the clock,' he said tightly. 'Are you as circumscribed when you lunch with your colleague, or is that extendable in the guise of a business lunch?'

She didn't meet his eye. 'It depends on my schedule; you know that.'

He leaned forward, laying a hand on her wrist. 'What I know is that I need to see you – *really* see you, Lindsey.'

His hand seemed to burn through her skin and she forced herself to speak lightly. 'Only in public, Hugh; that was the agreement. And if you were about to suggest your flat, that would be doubly unwise; Pops is renting one in Talbot Road from the end of the month.'

He sat back in his chair, staring at her. 'My block?'

'Rona says not. However, it's immaterial as far as we're concerned.'

He leaned forward urgently. 'When are you going to stop all this nonsense and marry me again?'

'Don't rush me,' she said.

In truth though, Lindsey reflected, as Hugh relayed their order to the waiter, she had no intention of remarrying him. They'd been at each other's throats before, and would be again. It was only physical attraction that kept them, unwillingly for the most part, still tied to each other.

Roland Allerdyce lived in an old farmhouse on the fringes of a village some five miles from the town. He'd sold off the surrounding land when he bought it thirty years ago, but its barn, large and airy, had been converted into a centrally-heated studio that suited him admirably.

The house was, of course, far too large for him, but he refused point-blank to consider moving, either to somewhere smaller, or to live with his daughter and her family. His devoted housekeeper, Doris Pemberton, who'd been with him from the start, ran the house with quiet efficiency, helped for the last five years by a woman from the village who came in twice a week to do the heavy cleaning. It was thanks to Mrs Pemberton's ministrations that Cynthia was able to worry less about her father than she might otherwise have done.

The old man came out to meet them as they turned into the cobbled yard, the stiff breeze ruffling his still-plentiful hair. As Max quickly got out of the car and went to greet him, he was aware of shock. Though his father stood ramrod straight and was still the same height as Max himself, he seemed to have shrunk inside himself, the skin on his face falling away to leave nose and cheekbones more prominent and his clothes hanging loosely on his frame.

'Father!' Max clasped the veined hand thrust out at him, wincing at the strength of the grip.

'So you've put in an appearance at last. Cynthia put the wind up you, did she? She's been clucking round like a mother hen for months.'

Cynthia wound down the car window. 'I'll be back at five,' she called. 'Enjoy yourselves!'

'Humph!' Roland Allerdyce turned back towards the house, Max at his side. Mrs Pemberton was waiting at the door, concerned that the old man had gone out in the cold without additional clothing.

'Mr Max! Welcome home!'

'Thank you, Mrs P. It's – good to be back.'

'There's coffee in the den. I thought it would be more cosy in there.'

Roland led the way to the small room that, in earlier times, had been known as the parlour, and Mrs Pemberton saw them settled with cups of coffee before leaving them to themselves. Max had forgotten how small the farmhouse windows were, and how low the ceilings. He and his father had both had to stoop when they came into the room. Small wonder it had been necessary to convert the barn into a studio. The room was already shadowed this winter after-noon, lit solely by the blazing open fire. The armchairs on either side of it were of worn leather, and Max settled back comfortably, coffee in hand.

'So, Father, what's the score? Honestly?'

The old man held his eyes for a minute, then looked away. 'Devil of a cough, that's all. Won't let me get a decent night's sleep.'

'Have you seen the doctor?'

'What's the point of bothering him? He has enough hypochondriacs on his books as it is.'

'What's this about not eating properly?'

'Good God, boy, when you get to my age, you don't need as much to keep you going. Mrs P, God bless her, can't see it, and keeps trying to force-feed me.'

'Will you do something for me, Father?'

'It depends.'

'I want you to promise to go to the doctor. You're losing weight, and that's not good at any age. Anyway, the world's awaiting several more masterpieces, so don't think you can slip away without anyone noticing.'

Roland Allerdyce smiled. 'I've missed you, boy,' he said gruffly. 'What are you working on at the moment?'

'I'll be delighted to talk shop, but only after I have your promise.'

'I tell you there's nothing wrong with me.'

'I trust you're right, but I'd like the doctor to confirm it.'

There was a silence, measured by the wheezing tick of the clock on the mantelpiece.

Finally the old man moved impatiently. 'Oh, very well, then. If you've taken the trouble to fly up here, I suppose it's the least I can do.'

'You'll go to the doctor?'

'I'll go to the doctor, dammit, for all the good it'll do. Now, can we talk about something more interesting? How's that independent young wife of yours?'

And Max, promise duly extracted, settled back to enjoy his father's company.

Rona was taking some fishcakes from the freezer when the phone interrupted her. She glanced at the clock. Just before seven; on the early side for Max. With a jerk of her heart, she hoped it wasn't bad news about the old man.

She caught up the phone. 'Hello?' she said quickly.

'Oh – hello,' replied a hesitant voice. 'Could I speak to Max, please?'

'I'm afraid he's not here. Who's speaking?'

Another pause. Then: 'It's Adele Yarborough, Rona. Sorry to trouble you, but I thought he'd be home by now.'

'Afraid not,' Rona said crisply. She would *not* explain where Max was; it was no business of Adele Yarborough's.

'What time are you expecting him?' she persisted.

'Not until tomorrow lunchtime, actually.'

'Oh. I thought Friday was one of his home nights?'

His *home* nights? Max, Rona remembered uncomfortably, had used the same expression. How much did this woman know about their domestic arrangements?

She maintained a steely silence, and after a minute Adele

45

said, 'Right. Well, sorry to have troubled you. It's – not important.'

She waited for Rona to make a comment, and when she did not, added, 'Goodbye, then.'

'Goodbye,' Rona said, and put down the phone.

Four

Max did not open his newspaper on his return flight. Instead, he stared out of the window at the massed clouds below, his mind full of impressions of the last twenty-four hours. It had given him a jolt to see how frail his previously invincible father had looked, and the cough that rattled in his chest from time to time was alarming. It was to be hoped he'd fulfil his promise of seeking medical advice.

Max had enjoyed their masculine tête-à-tête by the fire; God knows when they'd last had one, and he'd been increasingly aware of guilt at his long absence. The evening at Cynthia and Paul's had been relaxed and informal, and to his surprise he had found himself enjoying his family's company. His nephews, both in their early twenties, were pleasant, self-confident young men, one an accountant, the other following his father into the Inland Revenue, which elicited the usual quota of jokes. Neither seemed to have inherited their grandfather's artistic tendencies, though in Cynthia the creative urge had manifested itself in exquisite embroidery – on tray cloths, cushions, bedspreads and framed pictures throughout her house. Max had always marvelled that her short, stubby fingers could achieve such miracles of precision.

'Thanks for coming, Max,' she had said at the airport. 'I've been on at Father for weeks to go to the doctor, but one word from you, and he caves in!'

'Perhaps it had got to the stage when he was worried himself, even if he wouldn't admit it. And thank you, Cyn, for stirring my dormant conscience. I've been very remiss about coming up, but if you'll have me, I'd like to pay regular visits from now on. Say every couple of months?'

47

'That'd be great. We'd love to see you, and I know Father would be delighted.'

'You'll let me know what the doctor says?'

'Of course. I'll fix an appointment as soon as I get back. Take care of yourself, and love to Rona. Bring her up with you next time.'

His father had made the same request; Rona had always been a favourite of his. Max hoped devoutly that this renewal of contact had not come too late for them to enjoy many such reunions. If it had, it would be a burden he'd have to live with for the rest of his life.

It was one o'clock by the time he reached Lightbourne Avenue, and Rona had laid the kitchen table with a selection of breads and cheeses, while a pan of artichoke soup, made by himself and stored in the freezer, simmered on the hob.

As they ate, he related the details of his visit and passed on the various messages. 'I should have listened to you, love, and gone up much more regularly,' he concluded. 'I won't make the same mistake again, and your presence is requested on the next visit.'

'I shall be delighted.' She paused, crumbling the bread on her plate. 'By the way, there was a phone call for you last night.'

'Oh? Who was it?'

'One of your admirers.'

He smiled. 'That narrows it down to about a thousand!' Then, seeing her face, his smile faded. 'Adele?' he asked flatly.

'Adele.'

'What did she want?'

'You. She thought you'd be here, as Friday is one of your home nights.' Rona strove to keep her voice level but accusation seeped through, and when he made no comment, her anger, simmering ever since the call, boiled over.

'What the hell has it to do with her, which are your *home* nights? How does she even *know* you sometimes sleep at Farthings?'

48

'Rona, for God's sake!'

'Well? How does she? Do you discuss our marital arrangements with your students? Or only with specific ones, like Adele?'

'Now you're just being stupid.'

'Humour me.'

'I don't *know* how she knew. I certainly don't recall mentioning it. Damn it, I never even *see* her except in class, so how could I have?'

'Then it follows that the whole class knows which nights I sleep with my husband.'

Max lowered his head into his hands, his fingers deep in his hair. 'What is it about Adele that winds you up so much?'

'That's a good question.' Rona spoke more calmly, but her breathing was still uneven. 'What *is* it about Adele, Max? She's able to push buttons with both of us, isn't she? Though they're different buttons. You seem to have appointed yourself her Lord Protector, and she's taking full advantage of it. I suppose that's what riles me.'

Max raised his head and ran a hand over his face. 'Can we drop this? It's not getting us anywhere, and I've had enough emotional roller coasters over the last twenty-four hours.'

As quickly as it had arisen, Rona's anger died and she laid an impulsive hand on his arm. 'Max, I'm sorry. That was lousy timing, but—'

'I know,' he said quietly, patting her hand. 'I know.' After a moment, he added, 'Our friends all know I stay over at Farthings. These things get round, whether or not it's anyone else's business. She must have picked it up somewhere.'

Rona nodded. 'Will you phone her back?'

'Would I dare?'

Their eyes held, then, almost against their wills, they both smiled. It was the way most of their rows ended, and they leaned simultaneously towards each other for a placatory kiss.

'And now that's settled,' Rona said, 'you can take me to Tarlton's to buy my Christmas present.'

*   *   *

49

Rona saw Kate as soon as they walked into the shop, but she was already serving someone, and it was another assistant who came forward. Rona wondered if she was part-time or one of the family.

'Good afternoon. Can I help you?'

'We'd like to look at some ladies' gold watches,' Max told her, and they were led to a cubicle containing chairs and a table covered with a velvet cloth. Purchases at Tarlton's were conducted in privacy.

'If you'd like to take a seat, I'll bring a selection through. Can I offer you tea or coffee while you choose?'

'No thank you, we've just had some.'

The girl smiled and withdrew. 'Is all this recouped in the prices they charge?' Max asked in a whisper, and Rona reprovingly shook her head.

As Kate had intimated, there was plenty of choice in a variety of sizes and designs, but after narrowing them down, one emerged as the clear favourite. Max was discreetly shown the price, and, to Rona's relief, nodded confirmation.

'Fine. We'll take it,' he said.

'Would you like it gift-wrapped, sir?'

'Yes, please. Then there's no way she can look at it again before Christmas!'

They followed her out of the cubicle, and while Max busied himself at the till, Rona moved slowly along the various display cases, admiring bracelets, earrings, brooches and necklaces, all glittering under strategically placed lights. Mrs Tarlton senior certainly knew a thing or two about displays, Rona thought.

Max put away his credit card, the assistant handed him the distinctive carrier bag striped in silver and gold, and, looking up as they came towards her, Rona's eyes fell on a carved wooden musical box on top of a cabinet.

'Oh Max, look! Isn't that pretty? It would make a lovely present for Lindsey.' She turned to the girl, who was waiting to accompany them to the door. 'What tune does it play?'

'I'm afraid I don't know; they only came in this morning. Shall we see?'

She lifted the lid, and Rona watched in delight as two

50

small figures began to rotate in time to the tune that spilled out, filling the shop with its lilting melody. Several people turned with a smile, but a stifled sound made Rona glance quickly at the girl beside her. Her hands had flown to her mouth, her already pale face had taken on a greenish tinge, and she was staring as though mesmerized at the revolving figures. Then, before Rona realized what was happening, the girl's eyes closed and she slid bonelessly to the floor.

Rona dropped to her knees, but was moved politely aside as members of the family hurried to the girl's aid.

'Freya! Freya, it's all right, honey! Get some water, someone! If everyone could just stand back, please?'

Lewis's sister, Rona thought in bewilderment, as Max helped her to her feet. Whatever had caused that reaction? Freya's eyes were already flickering and she gave a little moan, shaking her head from side to side. Lewis himself had now appeared, and, bending down, picked up his sister with ease and carried her to one of the offices at the back of the shop. And all the time, the musical box played its catchy, innocent little melody and the tiny figures continued to rotate. No one had thought to turn it off, but then only Rona and Max knew it had been the trigger for the attack. As the shutting of the office door ended the drama, Rona reached forward and gently closed the lid. She didn't think she'd be buying it after all.

An older man held up a hand, raising his voice above the general concerned murmur. 'I'm so sorry, everyone; it must be one of these bugs that are doing the rounds. She's already recovering, so do please return to your browsing. The staff are ready to help, if you need any assistance.'

Max took Rona's elbow and steered her out of the bright warmth of the shop on to the already darkening pavement.

'What the hell was that all about?' he asked.

Rona shook her head. 'I'm not wrong, am I? It *was* the tune that sparked it off?'

'Well, I can't imagine it was the little figures.'

'What was it, anyway?'

'"Auprès de ma blonde". Didn't you recognize it?' He began to sing softly:

Auprès de ma blonde,
Qu'il fait bon, fait bon, fait bon,
Auprès de ma blonde,
Qu'il fait bon dormir

'Surely you learnt it at school?'

Rona laughed. 'We most certainly did not. Mademoiselle would have had the vapours!'

'Well, enough of all that. At least we've got your Christmas present, so let's go home and have a quiet, relaxing evening. What with one thing and another, I feel in need of it.'

In her father's office at the back of the shop, Freya lay in a reclining chair and let the hot tears slide unchecked from under her closed lids. Her mouth was dry and her heart hammered sickly in her chest. The tune existed, then, she thought numbly. It wasn't just something she'd conjured up in her dream; it was known to other people. *Why* was it haunting her so?

'Drink this, darling.' Aunt Jan was holding a cup of water to her lips and she obediently sipped it.

'I'm – sorry,' she said weakly. 'I don't know what came over me. I'm all right now.'

She made to sit up, but Jan pushed her gently back against the cushions. 'Stay there a while and regain your equilibrium. There are plenty of others to see to the customers.'

She turned to Kate and Susie, who were hovering anxiously in the background. 'At least, there will be, when these two get back to work. Off you go now, the crisis is over. You too, Bruce. She needs a little space. I'll see to her.'

Her husband hesitated. 'Should I nip up and tell Robert?'

Jan shook her head. 'He'll hear in due course, but there's no urgency. Let him enjoy his Saturday off.'

Since handing over the family home to Lewis, Robert Tarlton had taken up residence in the flat above the shop. Ignoring his family's cries of protest, he'd insisted it was warm, comfortable, convenient and amply big enough for his needs. He also liked being on Guild Street – in the middle of things, as he put it, and only yards from his club.

When they were alone, Jan said quietly, 'Are you going to tell me what happened?'

Freya's eyes flew to her face. 'I – don't know,' she faltered.

'I think you do. You're not ill; you haven't a temperature, and you've not mentioned a headache. Healthy young women don't suddenly keel over for no reason.'

Freya was silent, wondering how much to confide. Only Matthew knew the full extent of the havoc her recurring dreams were causing, and she was unwilling to involve anyone else. But Jan Tarlton wasn't 'anyone else'. Freya had been three when her mother left them, and Jan, who'd been able to have only one child herself, had taken both her and Lewis under her maternal wing. She had in effect been a surrogate mother, and Freya loved her accordingly.

Seeing her hesitation, Jan laid one of her large, capable hands over Freya's. 'It won't go any further, if you don't want it to.'

So, stumblingly, Freya told her about the onset of the night-mares, about the way they were slowly developing, little bits seeming to be added on each time, and of the tune, which she'd been sure was a figment of her own imagination.

'The one the musical box played?'

Freya nodded. 'What terrified me was discovering it actu-ally existed, even though I'd never heard it before outside my dreams. Because if the tune's real, perhaps the rest of it is too.'

'The most likely explanation is that you *have* heard it somewhere, without being aware of it, and for some reason it lodged in your subconscious.'

Freya said in a whisper, 'But *where* did I hear it? That's the question. What is it, anyway? Do you know?'

'It's an old French song, "Auprès de ma blonde". Ring any bells?'

Freya shook her head.

'Well, the thing to do, honeybun, is keep a sense of propor-tion. Nothing you dream can possibly harm you, so though the nightmares are unpleasant at the time, you mustn't let them rule your life. And if you can force yourself to react

to them calmly, they'll just fade away, as they did last time.'
She paused. 'Of course, they might be indicative of some
other worry. Is there anything on your mind?'

Freya shook her head. 'I love my job and my family, I
love living with Matthew, and, as you said, I'm in perfect
health. Positively no worries,' she added in an Australian
accent, and Jan laughed.

'That's the spirit. Well, it was a nasty little upset, but
there's no lasting harm done. You can tell people it was
something you ate. OK?'

'OK,' Freya repeated gratefully, and almost believed that
it was.

Freya's collapse was the subject of several conversations
over dinner that evening.

'You missed quite a drama this afternoon,' Susie Tarlton
told her husband, as he returned from kissing their daughter
goodnight.

'Come to that, the match was pretty dramatic,' Nicholas
countered, pouring wine into their glasses. 'Murray scored
a fantastic try in the last minute of the game, from more
than halfway down the pitch. Can you top that?'

'Freya fainted dead away on the shop floor.'

'*What?*' She had his full attention now.

'Out for the count, with the place full of customers. Believe
me, it caused quite a stir.'

'But – you mean she was taken ill?'

'You tell me. One minute she was calmly handing someone
his purchase, the next she was flat on the floor.'

'Good God! What happened?'

'Lewis carried her to Robert's office. She was already
coming round by then, but Jan did her mother-hen act and
shooed the rest of us out. And about twenty minutes later
she was serving customers again.'

'But – there must have been some explanation?'

Susie shrugged. 'We weren't given one. Or at least, not
one I believed. When I asked if she was all right, she just
said yes, thanks, it must have been something she ate.'

'But surely that's feasible?'

54

'It wouldn't have come on so abruptly, Nick. One minute she was fine, the next not. No sickness or stomach cramps. Something gave her a fright, if you want my opinion, but God knows what.'

'I'll have a go at Mama and see what gives.'

Susie smiled and picked up her knife and fork. 'The best of luck,' she said.

'I'm worried about her,' Lewis said abruptly.

Kate nodded. 'I know you are.'

'She's not been right for a week or two, but she keeps insisting there's nothing wrong. God, I got the fright of my life, seeing her lying there on the floor. I thought she'd been stabbed or something.'

'You watch too much television.'

'You can scoff, but jewellers are more vulnerable than most.'

'Not on a Saturday afternoon, with the shop full of customers.'

Lewis pushed his plate away. 'She used to talk to me, you know, until Matthew came along. Now, he gets all her confidences. She's always been vulnerable, Kate, right from way back.'

'I know, darling, but she's a grown woman now. As to this afternoon, it was too hot in the shop – I said so at the time – and she'd been on her feet all day.'

'So had you all,' Lewis pointed out, unconvinced, and Kate, seeing nothing she said was going to satisfy him, determinedly changed the subject.

Sophie Fairfax learned of the incident from overhearing a conversation in the restaurant.

'Went down as if she'd been pole-axed,' said a florid-faced man with relish. 'The place just about erupted. Then Lewis Tarlton charged to the rescue and bore her off to the nether regions.'

Sophie's attention, already caught, quickened at the name of her ex-husband, and under the guise of checking the bookings, she paused to listen.

55

'Which of them was it?' asked one of the women at the table.

'The youngest, who looks as if she wouldn't say boo to a goose. She's always pale, but she went positively green. I kept well clear of her, I can tell you. It was the suddenness of it that was so startling. She'd walked past me only a minute before, as right as rain.'

There seemed to be no further information forthcoming, and Sophie left the restaurant and went in search of her husband.

'It seems Freya collapsed in the shop today,' she told him anxiously. 'Do you think I ought to phone and see how she is?'

Chris hesitated, trying not to allow his jealousy of Lewis to cloud his judgement. 'They wouldn't like to think it's the talk of the town,' he said. 'It probably caused enough embarrassment at the time.'

'But I'm concerned about her, Chris. I still think of her as my little sister.'

'You're not still in touch, are you?' Again that stab of insecurity.

'We phone each other from time to time.'

He hadn't realized that. After a minute, he said carefully, 'Well, if I were you, I'd wait a day or two, then just ring up casually, as though you hadn't heard anything. If she seems OK, that'll set your mind at rest, and if she isn't, no doubt she'll tell you.'

'Good idea,' Sophie agreed. 'Thanks, beloved.' And, dropping a kiss on his head as she passed the sofa, she went back to her duties, leaving him, had she known it, more anxious than she was.

Over dinner in Cricklehurst, Catherine also had something on her mind. She'd driven over that morning, but so far there'd not been an appropriate moment to tell her son and daughter-in-law her news. They'd gone out for a pub lunch, then walked across wintry fields that were crisp with frost and crunched beneath their footsteps – ironically enough, how she and Tom had planned to spend the day. And as they walked, hands deep in pockets to keep warm, Daniel had told her about his computer courses and how the scope of his job was changing. Then Jenny had taken over and regaled her with problems at the flower shop that she managed, and how their suppliers had suddenly announced they couldn't guarantee delivery of their order before Christmas.

'I played merry hell with them,' Jenny said, 'and after a lot of wrangling, finally managed to wring out the promise that it would be with us by the tenth at the latest. Even that's cutting it fine.'

'She's a dragon when roused,' Daniel said fondly, slipping an arm round his wife's shoulders.

On their return home, Daniel, with a token apology, had settled down to watch the post-mortems of the afternoon's sport, while Jenny disappeared into the kitchen to prepare the evening meal. At dinner, Catherine promised herself; that's when I'll tell them.

She'd gone upstairs, a knot of apprehension in her stomach, and as she turned into her room, her eyes lingered on the closed door at the top of the stairs. Behind it, she knew, was a fully equipped nursery, still awaiting the arrival of the baby that, tragically, had never come home. Nearly six months ago; was it too soon to hope another might be on the way?

And now they were sitting round the table in the small dining room, two-thirds of the meal behind them and one of Jenny's delectable desserts on their plates. There were candles on the table, and in their gentle light Catherine glanced at the faces of her family, aching with love for them. Please, she prayed, please let them be happy for me. Don't let Daniel think I'm betraying his father.

His voice broke into her musings. 'You're very quiet, Ma. Feeling all right?'

She looked up, bracing herself. 'Actually, I'm trying to pluck up courage to tell you something.'

Daniel's hand stilled, fork poised over his plate. 'There's something wrong? Ma – you're not ill?'

'No, no, darling, nothing like that. I've never been better. In fact, I'm – thinking of getting married again.'

The silence that followed her announcement seemed

endless measured in heartbeats, but could only have lasted seconds. Then, as Jenny exclaimed in delight, Daniel pushed back his chair, came quickly over to her, and put his arms round her.

'Well,' he commented, 'you've kept that pretty quiet!' He bent to kiss her cheek and she caught hold of his hand, her eyes full of relieved tears.

'You – don't mind?'

'Mind? How could I mind? I'm delighted for you. We both are.'

Jenny in turn jumped up to kiss her. 'It's wonderful news, Catherine! Do we know the lucky man?'

'Daniel does. At least, he's met him. His name's Tom Parish.'

Daniel frowned for a moment, then his face cleared. 'Oh, the chap who drove you to the hospital when Jenny had her miss?'

'That's the one.'

'And when did all this blow up?' he asked, returning to his seat.

'A couple of months ago, but things aren't exactly straight-forward.' Her hands gripped her napkin. 'Tom's still married. He'll be getting a divorce, but we're letting things take their course. Two years' separation, then it goes straight through. And darlings, please believe me: I wasn't the cause of the divorce. Things had been bad for some time.'

'So what will you do for the next two years?' Jenny asked, finally starting to eat her dessert. 'Live together?'

'No.' Catherine smiled. 'I'd be quite happy for Tom to move into the bungalow, but he wants to spare me unpleasant gossip, so he's renting a flat in the next road till we're free to marry.'

'When are we going to meet him?'

'I don't know. Things are a little fraught at the moment. He retires from the bank next week – he's the manager there – but once that's over, it'll come more into the open. I'm sorry I didn't tell you earlier, but you've had a lot on and it's not something I could say on the phone.' She laid a hand

58

on her son's. 'Darling, he'll never take the place of your father. You know that, don't you?'

'Of course I know that. But I've been hoping for years that you'd meet someone; I've hated thinking of you alone.'

'Bless you for that.'

'And now,' Daniel said, getting to his feet again, 'I think champagne is called for. I was keeping it for Christmas, but there's plenty of time to replace it.' He paused. 'You are still coming to us for Christmas?'

'Of course I am.'

'That's all right, then.'

He lifted a bottle out of the wine rack and began to unwind the gold wire, while Jenny took three champagne flutes from the cupboard. With a satisfying pop the cork came out and the foaming liquid was poured into the glasses.

Daniel raised his. 'To Ma and Tom,' he proposed. 'Long life and happiness! It'll be good to have another man around!'

'To the enlargement of the family!' Catherine toasted in her turn, and pretended not to see the swift look that passed between husband and wife. Perhaps, she thought, her heart swelling with happiness, there would soon be another reason to celebrate.

Five

'This time next week, Pops will have retired,' Rona remarked to Max over Sunday breakfast.

'And presumably left the marital home.'

'Yes. I wonder if he'll need help, moving his things out.'

'It might be wiser, in the circumstances, not to offer your services.'

'Possibly; though, according to Linz, Mum and Pops are on better terms than they've been for ages.'

Max said reflectively, 'It'll be worse for Avril; she hasn't a lover waiting in the wings. I can't help feeling sorry for her.'

Rona looked at him with a mixture of surprise and indignation. 'You're not changing sides, are you?'

'There shouldn't be any sides,' Max said gently. 'Let's say I'm particularly parent-conscious at the moment, and in fence-mending mode. But it's just occurred to me – you know how we're always being invited over for Sunday lunch?'

'Don't I just?'

'Well, wouldn't it be a nice gesture if we took her out somewhere? To the Clarendon, for example? Ask Lindsey along too, perhaps? It would show there are no hard feelings.'

Rona stared at him for a moment, then her eyes dropped. 'You put me to shame,' she said quietly. 'It's a lovely idea, darling. Shall I put it into effect?'

'As long as she wouldn't object to short notice.' He paused. 'But what about your father? Can we ask one without the other?'

'He's gone off on a golfing weekend – last-minute decision, apparently – so no feathers need be ruffled.'

Avril received the invitation with surprised delight, Lindsey a little more cautiously.

'What is this? Let's-be-nice-to-Mum-for-a-change week?'

'You're only miffed because you didn't think of it,' Rona retorted. 'Do you want to come, or not?'

'Of course I'll come. I wouldn't miss out on a free lunch, even if there's not supposed to be such a thing.'

'Gracious as always. Now we have to see if there's a table free. If you don't hear to the contrary, let's meet in the bar at twelve thirty.'

Their luck held. There'd been a cancellation five minutes earlier, and the Clarendon was able to accommodate them with a table for four at one o'clock. Fleetingly, Rona wondered what her father would think. Then, acknowledging that he was more forgiving than herself, she reckoned he'd be pleased.

Avril stood in front of her wardrobe, surveying the clothes she'd bought over the last month or so. Which outfit, she agonized, would be the most appropriate? Something smart, but not too eye-catching. After holding several up against herself in front of the mirror, she selected a sage green suit with a boxy jacket and knee-length skirt, and a tailored cream blouse. She was lucky that during the years of self-neglect she had neither gained nor lost weight, and her legs were still good.

Fortunately, she'd washed her hair that morning. She was still not used to the new style – short and layered, framing her face – and on her last visit to the hairdresser, had daringly agreed to blonde highlights to lift the general mousiness. Luckily, the girls had inherited their father's thick, dark hair, though his was now grey.

When, ten minutes later, she surveyed her reflection – a faint touch of green on her eyelids and softly pink lips – she felt a lift of pleasure, the more so since the metamorphosis had been not to please Tom or any other man, but herself. Even so, she admitted with a touch of bitterness, if it had come a year or so earlier, they might still be together. Her

61

general sloppiness had, she was sure, combined with her astringent tongue to drive him away.

Well, that was all in the past now, and after next week she'd have the house to herself and could start putting her plans for the shower room into effect. In the meantime, it would be good to be taken out for a meal, and Rona was a dear to have thought of it.

Feeling happier than she had for months, Avril picked up her handbag and went downstairs.

Rona, who had seen little of her mother over the last month, felt a jolt of surprise as she appeared in the doorway to the bar.

'Mum, you look stunning!' she exclaimed, and Avril flushed with pleasure as Max led her to their table.

'Thank you, dear. This is really very good of you.'

'Our pleasure,' Max said smoothly. 'And here's Lindsey, to complete the party.'

Lindsey, elegant in black and cream, greeted everyone with a kiss before seating herself next to her mother.

'Now,' Max said, 'what's everyone drinking?'

'Max!'

They all turned as a tall, thin man came into the bar, holding out his hand. 'Good to see you again!'

'Hello, Stephen.' Max turned to his seated family. 'This gentleman's the owner of this magnificent establishment – Stephen Fairfax. Stephen, may I introduce my mother-in-law, Avril Parish—'

'I believe we've already met,' Fairfax said, with a little bow in Avril's direction. 'Your husband not with you today, Mrs Parish?'

Rona held her breath, but Avril answered calmly, 'No, he left me on my own, so my family took pity on me.'

Fairfax laughed. 'Quite right, too.'

'—my wife, Rona,' Max continued smoothly, 'and sister-in-law, Lindsey.'

Hands were shaken and smiles exchanged. Rona, having met his son Chris, surreptitiously studied the newcomer. Though he had a high forehead, his hair, steel-grey, was still plentiful over his crown and above his ears, while the brows over deep-set eyes remained dark, giving an impression of authority that was emphasized by the firmness of mouth and chin. Not a man to be trifled with, Rona guessed, concluding that Chris must have inherited the gentler features of his mother.

'Allow me to see to the drinks,' Fairfax was saying, waving away Max's automatic protest. 'I insist. It's not every day a famous artist graces my bar.'

He took their orders, had a word with the barman, and, apologetically excusing himself, left the room.

'A forceful character,' Lindsey murmured. 'Attractive, though.' She turned to her mother. 'I didn't know you knew him?'

'He banks at the National; we met briefly at one of their functions. I'm surprised he remembers.'

'Sign of a good hotelier,' Max said. 'Though he's usually behind the scenes, keeping his finger on the pulse. Front of the house is left to his son and daughter-in-law. And of course, his mother, who's the power behind the throne.'

'Aren't there two sons?'

'Yes, Chris and Gerald, who's the chef. He lives in one of the cottages down the road from Farthings. A bit of a loner, from what I've heard.'

'It's odd to think I've been coming here on and off for most of my life,' Rona remarked, 'yet everything I know about the family, I've learned in the last week.' Starting, she remembered, with Kate, and then Coralie. And thinking of Coralie, Rona wondered if she would in fact ever hear from her again.

That doubt was settled the next morning. Rona was at her desk, writing up the latest parent-search article, when the phone interrupted her.

'Rona? It's Coralie Davis. Have you thought any more about what I told you?'

'Yes, I have, Coralie, and I'd like to include it in the series, if you're willing?'

'That's why I'm ringing; I've discussed it with Brad, and

he agrees I should go ahead. It'll be good to have it all down in one piece, instead of on different scraps of paper, and as you said, it'd be something to hand on. So what's the next step?'

'I come round and go through it all with you in detail, using the tape recorder. It would help if you could have everything you've managed to find out to hand, and any photographs, birth or death certificates and so on.'

'You said you have several other cases to consider.'

'That's right.'

'So mine still mightn't make it into print?'

'From what you've already told me, I'd say it was a safe bet. One of the pluses is that you were older, and could remember things about your mother. So, when would it be convenient for me to call?'

'Well, it would have to be evenings or weekend.'

'An evening would be best.' One when Max was at Farthings. 'Would tomorrow suit you?'

'Sorry, we're going out tomorrow. How about Wednesday?'

Max's mid-week return. 'And I can't manage Wednesday. Thursday any good?'

Coralie laughed. 'Bingo! Let's make it Thursday. Straight after work would be best. I live out at Shellswick, so I don't get back till after six. Shall we say six thirty?'

'Fine.' Rona took down her address. 'See you on Thursday, then.'

As she put down the phone, her eyes fell on the case history she'd been working on and she realized, a little to her surprise, that she was starting to lose interest in the series. Though there'd been a good response, there was inevitably a sameness about the stories that made it difficult to present them in different and interesting ways. The first two, as she'd told Kate, had ended with joyful reunions. The third, that she was just finishing, had been less happy; the mother had refused to meet her son, though he'd established contact with his father. The half dozen or so she'd put to one side were divided more or less equally between the two outcomes.

Barnie had stipulated a minimum of four, and in Rona's opinion that would be enough. With luck, Coralie's would be a good one with which to end the series.

Ten minutes later, the phone rang again.

'Rona – it's Kate. Are you by any chance free for lunch?'

'Oh – hello, Kate. Yes, I think so.'

'Could you meet me at the Gallery at about twelve thirty? It'll be busy, so I'll book a table. Sorry – can't stop now. I'll explain when I see you.' And she rang off.

Rona stared at the phone for a minute before replacing it. Kate had been speaking quickly and quietly, as though she didn't want to be overheard. Until their chance meeting in the street last week, they'd not spoken more than a few words to each other in years. Yet here she was, wanting to meet again. Still, Rona reflected, if she was serious about researching local firms, Tarlton's would be as good a starting place as any.

At a quarter past twelve she completed the last page of the article, saved it on to a CD and switched off the computer. That, she thought with satisfaction, cleared the decks for the Coralie article, and after she'd done that, she'd approach Barnie with her idea of local family histories. The more she thought about it, the more pleased she was with the idea. She'd been feeling for some time that she should return to biographies, and this series could break her in, since each article would be a mini-bio. 'The Tarltons of Marsborough', for example. And if, she told herself, enthusiasm growing, one person stood out more strongly than the rest, perhaps she could make him or her the subject of a proper, full-blown biography.

'Gus!' she called, running down the stairs. 'We're going out for lunch!'

There was no sign of Kate when Rona and Gus arrived at the café, but a waitress showed her to the table Kate had reserved – one of the favoured window ones overlooking Guild Street. Gus, used to the procedure, went straight under the table, turned round a few times to settle himself, then lay down and went to sleep.

65

'Sorry!'

Rona looked up from the menu as Kate flopped into the chair opposite her. 'I was just about to leave when there was an influx of customers. Have you chosen what you're having?'

'I'm tempted by the steak and kidney pie. They're renowned for it here.'

'Right, let's go for it. And a bottle of red wine?'

'Why not?'

Once the order had been given, Kate settled back in her chair. Her eyes met and held Rona's. 'If you're wondering why I wanted to meet again so soon, it's because of Freya. You were with her when she collapsed, weren't you?'

'Well, yes, but—'

'We're all really worried about her; she's been getting progressively more edgy over the last few weeks, but keeps insisting there's nothing wrong. How did she seem to you, on Saturday?'

'Up to the time she fainted, perfectly fine. As you probably gathered, Max and I were choosing a watch, and she was very helpful, showing us lots of different styles, pointing out special features and so on.'

'And during all that, she didn't give any sign of not feeling well, or being under a strain?'

'No, not at all.'

Kate shook her head worriedly. 'I've a feeling Jan knows something, but she won't be drawn.'

Rona moved uncomfortably. 'Max and I thought it was the tune that upset her.'

Kate looked at her blankly. 'The tune?'

'From the musical box. I caught sight of it on the way out, and asked – Freya – what tune it played, but it had only just come in, and she didn't know. So she opened the lid, it began to play, and she just gave a little gasp and slid to the floor.'

Kate looked completely nonplussed. 'That must have been sheer coincidence, surely? I mean, how could a tune upset her?'

Rona shrugged.

66

Kate picked up the little glass pepper pot and began turning it round and round in her fingers. 'I've always thought the family was overprotective of her, but I'm beginning to wonder if something's really wrong.'

Their wine was brought and, after the usual procedure, poured into their glasses. As the waitress moved away, Rona asked curiously, 'Why should they be protective at all?'

'Because of what happened when she was little. She was only three when her mother left them, and it had a traumatic effect on her.'

'You say her mother "left". Do you know why?'

'I haven't liked to probe too deeply – Lewis is still a bit touchy about it – but I gather Velma was always flighty, and this wasn't by any means the first affair she'd had.'

'She went off with another man?'

'Oh yes. I think, from what Jan let drop once, that she'd left Robert before, when Lewis was about five, and that time she stayed away for a couple of months. I don't know whether she came back of her own volition, if her lover dumped her, or if Robert went in search of her.'

She paused and took a sip of wine. 'The sad thing is that I think he still loves her, even after all this time. Lewis said he kept hoping for years that she'd come back.'

'Did they know who she'd gone off with?'

'No. Years later, Robert told Lewis she'd left a note saying she was in love with someone else, that this time she was leaving for good, and not to try to find her, because they were going abroad.'

Rona was silent for a moment. Then she said tentatively, 'You say this had a traumatic effect on Freya. In what way?'

'Apparently she turned overnight from a happy, confident child to a timid little creature who hid in corners. Lewis said she didn't even *speak* for weeks. Eventually they took her to a child psychologist, who gave the opinion that she was suffering trauma over her mother's desertion.'

'Feasible, I suppose.'

'Personally,' Kate said slowly, 'I'm not convinced. From what Lewis says, Velma was never a doting mother, and they were largely brought up by Nanny Gray, who'd been with the Tarltons when Bruce and Robert were born. Velma's going didn't alter Freya's routine in the slightest: she was still in her own home, still had her father, who, then as now, adored her, and Nanny, who was her anchor. So why should she have reacted so violently?'

'But surely all this can't have any bearing on what's happening now?'

'According to psychologists, it can. Childhood traumas can be resurrected at any time, sometimes with disastrous results.'

'You say this edginess has increased over the last few weeks. What are the symptoms, exactly?'

'It's hard to pin down. I don't think she's sleeping well, though she hasn't actually said so, and now that she's moved in with her boyfriend there's no way of checking.'

'Could there be trouble with the boyfriend?'

'Doubtful. He's a nice guy, and they seem very happy together.'

'So what other symptoms are there, apart from not sleeping well, which you're not sure about?'

Kate smiled ruefully. 'If you're insinuating I've not much of a case, you're right. It's a nebulous feeling, that's all, but the whole family's suffering from it.'

'They've treated Freya with kid gloves all her life?'

'Not exactly kid gloves, but they do tend to tread softly round her, try not to upset her and so on. I think they're terrified she might have another relapse. She did have a rather rocky spell when she was twelve or thirteen, but it didn't come to anything.'

'What caused that?'

'They never found out, but again I think her sleeping was affected.'

'Nightmares?'

'Quite possibly, but everyone has them from time to time. We don't all go into a decline.'

A touch of waspishness, Rona noted, and steered her next question in a different direction. 'What about Lewis? Did his mother's leaving affect him?'

'Not to the same extent, but then he's ten years older.'

68

Rona raised her eyebrows. 'That's quite a gap! Was Freya an afterthought?'

Kate grimaced. 'More like a mistake, from what I gather. As I said, Velma wasn't exactly maternal; if Robert hadn't been so keen for a family, I doubt if she'd have had any.'

'And after she'd gone, Freya was looked after by the nanny,' Rona recapped thoughtfully.

'Just as she always had been. Jan stepped in, too, and became a mother-figure for both children. That's why there's a close bond between them.'

Their lunch finally arrived, and they began their meal in silence.

Thinking over their conversation, Rona wondered guiltily if she'd asked too many questions; an occupational hazard, she knew. To remedy matters, she now changed the subject.

'I'm considering a series of articles on long-established family businesses here in Marsborough. There's Tarlton's, of course, and the Clarendon, and Willows' Furniture, for a start. What do you think?'

'It's a great idea! Free publicity! What more could we ask?'

'I suppose you have archives or something, of how the firm began?'

'Bruce has sheaves of papers locked away, though I don't know exactly what they are. Probably just the bare bones – stock, prices, suppliers and so on, from year one – but he and Robert could fill you in on human-interest stories. They often talk about the old days and what a character their grandfather was.'

'That's exactly what I was hoping for. I'd have to clear it with my editor, but I'm pretty sure he'd give me the go-ahead. In a way, it would be doing for Marsborough what I did for Buckford, and there's been a very good response to that. People are more and more interested in local history these days.'

Talk moved on to other matters, and they were preparing to leave when Kate reverted to the topic that had brought them there. 'Well, it's been lovely seeing you. The only drawback is that we didn't get much further on what's wrong with Freya. I'll ask her about the tune, and see what she says.'

She looked up suddenly, her face brightening. 'Rona, I've just had a thought! Could *you* talk to her? As part of your research into the family? You're good at unearthing things, aren't you?'

'Oh, now look,' Rona began hastily, 'I don't want to intrude on people's private problems. I already feel guilty about asking so many questions.'

'Oh, nonsense. And, don't you see, it could help her! She might find it easier to talk to someone outside the family.'

'But even if I do start researching – and it's by no means definite – I'd begin, obviously, at the beginning, and it would be some time before I got down to the present generation.'

'You could get round that, I'm sure,' Kate said dismissively.

'I'm not a psychologist, Kate.'

'The one she saw didn't do her much good. I'd bet if anyone can find out what's troubling her, you can.'

'But you say she may have told her aunt. If so, she'll know what to do. I can't go butting in.'

'Well, we'll see what develops.' Kate smiled wryly. 'It seems I also find it easier to talk to someone who's not family. Sorry for the way I've been bending your ear.'

'I wish I'd been more help,' Rona said.

Rona made a detour on the way home, in order to call in at the offices of *Chiltern Life*. As usual, the receptionist welcomed them with a smile, willingly taking Gus's lead while Rona went upstairs to Barnie's office.

'How's my favourite journalist?' he greeted her. 'Dinah was asking at breakfast if I'd seen you lately; your ears must have been burning.'

The Trents, though older than Rona and Max, were good friends, and the two couples met socially on a fairly regular basis.

'How is she, and Melissa and the children?'

Barnie's married daughter, who lived in the States, was staying with them for a few months while her husband worked in the Gulf.

70

'Dinah and Mel are fine, and the kids are getting noisier by the hour. Or perhaps it only seems so!'

Rona smiled. 'You old grump! Mitch will be coming over soon, surely?'

'Yes, he has two weeks' leave over Christmas. Dinah was saying we must have a get-together while he's with us. Now, I'm a busy man, so enough of these pleasantries. Have you finished the parent-search articles?'

'I'll drop the third one in tomorrow – it just needs polishing – and I'm seeing a fourth possibility on Thursday. That should wrap it up nicely. What I wanted to speak to you about, though, is another series I'm contemplating.'

Barnie gave a gruff laugh. 'That's my girl – always one step ahead! All right, then, shoot.'

Rona explained her idea, emphasizing the interest in local history and the number of old-established firms in the town. 'It might work best as an occasional series,' she concluded, 'say an article every three or four months. But we could do a centre pull-out, as we did for the Buckford ones, in case people wanted to keep them. What do you think?'

'It sounds very promising, certainly. But could you gather enough information to make a go of it?'

'Oh, I think so, by the time you take in family histories. There should be plenty of anecdotes over the years. Anyway, they don't need to be very long, do they?'

'No, but if they're short, you'll need more of them to make it worthwhile.'

'I don't think numbers would be a problem. Many of the solicitors and accountants have been here since the year dot; I remember Lindsey going with Hugh to his firm's seventy-fifth anniversary.'

'Right, as long as you don't tread on any toes, you're on, but I'm not getting caught up in libel suits!'

Which, Rona acknowledged inwardly, was a timely warning before she took on the Tarltons. Velma's desertion and Freya's problems were likely to remain very definitely off limits.

*   *   *

71

Lindsey looked up from her computer as, following a cursory knock, Jonathan Hurst came into the room, closing the door behind him. He walked over to the desk, rested both hands on its surface and leaned forward until his face was only inches from hers.

Lindsey's pulse quickened. She knew she was playing with fire – she didn't need Rona to tell her that. Like herself, Jonathan was a partner in Chase Mortimer, the firm of solicitors where they worked, and if the other partners – or anyone else for that matter – learned of their liaison, both their careers would suffer. Quite apart from the fact that he was a married man with two children. Yet when she looked at him, at the quizzical grey eyes, the fair, greying hair falling over his brow as he bent forward, the humorous twist to his mouth, her resolutions faltered and she made no strenuous effort to resurrect them.

'Free this evening?' he asked.

She hesitated. Hugh had mentioned phoning, but no definite arrangement had been made. And Hugh, she thought with a sigh, was an added complication. Why *did* she allow herself to get into these situations?

'I think so. Why, are you?'

'I've managed to wangle a couple of hours, time enough to go back to your flat.'

'But not stay for dinner?'

'Sorry, sweetheart, my presence is required at home. We've some people coming; it wasn't easy getting the couple of hours.'

Lindsey said stiffly, 'Well, if you're sure you can spare the time.'

He gave a low laugh and, reaching forward, brushed his fingers lightly across her breast.

'I'm sure,' he said.

Since Gus had had little exercise that day, Rona delayed her return home still further and took him to Furze Hill Park, where they passed a pleasant hour in the large, uncultivated section at the upper end, Gus romping over the grass and sniffing out new scents, and Rona, not having his ball to hand, throwing sticks for his retrieval.

It was beginning to get dark when they finally turned into Lightbourne Avenue, and she was surprised to find a van parked outside her gate. As they came nearer, she saw it belonged to the florist, Camellia, and the delivery man was just returning down the path. He nodded towards the house.

'I couldn't get round the back, so I left the flowers on the step.'

'Thank you, but are you sure they're for me?'

'Allerdyce? That the name?'

'That's right.'

'They're yours, then. Enjoy!' And he climbed into his van, switched on his headlights, and drove away.

Rona let herself and Gus into the house, and bent to pick up the bouquet. Who could be sending her flowers? She carried them down to the kitchen, laid them on the table, and extracted the tiny envelope pinned to the cellophane. It was addressed to Mr and Mrs Allerdyce. Curiouser and curiouser. Rona slit it open and withdrew the little card.

With apologies for any embarrassment caused, she read. And the signature was Freya Tarlton.

Six

Tom lay in bed for some time on Tuesday morning, staring up at the guest-room ceiling. The previous evening, he had hosted a reception for branch managers and the senior partners of key clients, all accompanied by their wives, in order to bid each of them a personal farewell, and had been touched by the expressions of thanks and appreciation he'd received. Dorothy, Stephen and Ruth Fairfax had been among the guests, and he'd been caught off guard when Stephen mentioned seeing Avril at the Clarendon.

'She said you'd left her alone, so the family was taking pity on her,' Stephen reported with a smile.

Tom had managed to smile back and make a non-committal reply, surprised Rona hadn't warned him in advance, till he realized she wasn't to know he'd be meeting Fairfax. All the same, Stephen must have wondered why, since Avril was obviously well the previous day, she was not with him that evening, and the remembered comment about his leaving her might be given more weight. Ah well, by the end of the week all need for secrecy would have passed.

He stretched, letting his eyes move slowly round the room. Odd to think he'd spend only three more nights in this house, to which he had brought Avril as a bride. Come to think of it, he'd better make a start on packing up his things. Apart from clothes and personal items, there were a lot of official papers and documents in the desk in the dining room that would need sorting through. He'd make a start on them today, he resolved, since he wasn't going into the bank. No doubt a substantial amount could be thrown out, but most would need shredding first, and the only shredder he had to hand was a small electric one; it was to be hoped it would prove up to the task.

The eight o'clock pips sounded from the radio by his bed, and he swung his feet to the floor. Avril would be leaving for the library in under an hour, and she liked to clear away the breakfast things before she went.

'Good party?' she enquired, when he reached the kitchen twenty minutes later.

'Very enjoyable, thanks.' He paused. 'Stephen Fairfax was there; he mentioned having seen you.'

'Yes, Rona and Max took me out for Sunday lunch. Lindsey too. It was very pleasant.'

'I'm glad,' he said simply, sitting back to allow her to place a plate of scrambled eggs in front of him. How the hell did you scramble eggs? he wondered. Next week, in the flat, he'd be cooking for himself. He'd better have a few basic lessons from Catherine.

A thought occurred to him. 'If you're working at the library all week, the flu story won't hold much water.'

'Well, I'm certainly not going to stay off work,' she retorted, with a touch of the old asperity. 'Anyway,' she added more reasonably, 'it's highly unlikely that anyone coming into the library will be living it up at your receptions.'

He nodded, beginning on his breakfast. 'I think I'll make a start on packing up today.'

She turned quickly away, busying herself pouring water into the egg pan.

Misinterpreting her movement, he added awkwardly, 'Obviously I shan't be taking any of the ornaments or anything; only some books and the papers from the desk.'

'The ornaments are as much yours as mine,' she replied without turning. 'Take whichever you like.'

'They belong here,' he said gently. 'Avril, we shall be friends, shan't we? When all this has died down?'

'I don't know, Tom. I shan't be bitter and twisted – that's all over and done with – but friendship . . . I'm not sure if

I could cope with that. I certainly have no desire to meet your lady-love.'

Perhaps it had been clumsy of him to suggest it, Tom thought miserably. He didn't want to hurt her, but the mere fact of his leaving had already done that. He wanted it too easy, that was the trouble – to be with Catherine, but still be friends with Avril. Well, it looked as though that wasn't going to work. He just hoped to God that Lindsey would come round. He couldn't bear to lose one of his daughters as well.

'Rona? It's Kate. Just to let you know you were right about the tune, and I was right about the nightmares. They're linked, it seems, God knows how. When she saw how worried we were, she agreed to let Jan tell us, but personally I can't see what all the fuss is about. She dreams she's falling, which must be the most common of all dreams. Caused by a missed heartbeat, isn't it?'

'So where does the tune come in?' Rona asked.

'I'm not sure; I think it runs through the dream. And she's afraid someone else is there, just out of sight. Pretty standard stuff. The point is, though, she's dreaming it increasingly often and it's getting more detailed each time. The whole thing is spooking her, but she refuses point-blank to see anyone professional. Poor Matthew must be having a hell of a time with her.' Kate paused. 'Are you going ahead with the series, about the shops?'

'I think so, yes.'

'You will be starting with us, won't you? Please?'

'Kate, I really don't see what I can do. I'm not qualified in any way; if I started meddling, I could do her positive harm. Incidentally, she sent some flowers to apologize for fainting at our feet. It was very sweet of her – I've written her a brief note, hoping she's feeling better.'

'Suppose I invite you both to tea on Monday, when the shop's closed?'

'Kate—'

'Bless you, I knew you'd help. Three o'clock? We live

76

in Brindley Grove, a cul-de-sac off the Belmont Road. Brindley Lodge is at the far end, facing you; it backs on to woods.'

'I'd like to come to tea, thank you, but I don't promise anything else,' Rona said.

The phone call unsettled her. After an hour or so of making notes and promptly deleting them, she gave up and, wrapping up warmly, set off with Gus for an extended walk. There were a lot of things on her mind – Christmas and the parents, Freya and her disturbing dreams, and, particularly, Kate's conviction that she, Rona, could help her. Usually, the clear sharp air and exercise cleared her head, but today she felt as depressed when she returned as when she'd set out.

It was a pity Max wasn't coming home this evening; she was tired of her own company. She'd go to Dino's, she decided; that should cheer her up. The Italian restaurant was a mere five minutes' walk away, and though she hadn't booked, she knew Dino would find her a table. She was a regular customer, both with and without Max.

A cold wind had arisen by the time she and Gus set out, and the warmth of the restaurant met them with a palpable wave as she pushed open the door. At once she heard her name called and, turning, saw two couples she knew waving to attract her attention.

'Max not with you?' Patrick Kingston asked, as she walked over to them.

'No, it's one of his class nights.'

'Come and join us, then; we've only just ordered.'

Rona glanced at Dino, who, about to lead her to her own table, was awaiting her. 'Would that be all right?'

'But of course, signora. A chair will be brought at once.'

When they were settled and Gus had taken his place under the table, she turned to Hilary Grant. 'Thanks for your invitation; it arrived this morning.'

'Along with the Dawsons', I suppose? We had one from them.'

'It's that time of year, isn't it?' Georgia Kingston commented.

'We're also going to the Willows' do, so I've a good excuse to visit Magda's boutique!'

'You *do* move in exalted circles!' Hilary teased her.

'Don't you remember, Julian and I had a thing going, way back?'

'Lord, yes! I'd forgotten that.'

'You went out with Julian Willow?' Rona asked.

'In the year dot, yes. Do you know him?'

'No, but I'm . . . oh, it doesn't matter.' This wasn't the place to explain about her new project, and in any case she hadn't approached the Willows; if Georgia repeated the conversation, they'd have no idea what she was talking about.

'Come on, what were you going to say?'

'Only that I'm interested in the family at the moment. I'm hoping to write about some of the long-established businesses here.'

'And you want to know if John really started life as a barrow boy?'

Rona smiled. 'I haven't mentioned it to them yet, so please don't jump the gun.'

'My lips are sealed. But Julian will be useful to you; he's steeped in family lore. To be honest, he talked about it so much, he bored me rigid. At eighteen, ancestors are quite simply history. But I remember him showing me a diary kept by Sebastian, who was his great-grandfather, written in the most beautiful copperplate.'

'Sebastian Willow!' Hilary exclaimed. 'What a wonderful name.'

'It stood him in good stead,' Georgia said drily. 'He married an Honourable. Her family were scandalized at her marrying Trade, but she was an independent young lady and did as she pleased. I suspect it's because of that connection that the Willows give themselves airs.'

Their meal arrived and conversation became general. Simon Grant was an artist friend of Max's, and interested to know what he was working on at the moment.

'I saw the portrait he did of that MP chap. It was bloody good.'

'Well, he's reverted to landscapes at the moment, though

78

I did warn him it was the wrong time of year.'

Simon laughed. 'No doubt like me, he resorts to photographs and sketches, and does the main work in the warmth of his studio. Tell him we must get together sometime.'

The evening passed pleasantly, and as Rona made her way home through the cold streets, she admitted she was glad Coralie's story would close the present series. She was impatient to make a start on the next one.

Adele arrived as usual for the Wednesday class, and when Max made his round to check the students' work, he paused by her easel.

'I believe you phoned last Friday?' he said in a low voice.

She flushed a painful pink. 'It was stupid of me – I'm so sorry.'

'There's something you wanted to discuss?'

'Not really. I was just – panicking.'

He frowned. 'What about?'

'It was nothing, honestly. I was being neurotic.'

All his latent worries surfaced in a flood. 'If there's anything I can help with, you only—'

To his horror, he saw her eyes fill with tears. She shook her head blindly.

'Look,' he said quickly, aware of stirring interest among the rest of the class, 'stay behind at the end, and we'll try to sort this out.'

And he moved on, before she could protest again.

He was not at all sure she would stay, but she delayed over the gathering together of her equipment, and was still there when the last of the students had clattered down the stairs. As Max heard the front door close, he said quietly, 'Right, let's go down and have a cup of tea. I've half an hour before the next class.'

'I shouldn't impose on you like this,' she murmured, not meeting his eyes. 'You've already been more than kind.'

He motioned her ahead of him down the stairs and along the hall to the kitchen.

'Now, it's clear something's worrying you, so please tell me. Is it to do with your work?'

She shook her head. 'That's why I shouldn't inflict it on you.'

'On the contrary; if something's on your mind, it's bound to affect your painting,' he said, not sure how sound that assumption was. The kettle boiled and he made tea, poured it into mugs, and set them on the kitchen table, together with milk and sugar.

She glanced up at him beneath her lashes, then quickly down again, and Max remembered how this unwillingness to meet one's eye had irritated both Rona and Lindsey. Aware that time was passing and that he hadn't prepared for the next class, he was about to prompt her again when she said in a rush, 'It's just that I was feeling so unhappy, and I didn't know who to turn to.'

He studied her downcast face, the curve of her cheek and the creamy pallor of her skin, disturbingly aware of the protectiveness she aroused in him.

'Unhappy about what, Adele?'

'I don't know, really.' She took a quick sip of tea. 'After Daisy was born, I suffered from post-natal depression. It went on for years, and every now and then it – resurfaces. It's very hard on poor Philip.'

'But considerably harder on you,' Max returned sharply, and received another lightning glance. 'Can't your doctor help?' he asked more levelly.

'I get the impression he thinks I'm wasting his time.'

'That's totally unacceptable! If that's his attitude, you should change your GP.'

She drank her tea quickly, though it was still painfully hot. 'I'm holding you up; I must go.'

'You can't think what triggered this latest depression?'

'No, there's nothing.'

On a sudden impulse, Max leaned forward and, catching hold of her wrist, pushed up her sleeve. There was a minute's intense silence as he stared, horrified, at the livid bruises that covered her arm. Then, before he could move or speak, she gave a little sob, caught up her folder and handbag, and ran from the room. Seconds later, the front door banged shut.

* * *

'It's crystal-clear what happens,' Max said savagely, splashing whisky into his glass. 'She feels depressed, her husband can see no reason for it, and eventually loses his temper. She admitted it was "difficult" for him.'

Rona moved uncomfortably. 'That doesn't mean he actually *beats* her,' she pointed out. 'He might just seize her arms, give her a little shake—'

'And you think that's acceptable, when these "little shakes" leave such bruises?'

'I'm not saying it's acceptable, Max, just that it mightn't be as extreme as you seem to think. She has fair skin and might bruise easily.'

'At least admit I was right to be suspicious of the perpetual long sleeves.'

'It mightn't even be Philip who's responsible. She could have bumped into something—'

'*No*, Rona. You and Lindsey fobbed me off with that before. It won't wash this time.'

Rona sat back in her chair and stared at him belligerently.

'So what do you propose to do about it?'

For a moment he held her gaze. Then she saw the fight go out of him, and his shoulders slumped. 'God knows. I can hardly go round and read him the Riot Act.'

'Exactly.'

'So we all just turn a blind eye? Is that what you're suggesting? Walk by on the other side?'

'Oh, for God's sake!' Rona said irritably.

'Well? Is that what you're proposing?'

'I'm not proposing anything. You've made Adele your protégée; it's up to you how you deal with her.'

'Thanks for your support.'

'Well, what do you expect me to say?' Rona flared. 'You've been obsessed with that woman from day one, and frankly I'm sick of hearing about her and her problems. You have absolutely no evidence of any trouble between her and Philip, and you admit you can't storm round there and accuse him. You could end up being sued for slander. Nor can you report your suspicions to anyone,

81

since you've no basis for them other than occasional bruises.'

'Occasional? She *always* covers her arms, as you well know, and the only other time I saw one bare – five months ago, mind you – it was also covered in bruises. What do you deduce from that?'

Rona thought back to her meetings with Adele, visualizing the small, pointed face, the slatey eyes so unwilling to meet hers, the short, ash-blonde hair curving on to her cheek. Portrait of a born victim, she thought. If she hadn't been so petite and pretty, would Max still have played knight errant?

'Persuade her to see her doctor again,' she said at last. 'That is literally all you can do.'

The same advice, she reflected, as she might soon be offering to Freya Tarlton.

Having already delivered the third article to *Chiltern Life*, Rona spent most of the next morning preparing for her meeting with Coralie Davis. This case had raised several questions, and she hoped they'd be satisfactorily resolved. If not, or if the search was incomplete – as Coralie had half-hinted – it might not qualify for inclusion; in which case she'd have to resort to the half-dozen or so she'd discarded, in search of a substitute.

The phone rang, and a cheerful voice said in her ear, 'Hi, Rona! Where have you been hiding these last weeks?'

'Magda! Good to hear from you. How are you?'

Magda Ridgeway had been her closest friend since childhood, and was married to Gavin, to whom Rona had been briefly engaged before meeting Max. She was the owner of a string of highly successful boutiques scattered about the county.

'Oh, rushing from pillar to post, as usual – New York, Paris, Rome.'

'As one does!'

'The reason I'm phoning is that there's a concert at the Darcy Hall on Saturday. We were taking friends who should have been spending the weekend with us, but they've had to cry off, and we wondered if you'd like to join us? They're doing *Messiah*.'

'I'll check with Max, but I'm sure we'd love to. Two party invitations and now the *Messiah* too – Christmas is coming, and I've not even ordered my cards!'

'So what *have* you been doing? Are you still on this finding parents kick?' It had been at Gavin's birthday party that the whole idea had been born.

'Coming to the end of it, actually. One to go.'

'So no doubt you're already looking ahead. What next?'

'A series on long-established local businesses -- shops, firms, hotels, and so on.'

'Including me, I trust?'

'You hardly qualify, love; you've only been going six years!'

'I was afraid you'd say that. Sounds promising, though. It'll be interesting to hear how they all started.'

When she had rung off, all Rona's apprehension about Christmas returned in full measure. They'd still not decided how or with whom they'd spend the day, and she dreaded ending up by having to go to her mother's and sit round the table as they had every Christmas of her life, but without her father there to carve the turkey. She *must* tie Max and Lindsey down to a decision.

It was after eight o'clock when she arrived back from Shellswick. She dumped the photograph albums and papers Coralie had given her on the bottom stair, and ran down to the basement to give Gus his supper and prepare something for herself. Impatient to transcribe the tape with the interview fresh in her mind, she took out a frozen cottage pie and lit the oven, smiling at Max's imagined disapproval. Cooking was a chore to her, and she indulged in it as little as possible.

While the pie was heating through, she went upstairs, switched on the computer, and opened the document she'd already prepared for Coralie. So – what had she learned, and was it interesting enough to qualify for inclusion in the series? She thought that it was; the Hong Kong element lent an air of glamour, and the fact that Coralie could remember her early years singled it out from the previous accounts.

Rona switched on the tape, listening to the halting voice as Coralie related the traumas of her past, and mechanically transcribing them on to the screen.

Having learned from the adoption agency that she'd been abandoned in Woodbourne, she had gone to the town and driven round till she found the park and row of houses she remembered. There, by dint of ringing doorbells, she'd learned that a family named Craig had lived at number five at the relevant time, but they'd moved away and no one knew where they were. The electoral register, duly consulted, gave their names as Graham and Judith, and Coralie had then turned the information over to an organization specializing in that field, who traced them to Hertford.

Rona heard her own voice ask, 'Judith never tried to find you?'

'No.'

'You did meet her, though?'

'Eventually. She took a lot of persuading, terrified her husband would find out, but curiosity got the better of her. It wasn't much of a meeting, though. She cried the whole time, and kept saying how sorry she was. She'd never told Graham about me, which might be why he reacted as he did, and she insisted she'd have kept me if she could. To be honest, though, I didn't feel anything for her. She certainly didn't seem like my mother.'

'And Lena?'

Coralie's voice brightened. 'That was the one good thing to come out of it; Judith gave me Lena's address. We've been writing to each other, and I'm going out to Hong Kong in the New Year to stay with her and Jim, and to meet my father. He's married now with a family, so I have half-brothers and sisters, which is an exciting thought.'

The reason for taking the child to the Craigs was also explained; Jim Chan had been offered a government job in Hong Kong, and had panicked, thinking that if the irregular

84

arrangement over Coralie came out, he'd be in trouble. But once they were settled there, they'd written to Judith asking if they could have her back and adopt her formally, and were shattered to learn what had happened.

Rona again: 'Why didn't they take you out to your father, since they were all going to be in Hong Kong?'

'That was the first thing I asked her. She told me he'd been a very wild young man, and was in prison at the time. It would have been an added complication. So – that's the story, and I'm glad I went through with it. I now know who I am and exactly what happened, and the bonus is that I'm in touch with Lena again.'

The recording ended there, a fact Rona now regretted. Because, interesting though the parent search had been, their subsequent conversation, concerning the Fairfaxes, had intrigued her more. As her mind went back over it, she began to tap it out on the keyboard.

Coralie had come to Marsborough six years ago, when Andy, her boyfriend at the time, had moved here with his job, and she had worked at the Clarendon to help pay for the secretarial course she was taking at night school.

'Did you enjoy it?' Rona had asked idly, remembering the encounter in the hall.

'Yes, on the whole. As you know, it's family-run, so there were two Mrs Fairfaxes and three Misters – though Gerald was known as "Chef", if you please. Pretentious, or what? To avoid confusion we called them Mrs Dorothy, Mrs Ruth, and so on. I suppose it made sense, but it made me feel like a family retainer.'

She'd smiled reminiscently. 'It was quite an eye-opener, seeing how they interact. Mrs Dorothy's the queen bee, but she has her soft side and positively dotes on her grandsons, while Mrs Ruth is calm and efficient and makes the day-to-day decisions. Chris – well, Chris is just Chris, plodding along and doing his job, but the sparks often flew between Gerald and his father. Mr Stephen was always criticizing him, but then he's a moody so-and-so at the best of times, and drinks like a fish; though, give him his due, he can hold it. Occupational hazard, perhaps.' Coralie had shot her a glance. 'I probably shouldn't be saying this, but I wouldn't be surprised if Gerald batted for the other side, if you see what I mean. That could be what gets his father's goat.'

It seemed wiser not to comment, but Rona, intrigued by this insider view of the Fairfaxes, had decided to probe a little further.

'Didn't you say before that you were only there six months?'

'That's right.'

'And that was enough to fund your course? You must be a wealthy woman!'

Coralie laughed. 'Spot the deliberate mistake. You're right – I'd meant to stay longer, but fate intervened. No doubt you noticed the atmosphere between Chris and me.'

'I'm sorry,' Rona said belatedly, 'it's none of my business.'

'Oh, it's no secret, but you need to know the background. Chris and Sophie had been going out together for some time, but shortly before I started there, she met Lewis Tarlton at a family wedding, they had a whirlwind romance, and married within weeks. Chris was devastated, especially since she carried on working at the hotel. She couldn't have realized what it was doing to him, because she's normally so considerate of everyone's feelings. I suppose she was on cloud nine, and blind to everything else.

'Anyway, that was the state he was in when I arrived. Then, one evening when I was delivering room service, I met him in the upstairs corridor. He was very drunk, and since I didn't want any of the guests to see him, I helped him up to his room. Big mistake. You can guess what happened.'

'You had an affair with him?'

'Yes; I liked him, and my pride had been hurt by Andy dumping me. It was good to feel I was still attractive. But after a month or two we were discovered, and all hell broke loose. I was sent packing, with a handsome severance pay in lieu of notice. It was most efficiently hushed up – by Mrs Dorothy, no doubt – and none of the rest of the staff knew why I was leaving. It wasn't put into words, but the understanding was that I shouldn't darken their doors again. Hence Chris's reaction, when he saw me with you.'

'Did you feel unfairly treated?'

Coralie had shrugged. 'I don't see what else they could have done. I've no hard feelings.'

'And eventually Lewis and Sophie divorced, and Chris got her after all.'

'Yes. Happy endings all round.'

Rona sat back in her chair, reading over what she'd typed. Then, with a sigh, she deleted it. Though an intriguing insight into the Fairfax family, none of it could be used in an article, and, reluctantly putting it out of her mind, she went downstairs to her cottage pie.

Stephen Fairfax poured himself a stiff shot of whisky. What the hell was the matter with him? he wondered irritably. Everything was going smoothly, the restaurant full most evenings, a waiting list for all the Christmas meals, an excellent write-up in the latest food magazine. Gerald was good at his job, no denying that. If only the boy would be a bit more *manly*, stand his ground occasionally, instead of jumping like a startled rabbit every time he, Stephen, appeared.

He tossed the whisky back, feeling it burn the back of his throat, and immediately poured another. So what was needling him? Well, for one thing, Mother was getting a bit doddery, bless her; he'd seen her stumble a couple of times during the last week, and she'd knocked into an occasional table in her flat, sending a vase of flowers crashing to the ground. It had been a trifling accident, and he'd been startled to see her eyes fill with tears. Was she ill, perhaps, hiding something from them? He'd ask Ruth to have a word with her; it would come better from her, especially since it might be women's problems.

As always at the thought of his wife, he felt himself

relax. Thank God for Ruthie; she was more than he deserved. Though Mother liked to consider herself the matriarch, it was Ruth who was the linchpin, holding the family together.

Come to think of it, he reflected, cradling the glass in his hand, another concern, barely acknowledged, was his own health. He'd had an attack of palpitations last week, and, frankly, it had frightened him. God knew what it indicated – high blood pressure, probably – but no doubt the cure lay in his own hands: cut down on the hard stuff. He knew Ruth worried about his drinking; she'd hinted once or twice that he was overdoing it, and he'd bitten her head off for her pains, though he'd apologized later. A man had to have some vices, he'd said.

Time Chris and Sophie were starting a family, he thought suddenly. They'd been married over three years now, and not getting any younger. The sooner a new generation of Fairfaxes was in the pipeline, the better.

He turned as the door opened and his wife came into the room. She glanced at the glass he held, but all she said was, 'The Mayor and his wife are in the restaurant. It might be prudent to go and have a word with them.'

'Let's be prudent, by all means.'

She frowned. 'Is everything all right, darling?'

'You tell me. Sometimes it feels as if I'm balanced on a powder keg.' Then, seeing her troubled expression, he went on quickly, 'Don't mind me. Actually, I was just wondering when Chris and Sophie are going to make us grandparents. No hint of it, I suppose?'

'I haven't heard anything, but it's not something we can ask.'

'Well, we're on a hiding to nothing if we wait for Gerald.'

'Don't talk like that, Stephen. One of these days a nice girl will come along.'

If that's what he wants, Stephen thought darkly.

Ruth reached up and kissed him gently on the lips. 'So how about leaving the young to lead their own lives, getting off your powder keg, and going down to be civil to the Mayor?'

He laughed and put an arm round her. 'Right as always, my love. That's exactly what I shall do.'

Seven

Freya sat shivering at the kitchen table, a mug of hot chocolate between her hands. Though she made no sound, tears were streaming down her cheeks. Please make the dreams stop! she prayed, to anyone who would listen. I can't take much more!

She turned as Matthew came into the room. 'Sorry, Matt, I tried not to wake you.'

He sat down next to her, and she turned to him with swimming eyes. 'It was odd this time; I knew I was dreaming, and I was desperately trying to wake up, but I couldn't force my eyes open.'

He laid a hand on her knee. 'It progressed again?'

She nodded. 'There were angry voices, and then someone sobbing – horrible, deep sobs.'

She set her mug down so suddenly that the liquid slopped on to the table, and when she looked at him, there was horror in her eyes. 'Matthew, it was a *man* sobbing! Oh God, what can I do? I keep telling myself a dream can't hurt me, but when I'm actually dreaming it, that doesn't help.'

'Honey, you can't go on like this – really you can't. You're getting paler and thinner by the week. *Why* won't you agree to see someone?'

'Because I'm not having anyone messing with my mind! Anyway, what could I tell them? It sounds so pathetic, letting a dream upset me so much.'

'But they might be able to find out what's causing it.'

Freya shuddered. 'I'm not sure I want to know.'

She stood up abruptly. 'Definitely no psychiatrists, Matthew. OK? Come on, it's over now. Let's go back to bed.'

*   *   *

Friday morning, the twenty-fifth of November. His birthday, and his last day at the bank. Not much work would be done today, but he'd arranged to go in about eleven and clear the final things from his desk. He'd then have lunch with senior members of staff, before making himself scarce until the farewell reception at six.

Tom showered, dressed, and put his pyjamas and wash things in his overnight bag. They were the last of his possessions remaining in the house, and he'd take them with him when he finally left in a couple of hours' time.

He'd be glad when this series of goodbyes was over. On Wednesday, he'd taken the train to London for a presentation at Head Office, which had been followed by dinner with the General Manager and his wife. Two managers from other branches who, like himself, were retiring, were also present with their wives, and as on Monday, Avril's absence was explained by a dose of flu. He'd travelled back the next day, with a new carriage clock in his case. There wasn't a clock at the flat, so it would come in useful.

Snapping his bag shut, he went down to breakfast, where he was taken aback to find a pile of envelopes beside his plate.

'Happy birthday,' Avril said, and reached up to kiss his cheek.

'Thank you.' He riffled through the envelopes, recognizing the handwriting in most cases before opening them. Nothing, he noticed with a heavy heart, from Lindsey. Avril had slipped a couple of envelopes among the others, one containing a birthday card, the other a retirement card.

'Thank you,' Tom said again, unaccountably embarrassed. 'That's very sweet of you.'

'The girls are going with you this evening?'

'Rona and Max are.'

She made no comment, and he wondered if she'd spoken to Lindsey about it. The two of them had always been close, as had he and Rona. Families, he thought; divided, we fall.

Avril laid a package on the table. 'Just a little some-

91

thing to pass the time, since you'll be at a loose end.'

He looked at her quickly, unsure if she was joking, and her smile reassured him that she was. The package contained the latest novel by one of his favourite authors.

'It's hot off the press,' she told him. 'We had advance notice at the library.'

'That's very thoughtful of you. I'll enjoy that.'

The phone rang, and she went to answer it, returning a moment later with it in her hand. 'Rona,' she said.

'Many Happies, Pops! How does it feel to be almost a gentleman of leisure?'

'I'll let you know. Thanks for your card, darling.'

'There's more to follow when we see you this evening. What are the arrangements?'

'I have to be there by ten to six. I suggest we gather in the Clarendon bar at five thirty, and we can walk from there.'

'Fine. See you then. Lots of love.'

Breakfast was finished and all the cards opened. In a few minutes, Avril would be leaving for the library. Better to go now, when she did, instead of hanging round here in the empty house. He could drive to the flat to drop off his bag. Self-consciously he collected the cards together and put them in his briefcase. In previous years, they'd been arrayed on the sitting-room mantelpiece.

The final moment of leaving, which he'd been dreading for weeks, had arrived. What could he say to her? He'd been trying to think of something appropriate, but conventional phrases such as 'We must keep in touch' didn't fit the bill, since she'd indicated that she didn't want to. And he'd already given her his new address and phone number, to pass on as necessary.

In the end, it was she who took the initiative. As he hesitated in the hallway, overnight bag in hand, she said quickly, 'You asked if we could be friends, Tom. I – would like to, after all.'

'That's great, Avril,' he replied warmly. 'When we've shared so much, it would be a shame if—'

He broke off, unable to go on. Quickly she put her arms round him and he drew her close with his free arm. How

92

long since they'd stood like this? But now was not the time to look back. His throat tight, he bent his head and kissed her gently on the lips.

'Goodbye, Avril. Thanks for everything.' And, thank God, he could say it after all: 'I'll be in touch.'

As he turned for the last time out of Maple Drive, his eyes were full of tears.

Rona had tried to phone Lindsey the previous evening, to beg her to reconsider her boycott of the retirement party. There'd been no reply, and she'd left what she feared was an inadequate message on the answerphone.

That morning, she tried to reach her at Chase Mortimer, again without success. 'Miss Parish is with a client,' she'd been told.

'Please would you tell her her sister called, and I'm looking forward to seeing her this evening.'

'I'll see she gets the message, Miss Parish.'

A plethora of Miss Parishes, Rona thought in amusement as she replaced the phone, and neither of them strictly accurate. Lindsey had reverted to her maiden name on divorcing Hugh, while Rona herself, to her parents' horror, had refused to give up hers when she married Max. 'It's who I am!' she'd protested. 'And also the name I use professionally.'

Perhaps the Fairfaxes had a point, she thought, remembering what Coralie had told her. And, thinking of Coralie, she reached for the envelope and albums she'd brought back the previous evening.

As she'd been warned, there was only passing interest in the photographs. The tiny Chinese girl grew bigger page by page, as exotic as an orchid in the pleasant, typically English company of her adoptive parents. She knew virtually nothing about this couple, Rona realized; only that they had loved and supported Coralie, helping her to forget her disturbed past, but ready to back her when she attempted to resurrect it. Did they, she wondered, fear that when she met Lena again, they might lose her for ever?

She opened the large buff envelope and drew out certificates,

93

letters and search reports which, while confirming Coralie's story, added little to it. What she really wanted were photographs of Lena and Jim Chan, or Judith Craig – even Samuel – but, unless Lena had sent some from Hong Kong – and Coralie hadn't volunteered any – it seemed a vain hope.

With a sigh, she switched on the recorder and prepared to write her final article on the subject.

Since Max had no definite commitments on Fridays, he came back to the house at four to shower and change.

'Did you manage to contact Lindsey?' he asked, pulling off his sweater.

'No. I can't believe she's behaving like this, whatever she feels privately. It's like a slap in the face for her not to be there. Two lots of flu are too much to swallow.' Angrily, Rona tossed the dress she'd chosen on to the bed. 'I think the best policy is not to mention her at all, at least to Pops.'

Max held his peace. Lindsey's behaviour didn't particularly surprise him; he'd formed the opinion some time ago that, unlike her sister, Lindsey Parish seldom considered other people's feelings, and nothing she'd done so far had changed his mind.

Tom was waiting in the bar when they reached the Clarendon, and had their drinks lined up on the table. Rona handed over his birthday present – a pair of gold cufflinks – and despite his profuse thanks and the general chat and laughter, Rona noted with a tug of the heart that his eyes kept straying to the door. I could *kill* her! she thought savagely. How *dare* she not be here?

And then, suddenly, she was. They all spun round as a laughing voice said, 'Greetings, everyone! Happy birthday and happy retirement, Pops!'

Tom's face lit up as he returned her hug, took the parcel she handed him, and unwrapped an engraved silver hip flask.

'I've never had so much valuable stuff in my life!' he joked. 'Thank you so much, all of you, you've been more

94

than generous. Now, Lindsey, let's see about getting you a drink.'

As he went purposefully to the bar, Rona said softly, 'Thanks, sis.'

'You should know by now that my bark's worse than my bite,' Lindsey replied.

'We're going for a meal afterwards,' Max commented, hiding his annoyance with her. 'As you know, Tom won't be joining us, but if you'd like to, you'd be very welcome.'

Lindsey flushed. 'Sweet of you, Max, but I have a dinner date, thank you.'

'Tweedledum or Tweedledee?' Rona asked facetiously, and Lindsey did not reply.

Rona did not enjoy the retirement party, though she could not have said why. True, there were few people she knew, and she was constantly on edge, anticipating questions about her mother. Also, it felt like the end of an era. For as long as she could remember, her father had worked in this bank, and the fact that he would no longer be doing so seemed to her an intimation of mortality. Which, she told herself roundly, accepting another glass of wine, was plain ridiculous. He was not an old man; on the contrary, he was about to embark on what promised to be a very happy phase of his life. But the fact remained that he had suffered two heart attacks, and no amount of self-rallying could raise her spirits.

The presentation was duly made – in this instance, a crystal decanter – and there was an elaborately wrapped present for 'Mrs Parish, who, much to our regret, can't be with us this evening. Give her our best, Tom, and good wishes for a speedy recovery.'

Then, at last, they were free to go. They said goodbye to Tom, who was finding it difficult to break away from all the handshakes and back-slapping, thanked their hosts, and went out together into the cold and misty street. Across the road, the lights in Darcy Hall shone through the dark.

'We'll be there ourselves tomorrow,' Rona told Lindsey. 'We're going with Magda and Gavin to hear the *Messiah*.'

'Say hello to them for me. Where are you eating this evening? Dino's?'

'No, we're branching out. A new restaurant, at the far end of Guild Street.'

Lindsey looked at them sharply. 'Serendipity?'

Rona started to laugh. 'Is that where you're going with lover boy? Don't worry, Linz, we'll keep our eyes on our plates!'

'"Of all the gin joints . . ."' Max quoted softly.

'Very funny, both of you.'

'How are you getting there?' Max asked.

Lindsey nodded across the road, to Market Street car park. 'My car's over there.'

'So is ours.'

They crossed the road together. 'Lucky Tom's reception started early, or we'd have had trouble finding a place,' Max remarked, indicating the tightly packed cars. 'It's always like this when Darcy Hall has something on.'

He stopped as they reached their car.

'Mine's just over there,' Lindsey said.

'See you later, then.'

The new restaurant was nothing if not sumptuous. The main floor was laid out like an Elizabethan knot garden, with a continuous waist-high partition snaking in and out around the tables, giving the illusion of privacy, while in the centre a table displayed the magnificent figure of a dolphin, carved out of ice.

On either side of the room stood a counter, one displaying raw meat and the other fish, and set into the wall behind each was a charcoal grill. Beyond the counters, two galleries, accessed by a few steps, stretched to the far end of the room. Most of the tables on them, Rona noticed, were already occupied.

'Impressive, or what?' Max said sotto voce, as a waiter led them to their table. 'Dino had better look to his laurels.'

The waiter seated them with a flourish, shook large white napkins on to their laps, and handed each of them a glossy menu.

'The starred dishes,' he explained, 'offer you the choice of selecting your own cut of meat or fish and having it grilled individually to your taste. The wine waiter will be along in a minute. Enjoy your meal.'

'On reflection,' Max commented, 'I'm not sure Dino need be too worried. Have you seen the prices?'

'No, they're not shown on my menu.' Rona looked up, and was in time to see her sister hesitating just inside the door.

'Here's Linz now,' she said flatly, 'and look who's with her.'

'Your ex-brother-in-law, as I live and breathe.'

Hugh, tall, pale-faced and red-headed, was following Lindsey down the room, and for a heart-stopping minute Rona feared they might be seated near themselves. Fortunately, though, their table was further down the room, and as they passed them, Lindsey gave an ironic little wave and Hugh, catching Rona's eye, nodded briefly.

'Love you, too,' she said softly.

They ordered the wine and their first courses, and, having both opted for the grill, were advised to go up and make their selection.

'They won't be ready until you've finished your first course,' the waiter explained, as he motioned them to the front of the restaurant, 'but there are several orders ahead of you, and as it's cooked on a first come, first served basis, it's wise to place yours as soon as you've selected it.'

After studying the food on offer, Max elected to have lamb cutlets and Rona sea bass, and they were about to return to their table when the door behind them opened and Tom came in with Catherine Bishop. Even if they'd wanted it, there was no time to take avoiding action.

Tom was the first to find his voice. 'Well, well, we meet again! Catherine, you know Rona, of course, but I don't think you've met my son-in-law, Max Allerdyce. This, as you'll have gathered, Max, is my fiancée.'

Catherine smiled acknowledgement of Rona, and took Max's hand. 'I'm delighted to meet you. I've been an

97

admirer of your work for some time, as Rona might have told you.'

'And I ungraciously declined to speak to your Art Appreciation Society,' Max said, 'for which I belatedly apologize.' His mouth twitched. 'Possibly, now that you're almost family, I might reconsider.'

A waiter was hovering to show Tom and Catherine to their table, and as her father passed her, Rona said in a low voice, 'Incidentally, Lindsey's also here. With Hugh.'

Tom stopped in his tracks. 'Hugh? Good God, I thought all that was supposed to be in the past.'

'Not any more, it seems. Have a good evening, Pops. Nice to see you, Catherine,' she added – naturally, she hoped – and smiled at Catherine's murmured agreement.

'Bloody hell!' Tom said succinctly, when their waiter had left them with their menus. 'Here I was, hoping for an intimate *dîner à deux*, and I find it's to be conducted under the eagle eyes of both my daughters!'

Catherine laughed softly. 'Max is charming, isn't he? And so distinguished-looking, with that thick white hair. He can't be out of his forties, surely?'

'No; he apparently went white in his twenties. His sister is the same.'

'Darling, I don't want to search the room,' Catherine murmured, 'but have you located Lindsey?'

'No, and I don't particularly want to. Things have been a little strained between us, but she turned up trumps this evening, bless her, coming to the reception, and with a handsome present for good measure. If I see her with Hugh, my disapproval might show and we'd be back to square one. However, if we do catch sight of each other, of course I shall introduce you.'

'My God!' Lindsey exclaimed suddenly. 'There's Pops, with his fancy woman.'

Hugh looked up from his menu. 'Where?'

'Up on the gallery to your left, about the fourth table from the end. I wonder if they've seen us? Or Ro and Max, come to that.'

'Poor guy,' Hugh said, 'hoping to spend a romantic evening with his lady-love, and finding almost his entire family here. I'm experiencing much the same thing myself.'

'There's no point in our being secretive any more,' Lindsey agreed. 'Not,' she added, 'that there's really anything to be secretive *about*.'

'More's the pity,' Hugh muttered.

Her eyes had strayed back to the gallery. 'I can't *think* what he sees in her,' she said.

'Oh, I don't know; she has a certain something,' Hugh returned, studying the unaware Catherine. 'Poise, elegance, a charming smile.'

'Too long in the tooth for *you*, at any rate,' Lindsey said waspishly.

Hugh flicked her a glance, and his mouth twitched. 'I wouldn't say that,' he murmured consideringly. 'Sex appeal has no age limit, after all.'

'Men!' Lindsey exclaimed disgustedly, and Hugh, satisfied, let the subject drop.

'So what do you think of her?' Rona asked.

'Very attractive.'

She looked at him in surprise. 'Really? So do I, but I can't convince Linz. All right, she's not conventionally pretty, but she has a lovely smile – lovely eyes, too – and she's always so perfectly groomed, it's a pleasure to look at her.'

'You like her, don't you?'

'Very much. I always have. She helped me with my Buckford project, if you remember.'

'Oh, I remember, but I didn't realize you felt so warmly about her. Why didn't you say so?'

Rona shrugged. 'Almost as soon as I met her, I saw her with Pops that evening, which put the kibosh on everything. After that – well, divided loyalties, I suppose.' She paused. 'Will you really talk to her society? Won't it be starting a precedent, or opening the floodgates, or something?'

Max laughed. 'My darling girl, I'm not as avidly sought

after as you seem to think. I believe I can safely make an exception in Catherine's case. If, that is, she asks me again.'

'Oh, she will,' Rona said confidently. 'Believe me, she will.'

Since Lindsey and Hugh were still at their table when they were about to leave, Tom made a point of taking Catherine across to meet them. Hugh came to his feet, his eyes appraisingly on her, but after a quick, acknowledging glance, Lindsey's eyes dropped.

Aware of the embarrassment on all sides, Catherine said easily, 'Isn't this a splendid place? A real asset to the town. How long has it been open, do you know?'

It was Hugh who answered. 'About a month. Our firm received flyers, advising us of the opening. They don't serve lunches, incidentally; only dinners.'

'Very wise,' Tom commented. 'There'd be nowhere to park at lunchtime, whereas the meters are free after six. I'm sure they'll do well, particularly in the run-up to Christmas. Well, we must be on our way. Enjoy the rest of your meal.' And with his hand under Catherine's elbow, he steered her away from their assessing eyes.

'One more hurdle over,' he said, as they reached the car and he opened the passenger door for her. 'It'll be easier next time, I promise.'

Catherine wasn't so sure. There was a surly air about Lindsey very different from her twin's openness. She could, Catherine felt, hold grudges indefinitely.

Tom started the engine, and after a few yards, turned off Guild Street into Windsor Way.

'There's no need to drop me off, Tom,' Catherine said softly. 'If I may, I'd like to be with you your first night in the flat.' And at his exclamation, she added, 'Yes, I know; we said we wouldn't spend a night together till we're married, but this is a one-off. It's your birthday, your retirement and – to paraphrase – the first night of the rest of your life. You wouldn't mind, would you?'

'Mind?' Tom echoed, his voice choked. 'I can think of nothing more wonderful.'

*   *   *

On the Saturday morning, Max received a phone call from his sister.

'I promised to report back after Father had seen the doctor,' she began. 'I tried to ring you last night, but there was no reply, and I didn't want to leave a message.'

'How is he?' Max asked quickly.

'Actually, he seems a little better. His appointment was yesterday morning; I ran him there, of course, but he refused point-blank to allow me to go in with him, so I have only an edited version of what transpired. However, he seems to have had a thorough going-over and was prescribed some antibiotics, which, naturally, he scoffs at. But I made him promise to take them.'

'No sign of pneumonia?' That had been Max's secret fear.

'Not as far as I know.'

'Then let's hope the medicine gives him an appetite. He'd be a lot stronger if he ate properly.'

'I've been telling him that for weeks.'

'Thanks for letting me know, Cyn. I'll phone you next weekend, and hope for some positive progress.'

The Darcy Hall was packed for the performance of the *Messiah*, and judging by the continuing applause when it ended, the audience had enjoyed it to the full.

'It's only ten o'clock,' Gavin remarked as they filed slowly out of the hall. 'How about some wine and tapas at the Bacchus?'

'Excellent idea,' Max approved, and they walked the hundred yards or so to the wine bar along the road. It seemed others had had the same idea, and they were lucky to get the last vacant table.

'So,' Gavin began, when the food and wine had been served, 'what are you two up to these days?'

'Max has been commissioned to paint local landscapes for a calendar,' Rona volunteered. 'Talk about forward planning – it's for the year after next.'

'I'm trying to choose appropriate scenes for each month,' Max explained. 'They don't all have to be rural, and I've

101

made some preliminary sketches of Guild Street resplendent with its Christmas lights. With the old Georgian frontages, it should be very effective.'

'Put our name down for one!' Magda said, reaching for a stuffed squid.

Gavin turned to Rona. 'As for you, I can't open *Chiltern Life* these days without seeing your byline! Not thinking of a takeover bid, are you?'

'I'm still trying to get her back to biographies,' Max said ruefully. 'It seems a far less hazardous occupation.'

'Well, you'll have to put it on hold,' Magda told him. 'She's already planning a new set of articles, aren't you, Rona? On long-standing local shops and businesses.'

Gavin looked up. 'That should be interesting; who will you start with?'

Rona hesitated. 'I'll have to sound them out first, but I thought probably Tarlton's – the jewellers.'

'Good choice,' Gavin nodded. 'Not only a long-established business, but with interesting personal stories as well, if you can get them to open up.'

'Such as Lewis's ex marrying one of the Clarendon lot?' asked Magda, with her mouth full.

'That, of course, but also the flighty wife fleeing the marital bed.'

'Spare us the journalese, Gavin,' Max said. 'Elucidate.'

'Oh, it was years ago now, but old Robert's wife did a bunk with her lover and left him holding the baby. Two of them, in fact.' He bit into a prawn. 'Actually, I knew her – Velma Tarlton. My mother used to play tennis with her.'

'Gavin, that's fabulous!' Rona exclaimed. 'What was she like?'

'Pretty, in a blonde, blue-eyed way. In fact, very like her daughter, who works in the shop. Not as fragile-looking, though; she had bags of sex appeal. Too much, as it turned out. According to snippets I overheard, she'd had a string of lovers.'

'And who was the last one?'

'Ah, the million-dollar question! The prime suspect was

a bloke she'd had an affair with before. He left town about the same time she did.'

'I wonder if she stuck with him,' Max mused, 'or moved on to someone else. I suppose we'll never know.'

According to Kate, Rona remembered, Robert had hoped for years that she'd go back to him. Just as well all broken hearts didn't take so long to mend, she thought, with a guilty glance at Gavin. Thank God he and Magda were happy together. They made a striking couple, he just over and she just under six foot, Gavin ash-blond and Magda with her Italian mother's dark hair and eyes. Rona felt a rush of love for them both.

'What are you doing for Christmas?' Magda asked. 'Going to the parents, as usual?'

Rona took a deep breath. These were their closest friends, and after all, Pops had openly taken Catherine to Serendipity.

'It's not quite as simple as that,' she said quietly, aware of Max's eyes on her. 'My parents have just separated.'

'Oh no!' Magda exclaimed. 'Oh, Rona, I'm so sorry!'

Gavin said, 'Your father's retirement was in today's local rag. It said your mother couldn't attend because she had flu.'

'Only the diplomatic variety,' Rona replied.

'So – what's going to happen now?'

'Pops has moved out and is renting a flat in Talbot Road.' No need, yet, to mention Catherine. Rona didn't want him to appear the guilty party.

'Was it – amicable?'

'Not at first, but I believe things are easier now.' She paused, then carried on determinedly, 'Actually, Mum has blossomed in the last few weeks – new clothes, new hairdo, and she's taken a job at the local library.'

'Well, good for her,' Magda said uncertainly.

'How's *your* mother?' Rona put in quickly. 'I keep meaning to pop in and see her.'

Paola King had been an important figure in Rona's childhood, providing the warmth and tenderness that had been lacking in her relationship with her own mother.

'She's fine. Do call in, she'd love to see you.'

Mention of the separation seemed to have put a dampener on the evening, Rona thought sadly, and soon afterwards their party broke up and went their separate ways.

Max glanced at her as they got into the car, and laid a hand on her lap. 'It still hurts, doesn't it, love?'

'Of course it hurts. And oh Max, what are we going to do about Christmas?'

'As Gavin would say, that is the million-dollar question.'

On which unsettled note, they drove home.

Eight

On Monday morning, another invitation dropped through the letter box and Max, about to leave for Farthings, opened it.

'It's from the Trents,' he reported. 'Supper on Saturday the seventeenth.'

'Barnie said he'd arrange something while Mitch was over. That's every Saturday till Christmas accounted for. At one time, I'd thought we might have a party ourselves, but there's been so much going on I haven't got round to it, and now it's too late.'

Max bent to kiss her cheek. 'Have a good day and I'll ring you this evening.'

'If you're going out sketching, make sure you wrap up,' Rona called after him, as he went down the steps.

Actually, it was slightly less cold than it had been, and after days of drizzling mist the sky was a welcome blue. Resisting its temptation, Rona went up to her study, determined to complete Coralie Davis's story. Then, she told herself, all she'd have to do would be to return the photographs and papers and deliver the article to *Chiltern Life*, after which she could draw a line under the whole project and move on to something else.

On the days when Max had evening classes, he was free during the day to attend to his own work, and that morning he had, as Rona anticipated, taken his camera and sketch pad to the Memorial Gardens on Guild Street. From there, he had a good view of the busy thoroughfare, without being jostled by its crowds. Although he preferred its more sober aspect, when the bow windows, uneven rooftops and painted railings gave an air of Georgian elegance, its present festive mood would, as he'd told his friends, look admirable gracing the December page of the commissioned calendar.

He worked steadily for a couple of hours, until his fingers were too cold to function properly, and he decided to take a break and go along to the Gallery for a warming coffee. And it was as he was crossing the road that a breathless voice behind him said hesitantly, 'Mr Allerdyce? Max?' and he turned to find himself face to face with Adele Yarborough.

His first reaction was embarrassment, remembering how he'd pushed up her sleeve to expose the bruises, and her subsequent flight from the house. But before he could speak, she rushed in with her own apology.

'I behaved very foolishly last week,' she began.

'On the contrary, I'd no right to do what I did.'

She gave him a tremulous smile. 'I know it was because you were worried about me.'

She'd fallen into step with him as he walked along the pavement, and he wondered uneasily how he was going to get rid of her before they reached the Gallery. Though he needed a physical break, he didn't want his line of thought interrupted, and had intended, over coffee, to plan the angles of the next set of sketches.

'Are you feeling better now?' he asked inanely.

'Not really. I'm not sleeping too well, which doesn't help. This morning I felt so tired I shouted at Nick, and he went off to school in a strop. I've had a conscience about it all morning.'

'He probably forgot as soon as he was out of the door.'

They'd reached the iron staircase leading up to the café, and he cast about for some way of ending the conversation. 'Try taking a sedative,' he suggested. 'I'm sure that'll help. See you on Wednesday, then.'

But she did not, as he'd hoped, walk on. 'Are you going up for a coffee? I'm on the way there myself.'

Max swore silently, but there was no escape. 'Then we'll have one together,' he decreed with false heartiness, and motioned her ahead of him up the staircase.

Once in the Gallery, he instinctively chose a table half-hidden behind a pillar; worried as he was about Adele, he'd no wish to be seen with her in public. Meanwhile, she'd slipped off her coat with its fur collar, to reveal a pale blue angora sweater. As always, she wore no jewellery apart from a watch and her wedding ring. The cool air had stung colour into her usually pale cheeks, her hair was wind-blown, and it struck Max uncomfortably that she looked very pretty.

She ordered café latte, he espresso, and they sat in a pool of silence, surrounded by laughter and chat from the adjacent tables. Please, Max prayed silently, don't let me see anyone I know!

But even as the thought formed, a voice above him said acidly, 'Well, *hello* Max! And Adele, too!'; and to his horror, he looked up to meet Lindsey's accusing gaze.

Unwelcome colour seeped into his face, but before he could speak, Adele rushed into an over-abundance of explanations that would have aroused suspicions in the most trustful of minds – which Lindsey's certainly was not.

'We just bumped into each other in the street,' she gushed. 'Wasn't that a coincidence? I'd no idea Max would be there – I thought he'd be ensconced in his studio, painting furiously! But it turned out he was coming for a coffee, and as I was too, it – well, it just seemed natural to join up.'

Max found his voice at last. 'And why aren't *you* at your desk, Lindsey?' he asked drily.

'I'm on my way back after visiting a client, but they make better coffee here than they do in the office. Well, I must be on my way. Give my love to Rona,' she added pointedly, and with a nod to them both, she walked quickly out of the café.

Damn and double-damn! Max thought. He glanced at Adele, who was watching him with an amused glint in her eye.

'Will you get into trouble?' she asked with mock concern.

He said stiffly, 'I don't have to account for my movements.' Which, he realized as soon as he'd spoken, was hardly a wise comment.

She leaned across the table and put a slender hand on his

107

wrist. 'I'm sorry, Max. I realize I've made things awkward for you. Put the blame on me.'

'There's no blame attached to anyone. We're having a cup of coffee, that's all.'

'Yes,' she said, eyes demurely dropping again as she sat back in her chair. 'All the same, I do feel better after seeing you. I always do. Would it be possible, do you think, for us to meet every now and then, just for coffee or a drink or something? There wouldn't be any harm in it, would there?'

'It wouldn't be very sensible, though. If you're really in need of help, there are professional people you could contact.' He paused. 'Look, about those bruises—'

In an instant she was on her feet, shrugging on her coat. 'Thanks for the coffee,' she said rapidly. 'See you on Wednesday.'

And before he could draw breath, she was gone.

Max's coffee was ice-cold before he finally looked up and asked for the bill.

The promise of early morning was upheld, and mellow sunshine lit the last leaves to russet and gold as Rona and Gus walked down the road to collect the car.

Once out of the confines of the town, Guild Street metamorphosed into Belmont Road, leading eventually to the suburb where Rona had grown up and where her mother still lived. On its way there, it passed occasional small groups of houses, one or two shopping parades and the odd school, and just beyond one of these clusters was the turning Rona was looking for.

As Kate had said, Brindley Grove was a cul-de-sac, though a footpath alongside the house facing her gave pedestrian access to the road behind. The gates of the house were open, and Rona drove through them, parking next to a small red sports car. Kate came out to meet her, followed by Freya Tarlton.

'Good to see you, Rona. You've met Freya, of course.'

'Yes.' Rona smiled at the girl. 'It was sweet of you to send flowers.'

'I was highly embarrassed by the whole episode.'

Gus, recognizing Kate, was scratching at the side window and wagging his tail. It had the desired effect.

'I see his paw's better,' she commented. 'Do bring him in with you.'

'If you're sure.' Rona opened the rear door and Gus bounded out, licking the hand Kate held out to him. Rona was looking up at the stone house in front of them. 'I didn't know you lived in such grand surroundings.'

'It's the family home,' Kate replied. 'Soon after we were married, Robert made it over to Lewis and Freya, and since she didn't want to live here, Lewis bought her out. Come inside.'

'Where does he live now, your father-in-law?' Rona asked, as they went up the steps.

'Above the shop, would you believe, and no one can shift him. He loves it there.'

Kate led the way into a large sitting room overlooking a long back garden. Beyond the far wall, Rona could see the woods she'd mentioned. A trolley bearing cups and saucers stood by the open fire, and Kate excused herself to bring in the tea.

Rona turned from the window to find Freya watching her.

'Did Kate tell you I'm hoping to do some articles about family businesses?'

'Yes. It should be . . . interesting.'

'And I also told her,' continued Kate, coming in with the teapot, 'that you might be able to help with her dreams.'

'Oh Kate, I did say—'

Kate waved an airy hand. 'It can't do any harm, and Freya wouldn't have come if she'd not been prepared to talk about it.'

Rona glanced uneasily at the girl, but she replied quietly, 'I've told them I won't see a doctor, but I'll try almost anything else. And through no fault of your own, you're already involved.'

'I have to warn you, I'm not even remotely qualified in this field.'

'But you're good at working things out,' Kate argued. 'Go on, Rona, give it a try. You can see it's getting Freya down.'

109

'All right, I'll try, but I honestly don't think it'll do any good.'

Kate passed her a cup of tea and a plate of sandwiches. 'Off you go, then.'

'I suppose the first thing to ask,' Rona began reluctantly, 'is how long you've been having these dreams?'

'For a couple of months this time, but I had a bout several years ago, and as far as I remember they were much the same.'

'What helped you over them last time?'

'They just fizzled out. But they weren't nearly as detailed as they are now, and what's frightening is that each time I have the dream, it unfolds a bit more.'

'You think you're falling, is that right?'

Freya said slowly, 'I'm hiding somewhere quite high up – in a hay loft, perhaps, or at the top of a ladder. I can hear this tune—'

'"Auprès de ma blonde"?'

'You know it?'

'My husband recognized it. How exactly do you hear it? Is it on the radio, for instance, or is someone humming it?'

'Do you know,' Freya said slowly, 'I've never stopped to analyse that; it's just a sound in my head. But . . .' she frowned in concentration. '. . . I *think* someone is whistling it. Anyway, it goes on for some time, and then there are voices, getting more and more angry.' She closed her eyes tightly, and Kate and Rona sat immobile, waiting for her to continue. 'Then there's a gap,' Freya went on at last, 'and after that, I can hear a man sobbing.'

'How do you know it's a man?'

'I'm not sure – I just do. Then I want to sneeze, which I know would give me away, so I pinch my nose to try to stop it, but because I'm only hanging on by one hand, I start to slip.' There was another silence, then she said flatly, 'And that's about it, really.'

'You said there was a gap before you heard the sobbing. You mean you can't remember that bit?'

'No; I've tried to, but I get very upset and start shaking like mad, so I have to stop.'

110

Rona took the sandwich Kate was offering her. 'When these dreams started, can you think of anything that could have triggered them off?'

Freya shook her head. 'They came out of the blue.'

'And you have them every night?'

'Yes; probably because I now expect to.'

'Aren't dreams like this caused by childhood traumas?' Kate prompted.

'That's one interpretation, but I read somewhere that the mind is trying to make sense of something, and often misinterprets it.'

'The theory last time was that they were caused by her mother leaving her; could there be any truth in that?'

'Kate!' Rona protested helplessly. 'I've no more idea than you have!' Then, since they were both looking at her expectantly, she continued, 'I was told you were quite ill when she went. Can you remember that?'

'No, I only know what I've been told.'

Kate topped up her tea. 'Lewis says you changed overnight from an outgoing little tomboy to jumping at shadows.'

'I know.'

'And that you either wouldn't or couldn't speak for weeks afterwards. But Freya, from what I've heard your mother didn't have much to do with you anyway. So why should her going have such an effect?'

'I've no idea,' Freya said woodenly.

'You were close to your nanny?' Rona asked, and the girl's face brightened.

'Yes, very. I still see her from time to time.'

'Where's she living now?'

'In a residential home; Stapleton House, near Chesham.'

'I know it,' Rona said. It was an expensive establishment, and she guessed the Tarltons must be footing the bills. 'Have you asked her why it should have affected you?'

'No, it upsets her to talk about it. She was Daddy's nanny when he was little, and she never forgave Mummy for going off and leaving him.'

'She might talk to you,' Kate said eagerly.

111

Rona had been thinking the same thing. 'Would you mind if I went to see her?'

Freya shook her head. 'Her name's Violet Gray – Miss, of course. But I don't think you'll get much out of her.'

After a minute, Rona said, 'Does the rest of the family know you're talking to me? I don't want to feel I'm going behind their backs.'

'Lewis knows, of course,' Kate replied, 'and I told Jan and Robert. They weren't too keen on the idea, but agreed anything's worth a try if it helps Freya.' Kate flashed her a glance. 'I also told them about the articles you're planning,' she added. 'I hope you don't mind?'

Rona would have preferred to make the first approach herself, but the damage was done. 'What did they think about it?'

'Generally in favour, though I gather some subjects would be off-limits.'

Rona nodded. 'Though if I'm to try to get to the bottom of the dreams, I'll have to ask about Mrs Tarlton.'

'I think they realize that, but it won't be for publication.'

'Understood.' She turned back to Freya, who was staring into the fire. 'Is there anything else you can tell me?'

'I don't think so.'

'Then we'll leave any more questions till I've spoken to Miss Gray and your relatives. With luck, we might have a clearer picture.'

When they'd finished tea, Rona's glance returned to the window. 'Could I have a look at the garden before it gets dark?' she asked. 'Ours is only the size of a pocket-handkerchief.'

'It's not at its best this time of year,' Kate answered, 'but you're welcome to have a wander. I'll come with you. Freya?'

'You go ahead, I'll clear away the tea things.'

'Oh, leave them; I'll—'

'Really, I'd like to. You two go – please.'

Kate shrugged, and as Freya began to stack the plates on the trolley, she unlocked the French windows and Rona and Gus followed her outside. Beyond the window was a wide terrace containing several terracotta urns, emptied now of

112

their summer flowers, and a black wrought-iron table and chairs.

'We really ought to put those in the shed over winter,' Kate commented, 'but Lewis says it's not worth moving them.'

The terrace was bounded by a low stone wall, and a flight of steps led down through a grassy bank to the lawn some four feet below. On either side of the garden, crescent-shaped beds held dwarf conifers and variegated evergreens, with, scattered among them, the bravely flying flags of a few late dahlias.

'I knew Freya wouldn't come,' Kate remarked, as they started down the steps. 'We can hardly ever get her into the garden, and when we do manage it, she'll never go more than a few feet beyond the terrace.'

Rona looked at her in surprise. 'Why is that?'

'Search me. She maintains that she's "been there, done that".'

'But a garden's changing all the time, from season to season.'

'She says she can see as much as she needs to from the house. I've given up trying to persuade her, though I thought she might make an exception today, since you're here.'

'Has she always been like that?' Rona asked curiously.

'You'll have to ask Lewis, but certainly for as long as I've known her. And the odd thing is that she loves Matthew's garden; the two of them work in it together.'

'I wonder if it's part and parcel of the same thing,' Rona mused. 'A leftover of being timid, and so on. What time of year was it that Mrs Tarlton left?'

Kate looked surprised. 'What's that got to do with anything?'

'I'm trying to build up a mental picture.'

'Actually, it was September. I know, because Lewis told me it was the week after his thirteenth birthday.'

They walked slowly down the garden, and Gus, running ahead, lifted his leg against some bushes. Rona apologized, but Kate only laughed.

'No inhibitions!' she said. 'Mustn't it be wonderful?'

Rona was revelling in the spaciousness of the wide lawn and spreading flower beds, the gazebo and the little water feature. But shadows were already gathering round the edges, the sun was low in the sky, and a breeze had sprung up, making them shiver. As they reached the bottom of the garden, Kate turned to go back.

'Do you ever go through there?' Rona nodded towards the gate in the wall.

'No, the bolts are rusted solid. I keep meaning to have them freed, because in spring, the bluebells out there are spectacular.'

They started to walk up the darkening garden to the lighted windows of the house.

'What do you think?' Kate asked abruptly. 'Will you be able to do anything?'

'I can ask questions, but so could anyone else.'

'But you'd have a new slant on it, not being personally involved. We really are very grateful, Rona.'

'I'll do what I can, but no promises and no guarantees.'

'That's as much as anyone can ask,' Kate said, and they went back into the welcome warmth of the house.

Rona was surprised, when the phone rang at six, to find Max on the line. He usually phoned after the class, about ten o'clock.

'Hi, there,' he said.

'Hello! I wasn't expecting you so soon.'

'Well, I've got the studio all set up, so I thought I'd ring now.' A pause, almost as though he was waiting for her to say something. Then, 'How was your day?'

'Quite interesting. Kate invited me to tea to meet Freya, and she was telling me about her dreams. I'm not long home.'

'I shouldn't get involved, if I were you. Minds are tricky things, and you could end up doing actual damage.'

'That's what I told them, but they're insisting I go ahead. I said I'd see the nanny, anyway. She might fill in a few gaps.'

114

When he made no further comment, she asked, 'How about you? Did you finish the Guild Street sketches?'

'Almost.' Another pause. 'I presume you've not spoken to Lindsey today.'

Rona frowned. 'No, why?'

'Just that on the way to the Gallery, I was cornered by Adele Yarborough, who invited herself to join me. And Lindsey was there.'

Rona felt herself go hot. 'You had coffee with Adele?'

'I've just said so. Obviously it was pure chance, meeting her in the street like that, but Lindsey seemed to put a different interpretation on it.'

Yes, Rona thought, she would; as she would have herself, she admitted, had she been the one to see them.

Max said a little impatiently, 'Rona?'

'What do you want me to say?'

'That you believe it wasn't premeditated. I know how you are about Adele.'

'You've said what happened, and I believe you.' Her voice sounded stilted, even to herself.

'No questions?' His had an edge to it.

'No.' *But if you've anything to tell me, I'm listening.*

'Right.' He drew a deep breath, and she realized he hadn't relished the prospect of telling her – in fact, probably wouldn't have done so, had Lindsey not seen them. And that was a less than comfortable thought. 'Well, I'd better get something to eat before the hordes descend.'

'Yes.'

'Speak to you tomorrow.'

'Yes,' she said again. 'Goodnight.'

'Goodnight.'

Lindsey was lying on the bed with Jonathan's arm round her, agonizing over the chance meeting.

'I don't know what to do!' she moaned, for the third time. 'Do I tell Ro, or not? Max will probably say something, thinking I will, and then she'll wonder why I didn't tell her sooner.'

Jonathan sighed. He regarded these interludes as a pleasant

way to unwind after the day's work, and was already bored with discussing Max Allerdyce. He was not, in any case, particularly enamoured of Lindsey's sister – understandably, he felt, since she had once tricked him into having lunch with her, in order to accuse him of murder.

'Jonathan?' Lindsey twisted her head to look up at him. 'What do you think I should do?'

'Oh, now if *that's* all you're worrying about, I've all sorts of ideas!' he said, propping himself on one elbow and running his finger down the length of her throat.

She caught hold of his hand. 'About Rona, idiot! Be serious!'

'I am. Very serious.' He bit her lip gently, but she turned her head away and he sighed. 'All right, we're obviously not going to get anywhere till you've sorted this out. So my advice, for what it's worth, is, before you go rushing in to report what you obviously consider a breach of faith, be quite sure Max hadn't told her in advance that he was meeting this woman.'

'Oh!' Lindsey sounded a little deflated. 'He looked very guilty,' she added in mitigation.

'With you glaring at him, I'm not surprised. On the other hand, it could be that you're not the only one who saw them, in which case, I'd guess she'd rather hear it from you than anyone else.'

'So you think I *should* tell her? But she'll still wonder why I didn't phone straight away. Damn it, it was this morning that I saw them! And Max rings her every evening; I really ought to get in first.'

'I trust you're not thinking of interrupting this idyll to phone now? As you know, our time is limited, and I've been patient quite long enough.'

Lindsey smiled. 'So you have, darling. I'll wait till you've gone, and then—'

But the rest of her intention was lost as his mouth fastened over hers.

Cicely Ryder, chief receptionist at the Clarendon, tapped on the door of the private sitting room where Stephen and Ruth Fairfax were relaxing over a pre-dinner drink.

'I'm sorry to bother you,' she began worriedly, 'but I'm afraid we have a problem.'

'What is it, Cicely?'

'Mrs Jacobs has just reported that her Jacqmar scarf is missing. She says she left it on a chair in her room when she came in this afternoon, and when she went back to change for dinner, it wasn't there.'

Ruth frowned. 'Who's the chambermaid on her floor?'

'Franny. She swears she hasn't seen it.'

'It's quite likely,' Stephen remarked, 'that she only *thinks* she left it there. It'll probably turn up in her handbag or shopping bag. Or, of course, she could have lost it while she was out.'

'But you can't tell her that!' Ruth put in with a smile. 'Has anyone else been in her room?'

'She says not.'

'Well, assure her we'll look into it, and ask Franny to search under the beds and behind doors when she does the room in the morning.'

Cicely nodded and withdrew.

Stephen watched her go, a furrow between his brows. 'I hope to God we're not in for a spate of missing articles. That kind of thing does nothing for our reputation.'

'Let's not anticipate trouble,' Ruth said comfortingly. 'I'm sure it'll turn up.'

Stephen looked across at her fondly. In the forty-odd years they'd been married, she had filled out a little and her dark hair had threads of grey, but essentially she was still the serious, sweet-faced girl he'd fallen in love with.

On an impulse he got up, went over to her, and dropped a kiss on the top of her head.

She looked up in surprise. 'What was that for?'

'Just to say I don't know what I'd do without you.'

She smiled. 'I've no intention of your finding out,' she said.

When Lindsey phoned, some forty minutes after Max, it was Rona who broached the subject.

'Well!' she said. 'Better late than never!'

117

'You know? Max told you?'

'Of course he told me. He seemed to think you'd have got in first. Why didn't you, Linz?'

'I've been agonizing over it all day. He swore there was nothing in it—'

'But you think there was?'

'Oh God, Rona, I don't know. What I *do* know is that they were sitting behind a pillar, and when I appeared, Max went scarlet.'

'I suppose you gave him a shock,' Rona said with a dry mouth.

'No doubt of it. And Prissy Miss immediately leapt to his defence with a catalogue of explanations. I could see he'd willingly have cut her tongue out.'

Rona said, 'If it had been an assignation, he would hardly have taken her to the Gallery. I never go there without seeing someone I know.'

'I'm sure you're right,' Lindsey said uncertainly. 'But what would *you* have done, if you'd seen Hugh with someone while we were still together?'

After a minute, Rona said flatly, 'I don't know. The same as you, I suppose.' But, she thought, Hugh really *had* been having an affair, which had ultimately led to their divorce. She felt suddenly cold.

'Your love life as complicated as ever?' she asked lightly.

Lindsey laughed. 'Gloriously so!'

'Just don't burn your fingers,' Rona said.

It took her a long time to go to sleep that night.

Nine

The following morning, Rona phoned Stapleton House and asked to speak to Miss Violet Gray. Minutes later, a frail voice came on the line.

'I don't know you, do I?' it demanded querulously.

'No, but I've been asked to see you by the Tarlton family,' Rona explained, stretching the truth a little. 'I'm writing an article on the firm, but what I really want—'

'The Tarltons?' The old voice brightened. 'How are they all? I haven't seen them for a while.'

'They're well, I think.' Rona hesitated, unwilling to embark on Freya's problems over the phone. 'Would it be all right if I come along this afternoon?'

'Very well, if you'd like to. I take a nap after lunch, but any time after three would be convenient.'

'Thank you very much, Miss Gray. I look forward to meeting you.'

After she rang off, Rona glanced at the very brief notes she'd made on Freya.

> Mother left home when she was three. Allegedly
> traumatized by this; character changed, didn't speak
> for weeks, etc.
> Brought up by Nanny Gray and her aunt, Jan
> Tarlton.
> Father adored her and still does.
> Brother Lewis ten years her senior.
> Nightmares started at age 12/13 but gradually
> stopped. Started again two months ago. They
> concern fear of falling, hearing sobs, and the
> French song.

119

Won't go down the garden at her family home.
Lives with boyfriend Matthew, and helps in his garden.

The garden thing was curious, she reflected. Could it have any bearing on the dreams? Freya herself had made no mention of it. Come to that, would Miss Gray even know about the dreams? It was unlikely; Freya was twelve or thirteen when she first experienced them, and the nanny would have been long gone. She might be able to shed some light on them, though.

Before she could stop it, Rona's mind veered again to Max, and the abrupt end to their conversation the previous evening. She was being unreasonable, she told herself. In the circumstances, there was nothing else he could have done. He was guilty only of concern for a woman he thought abused, and frustrated that he could do nothing about it. Adele, on the other hand, Rona had long suspected of deviousness, and it was quite likely she was playing on Max's sympathy. Rona had warned him of this before, but he hadn't believed her. Perhaps, in the wake of this latest embarrassment, he would take more notice.

She lifted the phone and pressed the number for Farthings.

'Max Allerdyce.'

'Rona Parish.'

'Ah! Not ringing up to chastise me, are you?'

'Far from it; I'm ringing to suggest we meet for lunch.'

'Sounds good to me.'

'At the Gallery,' she said deliberately.

'As in getting back on the horse?'

'Something like that. Twelve thirty? I'm due at Stapleton House at three.'

'That'll be a barrel of laughs. Fine, twelve thirty it is. See you.'

'See you,' she echoed.

Mrs Jacobs' scarf had not turned up, despite a thorough search of her room by her chambermaid. Ruth had asked tactfully when she last remembered seeing it, and been told uncompromisingly that it was when she had draped it over the back of the chair before going down for tea. Ruth instructed that a notice be put on the board in the foyer, describing the scarf, and asking anyone who found it to return it to its owner. Mrs Jacobs was not mollified, commenting that no one was likely to respond, since it would amount to an admission of being in her room.

The inference, as Ruth well knew, was since members of staff were the only ones with access, one of them must have taken it. If the scarf were indeed stolen, she was reluctantly led to the same conclusion, and asked the housekeeper, Margaret Bailey, to come and see her.

'Keep it low-key,' she instructed, 'but watch out for anyone behaving guiltily when the scarf's mentioned, or who might have been in the wrong place at the wrong time.'

It was all she could do, she thought helplessly. Mrs Jacobs would be leaving on Thursday, and whether or not the scarf was recovered, Ruth very much hoped that would be the end of the matter.

Gerald saw the notice when he arrived for the lunch shift, and added it to his list of worries; if the hotel gained a reputation for theft, bookings would drop off, and then what would happen?

But his main concern was still Coralie Davis. As is often the way, after not having seen her since she'd left the hotel, he'd caught sight of her a couple of times in the last two weeks, once in the street, and again in one of the shops. The first time she'd just smiled at him, the second she had asked, 'Are you following me, Chef?'

And when he'd started to protest his innocence, she'd laughed and said, 'Relax! I was only joking!'

You didn't know where you were with girls like that. Mind you, he didn't know where he was with girls, period. The ones he'd quite fancied treated him like a younger brother, while the few who'd made the first move had sent him scuttling for cover. He seemed to attract the wrong people, he thought miserably; he'd even been approached by one of the waiters, until his terrified withdrawal had clarified the position.

By the time he reached the kitchen, he had also reached his usual conclusion: life was a lot simpler if he confined himself to cooking.

Rona thought over her lunch with Max as she and Gus set off for Chesham. She was glad she'd suggested it: any coolness between them made her miserable, but during the meal no mention had been made of the contretemps and they were perfectly relaxed with each other. She'd been unable, though, to prevent herself from searching out the table behind the pillar where, according to Lindsey, he had sat the day before with Adele. Too bad, she thought caustically, that the pillar hadn't hidden him from her sister's eagle eyes.

At Stapleton House, she left Gus in the car and, remembering the procedure from her last visit, rang the bell and spoke into the intercom. Once inside, she signed the visitors' book with her name and the current time, and pressed a bell for assistance.

'Miss Gray?' said the pleasant-faced woman who answered the call. 'Yes, I believe she's expecting you.' And Rona was led down the thickly carpeted corridor to a door at the far end. The woman tapped, opened it, and said, 'A visitor for you, Miss Gray.'

Rona approved of the formality; these elderly residents were accustomed to courtesy, rather than the unthinking familiarity that addressed them by their first names. She was glad that here at least it was afforded to them.

Miss Gray was seated in a deep winged chair before an electric fire, though the radiators heated the room quite adequately. Her white hair was scraped into a bun at the back of her head, and her face was as crumpled and soft-looking as velvet. She wore a hearing aid, Rona noticed, but the eyes that surveyed her were still sharp and without spectacles.

'You're here on behalf of the Tarltons?' she asked.

'In a way. I should explain that I work for *Chiltern Life*, and am planning a series on some of the older firms and shops in Marsborough. I – believe you have a long association with the family?'

'Indeed yes. I went to work for them when I was eighteen.

And when Mr Robert married, he sent for me to look after his own children.'

'But not Mr Bruce?'

The nanny's mouth tightened. 'No, Mr Bruce's wife wanted to care for the child herself. And Mr Robert's, too, after their mother left them. I had to be quite firm with her.'

So there was jealousy there, Rona thought.

'They must have needed you even more then,' she said tactfully.

'They did indeed, poor little souls. Master Lewis was older, of course, but little Freya—' She broke off, her mouth working.

'It's actually Freya I want to speak to you about,' Rona began. 'Did you know she's been suffering from rather frightening dreams?'

Miss Gray looked at her sharply. 'We all have those from time to time.'

'But it's been suggested they might go back to her mother having left her at such a young age.'

Again the tightened lips. 'Mrs Robert was never one to fuss over her, nor over Master Lewis, either.'

'But Freya changed, didn't she? After she left?'

The old lady nodded. 'It broke your heart to see her.'

'Yet if she'd never had much to do with her mother . . . ?'

Miss Gray flashed her a quick glance. 'Children are complex little beings, Miss – Parish, is it? It's hard to fathom what will or will not upset them.'

'Can you think of any other reason why she should have reacted as she did?'

The gnarled hands twitched convulsively, but all she said was, 'No.' Then she looked up, meeting Rona's questioning gaze. 'Dreams, you said. What about? Does she remember them?'

'Yes; she's hiding somewhere high up, and she overhears angry voices and someone whistling. Then she wants to sneeze, and is afraid of being discovered. She pinches her nose to stop the sneeze and begins to fall.'

The old eyes filled with tears. 'It was I who taught her that – how to stop sneezes,' Miss Gray said.

'Does the dream make any sense to you?'

A shake of the head.

'I wonder,' Rona began, 'if you could take me through the day Mrs Tarlton left? Was there anything else unusual about it?'

The old lady stared at the bars of the electric fire. What was she seeing? Rona wondered.

'I took Freya to playschool as usual,' she began, 'and went back to collect her at eleven thirty.' She paused. 'There was one thing: while I was giving her lunch in the nursery, Mrs Robert came in and told me she'd be going out later that afternoon. I was surprised – she didn't usually tell me her plans – and then she bent down and kissed Freya's cheek – which was even more unusual – and put a parcel beside her plate.

'"Here's a little present," she said. "Don't open it till you've finished lunch. There's one for Lewis, too, when he comes home from school." Freya said "Thank you", as she'd been taught, and Mrs Robert hesitated a moment, said "Goodbye, then", and left the room. We didn't realize the goodbye was permanent.'

Lost in the past as they were, they both jumped when there was a knock on the door, and a woman in a flowered overall came in, carrying a tray with two cups of tea and a plate of biscuits.

'What was in the parcel?' Rona asked, when she'd gone.

'A little Dutch doll. Freya played with it that day, but she wouldn't touch it afterwards.'

Resentment against her mother? 'What did you do after lunch?'

Again the old hands tightened. 'Freya wanted to play in her Wendy house. She was a self-sufficient little thing in those days. Well, she had to be; her brother was so much older, it was like being an only child. She often played by herself in the garden; you'd see her chatting away to her toys. I used to take the chance to do some mending or knitting, sitting at the nursery window, where I could keep an eye on her.'

She broke off, and Rona saw she was struggling for composure. To ease her over it, she asked curiously, 'Did she always stay near the house?'

Miss Gray's head shot up. 'Near the house? No, why should she? There's a large garden at Brindley Lodge, perfect for a child to play in. Her Wendy house was set up in the far corner.'

'Near the back wall?' Rona asked sharply.

There was a long silence, broken only by the harsh, erratic breathing of the old lady. Then she said in a low voice, 'How much do you know?'

Rona stared at her, aware that how she responded was crucial to how much she would learn. 'I know that nowadays she hardly ever goes into the garden, and when she does, she stays near the house.' She paused. 'There's a gate leading into the woods, isn't there?'

Slowly, Miss Gray's trembling hands went to her face. 'I always knew it would come out one day,' she said in a whisper.

Rona bent forward. 'What would?' she asked gently.

'I didn't dare tell anyone at the time – I could so easily have been dismissed. I *should* have been! And as it happened, there was so much going on, what with Mrs Robert going off like that, that not as much attention was paid as would have been otherwise. And – and – oh, dear Lord – the explanation was handed to me neatly on a plate. But if my silence has harmed Miss Freya in any way, I'll never forgive myself.'

'Tell me what happened,' Rona said quietly.

'I fell asleep, didn't I? When I was meant to be looking after her. The sun was warm through the glass, and I'd finished my knitting and began to feel drowsy. When I'd last checked on her, she was playing with her new doll, down by the Wendy house. Then the next I knew, I woke with a start and it was a good half-hour later. I looked out of the window, and – I couldn't see her.'

She put her hands to her face again, and Rona, feeling some restorative was called for, handed her her cup of tea.

'So you went out to look for her?' she prompted, when the old lady had taken several sips.

'Yes; I ran down the lawn, praying she'd be inside the

125

Wendy house, but she wasn't. She wasn't *anywhere*. I searched the garden, then I thought she might have come back into the house. No one was home; it was Shelley's afternoon off.'

'Who's Shelley?'

'She did the cooking and light housework. Someone came in twice a week to do the heavy stuff.'

'There was a cook?' Rona said. 'How positively Victorian!'

Miss Gray shrugged. 'Mrs Robert never lifted a finger in the house; somebody had to do it.'

'So – Freya wasn't in the house either?'

'No.' She took a deep breath. 'I went back down the garden, and to my horror I saw that the gate wasn't bolted. That must have been down to Master Lewis; he and his friends used to play in the woods. Well, I panicked, of course, thinking of the little thing wandering there all alone. Anything could have happened to her; tramps and all sorts went in there, and if she'd walked far enough through the trees, she'd have reached the main road on the other side.'

Rona's heart was thumping painfully. 'And you found her there?'

'Eventually, yes. I called and called but there was no reply. I remember running through all the overgrown brambles and nettles and bushes – it was a total nightmare.' She stopped, as the word rang a bell in her mind. 'A nightmare. No wonder she still has them,' she finished in a whisper.

'What was she doing when you found her?'

'She was crouched at the foot of a tree, making herself as small as possible and rocking backwards and forwards. The Dutch doll was beside her. Well, I scooped her up in my arms and hugged her, almost crying with relief. But she was as white as a sheet, and she had bruises on her arms and legs and scratches on her face, and though I kept asking her what had happened and was she all right, she never said a word. It was as though she couldn't hear me.

'I ran back to the house with her, intending to phone the doctor. But first I took her upstairs and removed her dirty clothes – they were covered with mud and dead leaves –

126

and sponged the blood from the scratches, feeling all over as I went, to see if there was any real damage. There didn't seem to be, and no bumps on the head, either, which was my main concern. So I decided to say nothing but to keep a careful eye on her, and if there was any change, I'd own up at once.'

She was still holding the cup of tea, and she raised it to her lips again and drank. 'But when Mr Robert arrived home from the shop,' she continued, dabbing at the corners of her mouth with a lace handkerchief, 'there was a note in his room saying his wife had left him, and with all the upset no one really noticed Freya for a day or two. In the end, I just *had* to tell him she wasn't speaking, and he immediately took her to the doctor, who, to my great relief, confirmed she wasn't physically hurt in any way, and put it down to her mother going.'

'But you knew differently,' Rona said.

'Yes. I was still going to own up, but with Mrs Robert gone, Mrs Bruce came very much to the fore, always checking on the children, and wanting to take them to stay with her. I felt my position was precarious enough, without admitting to a dereliction of duty, and I loved those children as though they were my own. I couldn't have borne to be parted from them.'

'But Freya wouldn't play in the garden any more?' Rona guessed.

'You're right. I could just about get her beyond the terrace as long as someone was with her, but her Wendy house had to be moved up right beside the house. Again, it was put down to insecurity.'

'You think something in the woods frightened her?'

'Stands to reason. It's my belief she met some tramp or beggar. I was terrified at first she might have been – molested.' A flush stained the old face. 'But there was no sign of that when I examined her, and the doctor confirmed it.'

'I wonder if the tune and the shouting link into that somehow?'

'Who's to say? But I feel terrible, now you've told me

about it. When she started speaking again, I convinced myself no real harm had been done. I didn't know about these dreams. How long has she been having them?'

'They seem to have started when she was twelve,' Rona said. 'She was taken to a psychiatrist, I think, but the explanation was the same as before – that they were caused by her mother leaving.'

'Stuff and nonsense!' said Violet Gray roundly, giving Rona a glimpse of her nanny persona. 'The child wasn't *grieving*, she was frightened.'

'It must have been something pretty traumatic, to keep coming back after – what? – twenty-five years?' Rona paused. 'You say she never played with that doll again?'

'Never – wouldn't have it anywhere near her. It must have had associations with what happened in the wood.'

Miss Gray looked at Rona resignedly. 'You're going to have to repeat all this, aren't you?'

'I think I must; the family asked me to try to find the root of Freya's dreams, and this seems likely to have some bearing on them.' She looked at the old lady contritely. 'Would you mind?'

'Surprisingly, no, I don't think I should. In fact, it would be a relief to get it off my chest after all this time. My only hope is that they'll be able to forgive me.' She straightened her shoulders. 'And now, my dear, I wonder if you'd excuse me? It has been – tiring – to go through all that again, and I need to rest.'

'Of course.' Rona stood up at once. 'And I'm sorry if I've upset you.'

'I deserved to be upset,' said Violet Gray.

Avril stood looking out into the darkening street, and was filled with desolation. Soon, she'd have to draw the curtains, closing off all links with the outside world. There was no one coming home, for whom she could cook supper, no crumpled newspaper on the floor needing to be tidied away. If she dropped something as she was dashing out of the house, it would still be there when she returned. She did not, she decided, like living alone, and the sooner she could take in lodgers, have someone living and breathing in the house again, the better it would be.

She'd already received the first estimate for the conversion of the box room, and the second builder had been here today. Once she could compare the prices, she'd be able to go ahead. Both had assured her that business was quiet at the moment, and as it wasn't a big job, they could fit her in quite soon. However, 'quite soon' at this time of year invariably meant after Christmas, so she'd have to be patient for a few weeks yet.

Which reminded her: neither of the girls had given her a firm commitment for Christmas lunch, and she was becoming more and more worried that they'd make excuses. In a way, she couldn't blame them; the first Christmas without Tom was bound to be difficult. Unless, of course – horrendous thought! – they were planning to spend the day with him and his new 'partner'. Surely they wouldn't do that to her?

She turned despondently from the window. By now, she reflected, it would be common knowledge that Tom had left her. That afternoon, a friend from the bridge club had phoned with her annual invitation to a drinks party, and, about to make excuses as she had over the last six weeks, Avril had realized that diplomacy was no longer either necessary or possible. Though she'd dreaded having to break the news, in the event it had come as a relief, especially since Sue Parsons was the most level-headed and down-to-earth of her friends. No probing questions or exclamations of disbelief, just a quiet word of regret and the offer to pass the news on, if it would help – an offer Avril had gladly accepted. She had also, she thought with a touch of pride, accepted the invitation. They were more her friends than Tom's, and she had no intention of shutting herself off from them.

'Life will go on,' she said aloud. If she could just get over the hurdle of Christmas, everything, she was sure, would seem more positive – work on the house, selecting her lodgers, perhaps accepting more responsibility at the library.

Squaring her shoulders, she firmly drew the curtains and went to prepare her solitary meal.

*   *   *

129

On her return home, Rona hurried straight up to the study to write down everything she could remember that Violet Gray had told her. She hadn't liked to use her recorder during her visit; it might have worried the old lady and made her more reticent in her reminiscences.

And as she wrote, she could feel her curiosity deepening. It seemed beyond doubt that the missing half-hour, while Nanny slept, had been responsible for Freya's subsequent trauma. What had happened in the woods, to have had such a lasting effect on her?

The telephone shrilled, making her jump. It was Kate Tarlton.

'Did you see Nanny Gray today?'

'Yes, I did.'

'And?'

'It's a long story, Kate, but I think it has a bearing on things.'

'What did she say?'

Rona hesitated. 'Do you mind if I don't go into it over the phone? I've not had time yet to sort it out. There is something you could do for me, though.'

'Which is?'

'Have the bolts on your back gate freed, so we can open it.'

'For heaven's sake, Rona! What is this? A maintenance survey?'

'Humour me, Kate. It could be important. Then, if it's all right with you, I'd like to come and see you again, with your husband this time.'

'Sure, any evening—'

'No, it would have to be in daylight. The weekend, perhaps?'

'Well, Saturday, of course, is our busiest day; even more so since it'll be December.'

'Sunday, then?'

'Rona, stop being so mysterious! I can't wait till *Sunday* to hear about it!'

'Sorry, Kate, but I have to check out a few things first. I really am serious about the gate, though; we need to be able to open it. Would about two be OK?'

And despite Kate's continuing protests, she put the phone down. Almost immediately it rang again, and she caught it up, ready to repeat there was no more she could say at present. But the caller this time was not Kate but Jan Tarlton.

'Miss Parish, I apologize for phoning when we've not even met, but Kate tells me you've been to see Nanny Gray.'

'I have, yes. With both Kate and Freya's permission.'

'I'm concerned that you might have been given a somewhat biased account. Miss Gray has very decided views, on the family as on other things, and these can lead to misunderstandings.'

'I'm hoping, of course, to see you all in due course,' Rona said diplomatically. 'Did Kate explain that?'

'About the firm, yes, but I'm thinking now of Freya. As you must know, we're all worried about her. I really feel you'd have done better to come to me. After all, I played a fairly large part in bringing her up, after my sister-in-law left.'

That jealousy again. 'I was trying to find out exactly what happened the day she went,' Rona explained. 'And I don't believe you saw Freya that day?'

'Well, no. But—'

'Miss Gray was able to give me a detailed timetable.'

'And what use was that?'

'I wanted to know, among other things, whether or not her mother had actually said goodbye to her.'

'And had she?' Jan asked after a moment.

'Yes; and she gave her a farewell present. I think she also left something for her son.'

'None of which seems to have much bearing on Freya's dreams.'

'It's given me something to work on,' Rona said evasively. She had no intention of telling Jan about the missing half-hour. Not yet, anyway.

'I see. Well, of course, anything you can do will be very much appreciated.'

'Thank you,' Rona said.

She pulled her desk diary towards her and wrote down the Sunday appointment. She was, she realized, breaking her own rule of no work at weekends, which were strictly reserved for Max. However, with the dark evenings and both Kate and Lewis working all day, there was no alternative. She hoped he would understand.

Tom and Catherine were sitting over the candlelit supper table in her bungalow.

'Next time,' he said, 'we must eat at the flat. But you might need to give me some cookery lessons first!'

Catherine laughed. 'Any time. Are you beginning to feel more settled now?'

'I wouldn't say settled, exactly. I keep waking in the night, wondering where I am, and it takes me a minute or two to orientate myself.'

'But your boxes are all unpacked?'

'Such as they were, yes. I wanted to get everything straight, so I can invite the girls round.'

'Food courtesy of M&S?'

'Very definitely.'

She refilled his coffee cup. 'Tom, what are you doing about Christmas?'

He gave a short laugh. 'I'll buy a portion of turkey breast and an individual plum pudding. Don't worry, I'll be fine. There's always a lot of festive nonsense on the box to keep me amused.'

'Why don't you come to Cricklehurst with me?' she asked suddenly. 'I don't know why I didn't think of it before. I know Daniel and Jenny would love to have you; it'll be the ideal opportunity to meet them.'

He put a hand over hers. 'No, my darling, it would not. In fact, it would be the worst of all possible times. They've only just learned about us; they need time to get used to it. The last thing they'd want is for me to gatecrash what they planned as an intimate family Christmas.'

'I hate to think of you by yourself,' Catherine said.

'We can have our own celebration before you go, and I'm

sure we'll be speaking on the phone. The girls will be ringing, too. I'll hardly be on my own at all.'

She leaned over and kissed him. 'Next year, it will be different,' she said.

Ten

When Rona woke the next morning, she lay for several minutes, thinking over the events of the previous day: not only her visit to Stapleton House, but the two phone calls that had followed it. Jan had warned her Miss Gray's account might be biased, but there'd been no bending of the facts relating to the day Velma left, which was what had interested her. And when it came to bias, she suspected that Jan Tarlton might be equally guilty of it.

Nevertheless, she felt she should perhaps consult a senior member of the family before going any further, and the obvious choice was Freya's father, Robert Tarlton. He'd been informed of her brief and had accepted, if not welcomed, it. It would be a courtesy to contact him now.

Accordingly, after breakfast she made the call and Robert, sounding surprised and apprehensive in equal measure, agreed to see her.

'It would be better if you came up to the flat,' he said. 'We could be more private there. It has a separate entrance, next door to the shop. About eleven o'clock?'

'That would be fine,' Rona told him. 'Thank you.'

How would he feel, she wondered belatedly, discussing the day his wife went off and left him? Perhaps, after all these years, the memories had lost the power to hurt him. She could only hope so.

Deciding it was better not to invade the home of someone she didn't know with a large dog at her side, she left a reproachful Gus at home and set off, glad that she wouldn't have to brave Kate, Freya or Jan on her way up to the flat.

Robert opened the door immediately. 'Miss Parish? Please come up.'

She'd seen him in the shop over the years, Rona realized, making her way up the steep stairs ahead of him, but as far as she remembered, she'd never spoken to him. He was an imposing figure, tall and broad-shouldered, with a lined forehead and vulnerable mouth that gave his face in repose a gravity tinged with sadness. It was not difficult to understand why.

Her instinctive exclamation of pleasure, however, on reaching the top of the stairs, brought a smile to it.

'What a charming room!' she said.

'Thank you.'

Rona walked to the mullioned window and looked down on Guild Street, some twenty feet below her. As usual, crowds were thronging the pavement, and she remembered his reported comment that he liked being in the centre of things. Turning, she saw that the furniture was period, purloined, she imagined, from Brindley Lodge – a comfortable sofa, two easy chairs, a drop-leaf table. There was the inevitable television and music centre, but they did not hold pride of place, and the pictures on the walls were Dutch Interior, one of Rona's favourite periods. On a small table was a thermos of coffee and two mugs.

'A little plebeian in presentation, I'm afraid, but I thought it might be welcome.'

And Rona, who had finished a cup barely half an hour earlier, assured him that it was.

'I was thinking the other day,' she said, 'that Tarlton's has been part of our family life for as long as I can remember.'

'Mine, too!'

She smiled. 'Your son and daughter are the fourth generation, aren't they?'

'Yes; we've always been a family concern. On occasion, in more ways than one!' he added with grim humour. 'Which brings us to the reason you're here.' He motioned her to a chair as he poured out the coffee. 'I'm told you're trying to sort out Freya's dreams, though I confess I'm not altogether sure why you've been roped in.'

A polite way of putting it! Rona thought wryly.

'One reason, I think, was because I was actually there that

135

Saturday, when she fainted. And another, because I'm a journalist, and Kate thought I'd have a nose for digging out facts.'

'Ah yes; you've known Kate for some time?'

'Since school,' Rona confirmed.

'And *are* you successful at ferreting things out?'

Rona carefully put her mug on the little table beside her. 'I have managed to unearth one thing,' she said carefully. She looked up and met his eyes. 'I believe you were told the dreams resulted from Freya's mother's departure.'

A faint shadow crossed his face. 'That's the received wisdom, yes. Are you saying it's not right?'

She had to feel her way here. 'I suspect that's not the only cause.'

'Go on.'

'I went to Stapleton House yesterday, to see Miss Gray.'

'So I gather. It reminded me that I've been remiss; I've not visited her for a while.'

'I – wanted to take her through that day, to see if there was anything other than your wife's going that might account for Freya's extreme reactions.' She smiled slightly. 'I'm not questioning the doctor's conclusion – he's qualified in such things, and I'm obviously not. But it occurred to me that he mightn't have had all the facts; in which case, he made the only diagnosis open to him.'

The ghost of a smile. 'Most tactfully put. And you uncovered some of these facts?'

Rona took a deep breath. 'I discovered that Freya disappeared during that afternoon.'

He tensed. 'Disappeared? How could she? She was with Nanny the whole time, and a more conscientious and devoted carer it would be impossible to find.'

'She fell asleep,' Rona said softly.

Robert stared at her. 'I don't . . .'

'She was sitting by the window in the sunshine, and she fell asleep. When she last looked, Freya was playing by her Wendy house at the bottom of the garden. When she woke, half an hour later, there was no sign of her.'

His hands were clenched on the arms of his chair, and his

face had paled. 'What are you telling me? She wasn't—?'

'You had her examined, didn't you? A day or two later? It was confirmed she hadn't been physically harmed.'

He let out his breath slowly. 'What, then? How and where was she found?'

'Miss Gray searched the house and garden thoroughly. Then she discovered that the gate leading to the woods was unbolted.'

'Oh, my God!'

'Eventually she found her, crouched at the foot of a tree. She was scratched and bruised, and she either wouldn't or couldn't speak.'

'Why the devil wasn't I told at once?' he burst out. 'My God, what was the woman thinking of?'

'Your wife had just gone; she didn't want to add to your worries. She'd already examined Freya carefully and was keeping a close eye on her, but she was relieved when the doctor confirmed her own findings. And the other reason she didn't tell you was because she was afraid she'd be dismissed. Especially,' she went on, over his protest, 'since your sister-in-law seemed only too ready to take over the children.'

Robert Tarlton nodded slowly. 'Yes, Jan, bless her heart, took them under her wing. I was aware there was a bit of resentment there.' He took a long draught of coffee. 'So what happened to Freya, when she was alone in the woods?'

'Miss Gray thinks she was frightened by a tramp.'

'Possible, I suppose. But would the fright have been so long lasting?'

'That's what I wondered.'

He looked at her closely. 'So what do you think?'

'Frankly, I've no idea. But she dreams of whistling and loud, angry voices, and being high up. I was wondering if she could possibly have climbed a tree?'

'She was only three, for God's sake!'

'But a tomboy, I heard. Before all this happened?'

He sighed. 'That's true. Have you mentioned this to Freya?'

'No, I haven't told anyone. But I should like to go through that gate and see the woods for myself.'

'After all this time?'

'If Freya came with me—'

'No,' he said sharply. 'I absolutely forbid that.' And then, 'Not yet, anyway. Not till I've had time to absorb all this. In any case, that gate is rusted solid; it's impossible to get it open.'

'I asked Kate to have it freed before I go over again on Sunday. It has to be the weekend, because obviously we'll need daylight.'

'Well, God knows what you'll find. I can't think it'll be anything enlightening.'

Rona said hesitantly. 'This is really why I wanted to see you, before I go any further. I can stop now, if you like.'

He was silent for some time, staring down into his coffee. Then he said heavily, 'No. It's clear we can't go on as we are; Freya seems to be heading for a real breakdown. Better to exorcise this thing now, if that's possible, and put it behind us. In the meantime, I shan't mention her disappearance. It would only add to the speculation, and I need to come to terms with it myself. But you'll let me know before you do anything drastic?'

'You sound like my husband!' she said with a smile.

'We could have had lunch at the hotel, I suppose,' Sophie remarked, 'but I can never relax there. I always feel I'm on duty!'

'This is fine,' Freya assured her, looking around the Bacchus. 'I haven't been here before.'

'It's not been open long, but it's quite handy if I want to escape for a quick bite, where no one can come up to me with their problems.'

They ordered wine and pasta, then Sophie put her elbows on the table, resting her chin in her cupped hands.

'Now, Little Sister, what exactly is going on?'

Freya shot her a startled glance, then smiled. 'That's what you called me when you were married to Lewis.'

'It's how I still think of you. But you haven't answered my question. You managed to stall me when I phoned, but you're not getting away with it this time. Something's not right, Freya. You look like a ghost.'

Freya sighed. 'I suppose you heard of my dramatic collapse,' she said resignedly. 'I certainly chose a public enough place for it.'

'But what brought it on?'

Freya looked at the worried brown eyes, the soft, curly fringe, the wide mouth. She'd always felt closer to Sophie than to Kate, who, Freya suspected, was rapidly losing patience with her.

'Right,' she said. 'If you really want to know, I'll tell you.'

And she went through the sequence of events: the first dreams, their increasing frequency and explicitness, the tune in the musical box.

'So Kate asked a friend of hers to look into it,' she finished. 'She's a journalist or something. Anyway, she was going to see Nanny Gray yesterday. I haven't heard how she got on, but I doubt if she'd have much luck. Nanny would never speak of that time; she couldn't forgive Mummy for going off and leaving us.'

'I'm not sure I'd want a journalist nosing through such private things.'

'That's what I thought, but Kate says Rona's not like that, and she seemed very nice when I met her.'

'You never actually see these people in your dream?'

'People?' Freya repeated sharply.

'Well, there must be more than one, if you heard voices.'

'I suppose you're right. I've always just thought of the man, the one who was whistling and later sobbing.'

'Was the other voice a man's or a woman's?'

Freya shuddered. 'I don't know. As I said, there's a blank in the middle, like a radio being switched off.'

'Radio rather than television? You don't see anything?'

'Not that I remember.' She forced a smile. 'Poor Matthew's having a terrible time. I'm quite sure he never expected this, when he asked me to move in with him!'

'Can you remember your mother?' Sophie asked curiously.

'I have one or two mental pictures of her, but mostly I rely on photos in the old albums.'

'Lewis said your father kept her framed portraits out for

139

a year or more, hoping she'd come back, till Jan persuaded him to put them away.'

Freya's eyes filled with tears. 'Poor Daddy. Thanks to me, the whole thing's being raked up again.'

'I heard she led him quite a dance, even before she left.'

To Freya's relief, their meal arrived, interrupting their train of thought, and when the waiter moved away, she started another topic of conversation. Sophie was content to follow it. She'd learned what she'd wanted to, but there seemed little she could do to help.

Yet again, Max awaited Adele's arrival at class with apprehension. He'd never known Wednesdays to come round so quickly, he thought grimly. The whole thing was getting ridiculous; she'd made it clear her bruises were not a subject for discussion, and had twice thwarted his attempts to help her. On the other hand, she'd seemed to imply that she'd like to meet now and then to discuss her depression, which was another kettle of fish entirely. He could just imagine Rona's reaction to that. It was probably time to make a discreet withdrawal, revert to a purely tutor–student relationship – which, if he'd had any sense, he would have stuck to in the first place.

She didn't come. Nor did she phone, and she was usually punctilious about letting him know if she had to miss a class. Was this non-appearance a result of their meeting on Monday? Max tried to anchor his thoughts on the rest of his students, moving among them admiring, correcting, suggesting. What the hell was she playing at? he wondered impatiently. And then, before he could stop the thought, suppose she's been badly hurt this time? Should he phone to check? She'd 'fallen' down the stairs once before; suppose she was now lying unconscious at the foot of them?

He changed his mind about ringing her half a dozen times during the class, but when they'd all left, he made straight for the phone. It rang for a very long time before her voice said faintly, 'Hello?'

'Adele, are you all right? Why didn't you come to the class?'

'Max! I hoped you'd call.' A little life came back into her voice.

'Are you all right?' he repeated, a little less urgently.

'Yes, of course. It was just that everything seemed too much of an effort today, so after I'd taken the children to school, I went back to bed.'

He frowned. 'You've not been there all day?'

'No, no. I got up about eleven, but I hadn't the energy to go into town. I'm sorry.'

'You usually let me know,' he said accusingly.

'I'm sorry. I didn't realize you'd be worrying about me.'

This was leading back to the bruises, and he'd decided not to go there again. 'As long as nothing's wrong,' he said lamely. 'See you next week, then.'

'If not before,' she said.

Dorothy Fairfax took the express lift up to her apartment. She felt one of her headaches coming on, and intended to lie down for a while before changing for the evening.

The top floor of the hotel was the private domain of the family, and contained a small suite of rooms for Dorothy and a larger one for Stephen and Ruth. Though there was provision for the two boys, both now lived elsewhere, Gerald round the corner in Dean's Crescent North, and Chris, since his marriage, on a new estate up Alban Road. Chris and Sophie had, however, retained possession of his former rooms to relax in when off duty or between shifts, an advantage of which Gerald never availed himself. Admittedly his hours were more erratic and his home a mere two minutes' walk away, but for odd breaks he retreated only as far as a small room off the kitchen. Dorothy sighed. He was a solitary and private young man who preferred to keep to himself, and she worried about him.

If only, she thought, turning down her bed, he could find himself a nice girl and settle down. Not, of course, that it was always the fairy-tale ending. She sighed; love, or the lack of it, caused so many problems. Dear Henry had had a wandering eye in his younger days, causing her much heartache, and even Stephen and Ruth had gone through a

141

difficult patch – though how anyone could fall out with Ruth was more than she could fathom. Then there'd been Christopher, hankering after Sophie and having that deplorable affair with the waitress. *La Ronde de l'amour*, she thought whimsically.

She slipped out of her blouse and skirt and reached for her kimono, feeling some of her tension dissolve as its silken folds caressed her body. A couple of aspirins, she told herself, going to the bathroom medicine cabinet, and an hour or so's complete rest, and she'd be fine for the evening ahead.

But when she lay down and closed her eyes, another set of worries swarmed into her head, chief of which being the unpleasant fact that there appeared to be a thief on the premises. First, one of the guests had mislaid an expensive scarf, and then today, another reported the loss of a gold fountain pen which had, he swore, been on his bedside table. If neither object reappeared in the next day or so, Stephen would have to contact the police. Dorothy intended to tell him so over dinner. Ruth had already seen to it that the staff were being closely watched; the fact remained that fellow guests were unlikely to go into each other's bedrooms – which were, in any case, accessible only with a key card.

Mentally, Dorothy ran through the staff who would have the opportunity to steal. She'd known most of them for years, and could not believe they'd succumb to temptation. At the Clarendon, there was no excuse for theft; the staff were well paid, and encouraged to go either to Ruth or Mrs Bailey, the housekeeper, if they had any problems, financial or otherwise. There had always been a family atmosphere at the hotel.

Gradually, the circling anxieties began to fade, disintegrating into a misty blur, and she drifted into sleep.

'I had lunch with Freya Tarlton today,' Sophie remarked later that evening, as the family sat at dinner. It was their practice to eat in the restaurant when the last of the guests had gone, relaxing after the day's duties. It was the one time Gerald was able – or chose – to join them, and Dorothy always looked forward to it.

'Has she got over that upset?' Ruth asked.

'Not really. She's been having disturbed nights, and they're trying to find the cause.'

'She should try sleeping pills,' Stephen said. 'This is an interesting sauce, Gerald. What are its components?'

Gerald looked up, his eyes anxious. 'Basically redcurrant and red wine, as you'd expect, but I put a touch of ginger in, to give it a lift.'

'It's delicious, darling,' Ruth said, and Stephen nodded approval.

Dorothy noted her grandson's flush of pleasure. If only Stephen wouldn't be so hard on the boy, she thought. He blossoms when he's given a little praise, and goodness knows, he deserves it. Gerald's cooking was the reason the restaurant was nearly always fully booked.

Chris said, 'I don't agree about the sleeping pills, Dad. She's too young to get into that habit.'

Stephen shrugged. 'If she has trouble getting off, it would see her over the problem.'

'It's not that she can't get to sleep,' Sophie told them. 'She keeps having nightmares.'

'Shouldn't eat cheese before bed,' suggested Chris with a grin.

'You may laugh, but they were serious enough in the past for her to be taken to a psychiatrist.'

'Overreaction, wouldn't you say?' Stephen commented.

Sophie gave up. 'You're an unsympathetic lot, but I was sorry for her. She looked really washed out.'

'The dreams will pass, dear,' Dorothy said comfortingly. 'These things run their course, and then they're done.'

But Sophie, remembering the fear in Freya's voice when she spoke of them, was not so sure.

Friday afternoon, and Max, up in his studio, was engaged in transforming his sketches and photographs into a watercolour of Guild Street, *en fête* with its Christmas lights. He'd decided when embarking on the calendar that rather than maintaining a uniform style he would use different mediums and methods as each subject suggested. Guild Street he was executing in an Impressionist manner – lights fragmenting on the pavements – and he was hoping to experiment with cubism in a woodland scene for April. It would be a challenge, but he looked forward to trying his hand. If it came off, it could be very effective.

The sound of the doorbell clarioned through the house, and he swore under his breath. Having just begun his colourwash, he certainly did not want interruptions. With bad grace, and determined to dispatch whoever it was as soon as possible, he clattered down the stairs and went to open the door, staring in total disbelief at Adele smiling on the step.

'Hello, Max,' she said. 'May I come in?'

Annoyance, surprise and common politeness battled for supremacy. 'It's not very convenient at the moment, Adele. I'm just in the middle of—'

'I won't stay long, I promise, but I need to see you.'

'You could have seen me on Wednesday,' he said shortly.

'I did explain about that.'

Not, as he remembered it, very satisfactorily.

'Please,' she said again, as he still hesitated, and with a sigh, he stood to one side to let her in.

'It's just that I'm feeling down, and need someone to talk to,' she said, making her way, uninvited, into the sitting room.

'How about your husband?' he asked bluntly, and she flushed.

'He's at work.'

'So am I, and I—'

'Please, Max, don't be cross with me. For one thing, I wanted to apologize about Wednesday.'

'You've already done that.'

She looked down at her twisting hands. 'Could I possibly have a cup of tea?'

'Adele,' he exclaimed in exasperation, 'my colour-wash is drying as we speak. If I don't get back to it at once, I'll have to start all over again.'

'Just a quick one? Please? I always feel so much better after talking to you.'

144

'I don't do counselling, you know,' he said ungraciously, but he turned and reluctantly made his way to the kitchen, aware that she was following him. If she intended to make a habit of dropping in, he thought, he'd have to nip it in the bud straight away. The scent she was wearing filled his nostrils, warm and heady, and he was aware of discomfort. God, how could he get rid of her?

He purposely kept his back to her while he made the tea, and when he turned to put the mugs on the table, saw that she'd taken off her coat. So much for a brief stay. She didn't, he thought resentfully, *look* particularly depressed. In fact, her face was flushed and her eyes, before she lowered them, had been bright and sparkling. All in all, the young woman in front of him bore surprisingly little resemblance to the cowed and pale creature he was used to seeing.

'Sugar?' he asked abruptly.

'Yes, please.'

With bad grace, he set a packet on the table, and watched as she spooned some into her mug.

She glanced up at him under her lashes. 'Aren't you going to sit down?'

He shook his head. 'I really must get back to work, or the whole canvas will need redoing.'

She hung her head. 'I've spoiled everything. I always do.'

Perhaps, he thought guiltily, her untroubled appearance was her public face, masking the bleakness she felt inside. Come to think of it, how could she help feeling bleak, when her husband abused her?

'I'm sorry,' he lied gently, 'that wasn't what I meant.'

'I came,' she said in a low voice, still not looking at him, 'because when you phoned, I thought you were worried about me.'

'I was. But you don't seem to want me to help you.'

'Of course I do, but not in that way. I – thought you cared about me.'

'What I care about is your welfare. You refuse to discuss—'

She jumped up, and he thought for a moment she was going to run away, as she had twice before. But to his stupefaction she came swiftly towards him and, reaching up, put

145

her arms round his neck and pulled his face down to hers. Before he could collect himself and move back, her pointed little tongue had darted into his mouth, and as her small body pressed against his, an agonizing shaft of desire, as unexpected as it was unwelcome, shot through him.

Furious and obscurely ashamed, he caught hold of her arms and tore them away – possibly adding to her bruises in the process – and they stood staring at each other, both of them struggling for breath.

He was the first to find his voice. 'For God's sake, Adele!' he said forcefully. '*No!*'

'Admit it, Max!' she panted, her fingers reaching for the buttons of his shirt. 'You *do* care about me, you know you do! Make love to me! No one will know! I want you so much, and I know you want me. You always have – that's why I came.'

He pulled her fingers away, shaking his head violently. 'You've got it all wrong. I was worried about you, yes, because of the bruises on your arms—'

'You were fooling yourself – admit it! You've been fighting against it, and I have too, till I suddenly thought, "What's the point?" After all, you don't live properly with your wife, do you? And this place is ideal; we could meet here regularly, and as nobody would know, we'd be hurting no one.'

'Listen to me, Adele! You're wrong – quite wrong. I love my wife, and I've never thought of you in that way, I swear it. I was concerned about your welfare, that's all.'

She searched his face for a minute, then the fire seemed to go out of her, and in an instant she was again the pale, defeated little mouse who had first aroused his protective instincts. More fool him, he thought bitterly. Rona had been right all along.

'You're rejecting me, then?' she whispered.

'I'm simply putting you straight. This need never be referred to again. Now, go home like a good girl; it'll soon be time to collect the children.'

The great, swimming eyes came up briefly to meet his. Then she turned, shrugged quickly into her coat, and hurried out of the room and, a minute later, the house. Max put his hands flat on the kitchen table and leaned on them, staring down at the surface, aware that his heart was still thumping and that sweat was coursing down his body. My God! he thought, and then again, My God!

He straightened, more shaken than he cared to admit, went to the sink, and sluiced cold water over his face. Adele! he thought wonderingly; fragile, timid Adele! Who would have thought it?

One thing was for sure, he told himself, towelling his face dry. This was very definitely something he wouldn't be telling Rona.

Eleven

That afternoon, Barnie phoned to approve the last two articles on parent searches, one of them Coralie's.

'So that brings the series to an end,' he concluded. 'Well done, I think they've come over well, and they've been sufficiently different to hold the readers' interest.'

'Fine; if there are no queries, I can return the photos and papers I borrowed.'

'Still thinking of doing something on long-term businesses?'

'I'm bearing it in mind, certainly, but I'm a bit sidetracked at the moment.'

'Useful copy?'

She smiled. 'Sorry, no. Not for publication.'

'Pity! Well, remember I'm always ready to hear your ideas. In the meantime, I believe we're seeing you and Max on the seventeenth?'

'Yes, we're looking forward to it.'

Coralie had mentioned that she worked at an estate agent's in Windsor Way, and, anxious to clear her desk, Rona decided to return the envelope and albums to her there. She'd no wish to drive out to Shellswick again, and it would constitute a good walk for Gus as well as herself.

It had rained during the morning, and the sky was still overcast; it would probably be dark even earlier this evening. She wound a long scarf round her neck and pulled on a woollen hat, watched by Gus, wagging his tail in anticipation. Windsor Way, she reflected as they set out, was where Hugh had his office. She hoped they wouldn't bump into him.

148

Because of the dimness of the afternoon, all the shop lights were on, and the atmosphere as she walked up Fullers Way to Guild Street was celebratory rather than sombre. Most of the windows had imitation Christmas trees in their windows, decorated with baubles and coloured lights. The bakery displayed a selection of delectably iced Christmas cakes and pastries, and on the pavement outside the florist was a cluster of holly garlands and poinsettias.

Rounding the corner by Willows' Furniture, Rona came upon the town's main display of lights strung across Guild Street, blinking on and off in permutations of gold, silver, red and green. No wonder the spectacle had appealed to Max for his calendar, she thought. As they passed the iron staircase leading to the Gallery, Gus paused hopefully, but Rona tugged on his lead.

'Not at the moment,' she told him. 'Perhaps on the way home.'

Just short of Windsor Way was Tarlton's, and Rona paused to survey the extravagant display of jewels, watches, gold and silver. Jan Tarlton had surpassed herself, she thought; it took an effort of will to walk past. Still, she had her own watch to open on Christmas Day.

They waited at the kerb till the traffic lights changed, then crossed the road and turned into Windsor Way. Here, the atmosphere was more subdued, as befitted a business area, though one or two of the doors had holly wreaths pinned to them. Having no wish to catch sight of Hugh, she purposely did not glance in the windows of his firm, which, as luck would have it, turned out to be actually next door to the estate agent's that was her destination.

Rona could see Coralie seated at one of the desks, and was glad there was no prospective client opposite her. She tied Gus's lead to a convenient post and went inside, to be met with a wall of warmth. Coralie saw her at once, and raised a hand. Her oriental good looks stood out among her fair or brown-haired companions, and the vivid red jumper she wore added to her exotic appearance.

'I hope I'm not interrupting anything,' Rona said, setting

149

the albums and envelope on the desk, 'but I thought it was simpler to deliver these to you here.'

Coralie pulled them towards her. 'Were they of any use?'

'A bit, but mostly I used what you told me. And incidentally, the story's been approved.'

Coralie's face lit up. 'Oh, that's great! When will it come out?'

'I'm afraid I can't tell you that. As you know, it's a monthly magazine and there are one or two ahead of yours. Early next year, I should think.'

'Good salesmanship!' Coralie smiled. 'I'll have to keep buying the mag till it appears! Actually, it'll be interesting to read other people's stories, and when they do print mine, I'll be buying copies for Lena and Jim, and my father, and Mum and Dad, as well as keeping one for myself.'

'That'll increase the circulation!' Rona paused. 'Have you heard anything further?'

'I had a Christmas card from Lena – she'd posted it early – and as I said, I'm going out there in the New Year. Pity I can't take the story with me then.'

'Sorry, but the schedule's already mapped out. Anyway, I think yours should be last, because it's a strong one to finish with. I might even be able to add the odd para when you get back from Hong Kong, to round things off.'

'That would be cool.'

Rona stood up. 'Well, thanks for all your help, Coralie, and good luck.'

'See you,' Coralie replied.

Having noted the mug of tea on her desk, Rona decided she would indeed call in at the Gallery on the way back. True, she could make herself a cup when she got home, but there were no ready supplies of flapjacks or teacakes there. She unhitched Gus and had turned towards Guild Street when a thought struck her. Talbot Road was only ten minutes' walk from here. She took out her mobile and called her father's number.

'Tom Parish,' said the familiar voice.

'Hello, Pops. You're at home, then?'

'Rona! Good to hear from you. Yes, I'm here. Why?'

'I'm in Windsor Way, and wondered if I could come on and view your new premises, and perhaps cadge a cup of tea?'

'That would be lovely! I was going to invite you all round soon for an official viewing, but you're welcome to a sneak preview. I'll put the kettle on.'

Arriving at the block of flats, Rona could appreciate her father's wry amusement at the continuing use of the name Mulberry Lodge. The building was purpose-built in uncompromising red brick, at odds with the weathered stone of its neighbours as though, Rona thought, making an aggressive statement of some kind. Still, this was a temporary home, and its nearness to Willow Crescent, where Catherine lived, had not been lost on her.

Tom was at the door of his flat as she and Gus came up the stairs.

'There is a lift, you know,' he told her, kissing her cheek.

'Gus isn't too fond of them, and it's only one flight.'

He bent to pat the dog. 'Good to see you both. Come in, and see what you think.'

Rona looked about her at the slightly worn furniture and bland décor. Though similar in size, it bore no comparison to Robert Tarlton's elegant home; but then this was rented accommodation. Her father had done his best to personalize it with his presentation clock and some family photographs. A copy of the *Daily Telegraph* lay near one of the chairs, and his glasses case was perched on the arm.

She smiled. 'It's very cosy, Pops, and I can see you've already settled in.'

His slightly anxious expression lightened, and he eagerly conducted her round the bedroom – double bed, she noted – bathroom and minuscule kitchen.

'No garden to worry about!' he said, and Rona, knowing how he'd enjoyed digging and planting in Maple Drive, felt a tug at her heart.

'You can help Catherine in hers,' she suggested, and, aware that she'd seen through him, he laughed.

'So I can,' he agreed. 'Now, come and have some tea. It looks cold out there.'

'It is, rather.' Rona unwound her scarf and pulled her hat off, shaking her hair loose.

'What were you doing in Windsor Way?' Tom asked curiously, bringing in a brown teapot. 'Not visiting Mr Cavendish, I presume?'

'You presume correctly, though I was actually next door, returning some photos and things to someone I've done an article on.'

'When are you going to get back to doing a biography? You were so good at that, and though I always enjoy what you write, I feel you're not reaching your potential with this ephemeral stuff.'

She grimaced. 'Max feels the same. He also reckons I'd be less at risk on a bio, but that doesn't always follow.'

'No indeed,' Tom agreed soberly. 'Well, don't take any notice of me, you do what you want. I remember, though, the first time I met Catherine, she remarked on how impressed she was with your work.'

'How is Catherine?'

'Fine. I'd love you to meet again soon.'

'Soon,' Rona echoed, without committing herself.

She reported on the conversation to Max that evening.

'I didn't dare bring up the subject of Christmas again,' she finished, 'though I'm really beginning to dread it.' She gave a little laugh. 'Robert Tarlton referred to the jewellery business as "a family concern". *Our* family concern is the parents!'

Max poured her a drink. 'I suppose I'd better come clean,' he said. 'I actually booked a table at the Clarendon several weeks ago, as a safeguard. For five,' he added meaningfully.

Rona gazed at him wide-eyed. 'You did?'

'Well, I knew if we left it till everyone made up their individual minds, we'd never have a hope of getting in.'

'It's a lovely thought,' she said slowly, 'though whether we can talk everyone into coming is anyone's guess.'

'At least we'll *ask* them all, then no one can justify feeling left out. Whether they come or not is up to them.'

'We'd better tell Mum as soon as possible, before she

orders the turkey. I doubt, though, that we'll get a straight answer from any of them at first. Well done, anyway, for that bit of forward thinking.'

She reached up to kiss him, and was surprised by the intensity of his response.

'Wow!' she said, when he finally released her. 'I must thank you more often!'

'So,' Max said dismissively, picking up his own glass, 'what's on the cards this weekend?'

'It's the Dawsons' party tomorrow,' Rona reminded him, 'and I'm sorry, darling, but I've committed myself to visiting the Tarltons again on Sunday afternoon. It was the only possible time, and I think it could be important.'

He shrugged, not questioning its priority.

'For the rest,' she went on, 'we really ought to make a start on Christmas shopping, or we'll be in the final rundown, which is always murder. In the meantime, I'll give the family a buzz and sound them out about Christmas lunch.'

Their varying responses were much as Rona had foreseen: Tom and Avril were equally apprehensive about the wisdom of attending together, and Lindsey made no secret of the fact that she thought Max had jumped the gun.

'He can't just corral us like that, and expect us to fall into line,' she said.

'Frankly,' Rona retorted, stung, 'it's about time someone made a positive move. The split's now a fait accompli; we can't ignore it, but we can at least be civilized about it. You said yourself Mum and Pops are getting on better; they both know we can't choose between them, so they jolly well ought to play ball.'

'What have they said?' Lindsey asked.

'They're grateful for the invitation and are thinking it over.'

'Suppose only one of them will come?'

'They've both been asked; we can't force them. Whatever happens, Max and I are going, and we'd like as many as possible of you to join us.'

After a minute, Lindsey said, 'Sorry. I wasn't being exactly gracious, was I? I'm grateful too, and I – think I'd like to come.'

'Even if it's only Pops who joins us?'

'Yes, provided Mum had the chance.'

Rona breathed a sigh of relief. 'Thanks, Linz. That's a good start.'

'Avril?'

Her hand tightened on the phone. 'Is that you, Tom?'

'Yes. I presume you've had a phone call from Rona? About Christmas?'

She tensed. 'Yes, I have.'

'What do you think?'

She said hesitantly, 'I thought you might be spending it with . . .'

'No, she's going to her own family, in Cricklehurst. How do you feel about this?'

'I don't know.' She paused, then added frankly, 'I've been dreading it this year.'

'I think we all have. I know you suggested they went to you, but—'

'It wouldn't have worked,' Avril cut in. 'I really knew that all the time. Your empty place . . .'

Tom winced. 'Could we possibly put aside our differences, do you think? You did agree we could be friends.'

But not as soon as this, she thought achingly. Aloud she said, 'All right. After all, it's sweet of them to think of it. I'm game if you are.'

'That's wonderful, Avril. Thank you. And as Rona said, it will be easier being in a public place, and not cooped up together in one or other of the houses.'

'Except that everyone will know we're separated, and be watching us.'

'They'll have better things to do on Christmas Day; but if they want to watch us, let them. We'll show them all how amicable we are. Shall I ring Rona back, or would you like to?'

'You do it,' she said.

The Christmas shopping went well, and they were able to cross a number of names off their list. Max did, however, have one uncomfortable moment: in Netherby's Department

Store, he caught sight of Philip Yarborough, who was their sales director, and tensed, half-expecting him to come up and accuse him of upsetting his wife. No doubt, Max thought grimly, that was his own prerogative. But Philip, engaged with a manager, didn't see them, and Max was able to steer Rona quickly in the opposite direction.

He had not slept well, continually replaying in his head the incredible scene with Adele, which then wove itself into his dreams. One of the more disturbing aspects had been his own brief but powerful response, and he reflected that several of his friends would think him a fool for not seizing his chance with a willing and attractive woman. God only knew how he was going to deal with her, he thought despairingly; he could scarcely ban her from the class.

They spent the afternoon seated at the kitchen table writing Christmas cards, and by the time they changed for the party, Rona at least was in a thoroughly festive mood.

'I can really look forward to Christmas now,' she said happily, fastening a gold chain round her neck. 'Bless you for sorting everything out.'

She smiled at him in the dressing-table mirror. They'd made love last night and it had been especially good. Often, their love-making was leisurely and tender rather than passionate, but last night it had been as urgent and intense as in the early days, and she was left with a warm glow of well-being.

Ben and Louise Dawson lived in one of the roads at the top of Furze Hill Park, and as they drove up, the pavement was already white with frost. 'I hope it doesn't get icy,' Max remarked, 'or it could be tricky coming back down again.'

A large conifer in the garden was bedecked with coloured lights – a practice of which Max professed to disapprove – and already a line of cars was drawn up outside the house. They were ushered inside, and Louise came forward to kiss them. She was a tall, bony woman whose long face was transformed when she smiled. She wore extra-large glasses, and her straw-coloured hair hung down from a centre parting on either side of her face – a factual description that did not do her justice, since she was undeniably attractive. She

155

and her husband were both surgeons at the Royal County.

'You'll know most people,' she told them, 'so just introduce yourselves to those you don't. They're a nice bunch.'

The first person Rona saw as they went into the long drawing room was Chris Fairfax, and her eyes went immediately to the elegant young woman beside him. Ben Dawson, seeing the direction of her gaze, took her elbow.

'Do you know the Fairfaxes, Rona? If not, come and meet them.'

Rona saw the alarmed recognition in Chris's eyes as they approached. She had, after all, witnessed his meeting with Coralie, and might well mention it. But as she smiled and took his hand, she gave no indication that they'd met before, and sensed his relief.

'Rona Parish?' repeated Sophie. 'Are you the journalist who's helping Freya Tarlton?'

'Well, trying to!' Rona modified.

'Could we have a little chat, do you think?'

'Of course.' Rona took the glass of champagne Ben handed her, and, threading her way between chattering groups, followed Sophie to vacant chairs on the far side of the room.

'I've been wanting to speak to you ever since Freya told me you were involved,' she began. 'Have you any idea what's behind these nightmares?'

'Not really,' Rona fenced. She didn't know how much Freya had confided in Sophie, but the story of the woods must remain under wraps, at least till she'd spoken to Lewis and Kate, not to mention Freya herself.

'It's not idle curiosity,' Sophie assured her, sensing her reticence. 'I'm not sure if you know that I used to be married to her brother? I'm still extremely fond of her.'

She waited, and when Rona didn't elaborate, went on, 'Do you think her mother's desertion is at the root of it?'

'It won't have helped,' Rona said cautiously.

Unexpectedly, Sophie laughed. 'OK, you're not going to tell me, and that's fair enough. It's just that I'm really worried about her. She passed out at the shop the other day, and she still doesn't look well.'

'I know,' Rona said. 'Please don't think I'm being

awkward; I'm sure Freya will keep you in the picture, but I don't feel it's up to me to discuss what is a pretty delicate matter.'

'You're quite right, and I was wrong to try to pressure you. I'm sorry. Let's start again, by my saying how much I'm enjoying your articles on Buckford. I grew up there, and never appreciated what a long and interesting history it had. You should do the same for Marsborough.'

Rona smiled. 'Marsborough's a Georgian town, a mere three hundred years old. It can't compete with Buckford's octocentenary, though I am considering a different angle. In fact, at a later stage I'd like to talk to you about it.'

'How mysterious! Obviously, I'd be glad to help.'

Someone came over to speak to Sophie, and their tête-à-tête was brought to an end. Rona, seeing Georgia Kingston nearby, went over to join her, and the evening proceeded pleasantly in chatting with old friends. Magda and Gavin weren't here, Rona noticed, slightly disappointed; perhaps at this time of year they'd had conflicting invitations.

The buffet was served and they all migrated to the dining room to fill their plates. As usual on these occasions, she'd lost sight of Max; no doubt he was in some corner discussing art with Simon Grant.

It wasn't until the evening was nearing an end that he was brought forcibly back to her notice. She was standing in a group discussing a recent television play when, behind her, she heard a man's voice she didn't recognize say, 'By the way, Max, have you started giving private lessons?'

She didn't look round, but, while continuing to smile attentively at the spokesman in her own group, focussed on the conversation behind her.

Max must have replied in the negative, because the next thing Rona heard was the first voice continuing, 'Well then, who was the little dolly-bird who came rushing out of Farthings yesterday afternoon?'

Rona caught her breath, a wave of heat engulfing her as she strained to hear Max's reply. It seemed an inordinately long time coming. Was he aware of her presence?

'Had you been at an office lunch, Charlie?' he asked with

a forced laugh. 'If so, I'd advise you to take more water with it!'

'Seriously, I kid you not. Saw her with my own eyes.'

'Then she must have come from the next door along.'

Charlie, whoever he was, remained unconvinced. 'No way!' he insisted. 'I tell you, guys, old Max here has something going! There I was, driving past minding my own business, and this cute little blonde comes dashing out of his house as though the Furies were at her heels! What had you been doing to her, old man?'

Someone in her group had made an amusing comment, and Rona joined mindlessly in the general laughter. Then, feeling suddenly sick, she extricated herself and, still without glancing in Max's direction, left the room and made her way to the cloakroom. Having locked the door behind her, she stood stock-still, staring at her reflection in the mirror, cheeks hot and eyes burning bright.

Was this, she wondered painfully, how wives usually found out about affairs? From apparently harmless jocularity at parties? Because she had positively no doubt that the 'dollybird', the 'cute little blonde', was Adele Yarborough. Was it to salve his conscience that he had made love to her so passionately last night?

A sob rose in her throat and, mindful that someone might be passing outside, she hastily turned it into a cough. Did Max know she'd overheard the conversation? Would he refer to it, or wait until she did? What was the accepted norm in these circumstances? She should ask Lindsey, she thought hysterically.

She walked slowly to the basin and gripped its blessedly cold edges. Suppose he didn't mention it? Or suppose he did? Suppose he finally admitted that he found Adele attractive, and would prefer to be with her? Yesterday afternoon. While she'd been with Pops, perhaps. Too bad she hadn't called in at Farthings herself, and caught them *in flagrante*. Perhaps then she'd be able to believe it.

Someone tried the door handle, and Rona hastily flushed the lavatory, washed her hands, and, with a last, unseeing glance in the mirror, opened the door, blindly smiling at the person – man or woman, she didn't register – who waited outside.

People were starting to leave, thank God. She reached the door of the drawing room as Max emerged from it, clearly looking for her.

'Oh, there you are,' he said, not meeting her eyes. 'Are you ready to make a move?'

She nodded, not trusting her voice, and he searched through the pile of coats on the chair, extracting hers and helping her on with it. Mechanically, Rona thanked their host and hostess and allowed Max to lead her down the icy front path. Several other couples were leaving at the same time, and called goodnight to them as they went to their own cars. Then, as Max climbed in beside her, they were completely alone, with no one to mask the silence between them.

She felt him glance at her, perhaps not yet sure if, or how much, she had heard.

'Enjoy yourself?' he asked abruptly.

'Up to a point.' A very specific point.

'Give me a dinner party, any day.' It was an old refrain, and didn't require a reply.

The rest of the ten-minute drive passed in silence. Max found a parking space outside the next-door house. Rona went ahead of him up the path, waiting as he inserted his key in the lock. The heat of the hall felt suffocating, and she pulled off her coat and draped it over the banister.

'You heard, didn't you?' he said flatly.

'Yes.'

'I'm sorry.'

'I bet you are!'

'I mean I'm sorry you found out that way. I should have told you, but—'

She spun to face him, eyes blazing. 'Too right, you should have told me! How long has it been going on?'

He stared at her for a minute. 'Now look—'

'No, *you* look! I knew from the first that woman was trouble, but you wouldn't have it. I *told* you there was nothing wrong with her, that she was after the sympathy vote. But

159

I never dreamed you'd actually stoop to secret meetings so you could—'

Max slammed his hand on the hall table, making her jump.

'That's enough, Rona! Now just be quiet and let me explain.'

'Are you having an affair with her?' she interrupted.

'Of course not!'

'But you've at least kissed her. Haven't you?'

He hesitated a fraction too long, and she spun on her heel, ran upstairs into the bedroom and slammed the door.

Max sat down on the lowest step and put his head in his hands.

Twelve

It was a long time before Max came to bed. When she heard his footsteps on the stairs, Rona, who had lain, burning-eyed, staring at the ceiling, turned on her side and lay motionless. She heard him pause briefly in the doorway, go to the bathroom and, minutes later, climb into bed beside her.

'Rona?' he said softly.

She did not reply. She knew he was lying as rigid as she was, feigning sleep, but she was too hurt, too angry, to make the first move. Eventually, after what seemed hours, she fell into a deep sleep, and when she woke, daylight was seeping through the curtains and she was alone in the bed.

Nine o'clock, she saw, peering at the bedside clock. She showered, dressed, and went down to the kitchen. Max was sitting at the table, also fully dressed, the newspaper in his hands. On a normal Sunday, she thought with aching throat, they had a leisurely breakfast in their dressing gowns, working their way through the heavy wad of newspapers.

'Good morning,' he said tightly.

'Good morning.'

'There's coffee in the pot.'

She poured herself a cup in silence. Max watched her, but she didn't look at him.

'Are you going to let me explain what happened?'

'I know as much as I want to, thank you.'

'You know damn all,' he said harshly.

'I know that you kissed her.'

'*She* kissed *me*!'

'There's a difference?'

'Of course there's a bloody difference!'

161

'Well, I don't want to go into it now.' She picked up her cup. 'I told you I'm seeing the Tarltons this afternoon; I've some things to prepare, so I'm going up to the study.'

'Suit yourself.'

She stayed there, staring at the blank computer screen, until the smell of roasting beef drifted up the stairs. Max always cooked Sunday lunch, though she was unsure whether she'd be able to eat it today. She did, however, gather her things together and go downstairs, to find the kitchen table laid and Max in the process of carving. From the set of his jaw and the fact that he didn't glance in her direction, she knew he was now as angry as she was; though what right he had, she couldn't imagine. He had tried to 'explain', she hadn't let him, and now, as stubborn as she was, he was determined that she should make the next move. She was incapable of doing so.

He set her plate in front of her, she said 'Thank you', and that was the sum of their conversation. Max had the colour supplement open at his side, and pointedly read it throughout the meal. Rona simply concentrated on getting through it as quickly as possible, and, having eaten as much as she could, tipped what was left into the bin and put her plate in the dishwasher. This is *horrible*! she thought shakily. She and Max frequently had rows, but none had been as serious or lasted as long as this one. If she'd not been going out, she might have instigated some communication between them, but she was afraid she might burst into tears – which was the last thing she wanted – and she had to keep her mind clear for the coming interview.

He didn't look up when she walked towards the stairs, but Gus wagged his tail uncertainly.

'I don't know when I'll be back,' she said.

It was too early to drive straight to Brindley Lodge, so Rona turned down a country lane off Belmont Road and parked in a gateway leading to a field. Lack of sleep, she realized, was not conducive to clear thinking, and it was imperative that she push Max and Adele out of her mind and concentrate on the Tarltons. The appointment ahead of her might well produce some of the answers she was looking for.

She switched the radio to Classic FM, leaned back against the headrest and closed her eyes. Had Kate had the bolts freed? she wondered. Would Lewis resent her questioning? She felt herself drifting off and woke with a start some fifteen minutes later, to find it was almost two o'clock. She started the car and drove the remaining distance to the house.

Kate led her through to the sitting room where they'd sat before. Lewis was standing in front of the fire, and came forward. 'I don't think we've been formally introduced,' he said, holding out his hand, 'but we both know who we are. I'm grateful to you for helping with this problem.'

'Tell us what Nanny said,' Kate instructed, as soon as they'd sat down.

'This might come as a bit of a shock,' Rona began carefully. And she went on to relate the length of time the three-year-old Freya had been missing, and her eventual discovery in the wood.

They were both looking at her with horrified expressions. 'How the devil did she get in there?' Lewis demanded.

Rona said tactfully, 'Miss Gray thought the gate couldn't have been bolted,' and saw him flush.

'Mea culpa, no doubt. My friends and I often played in the woods.' He paused. 'Is that why you wanted the bolts freed?'

'Yes; I thought it might be helpful to have a look for myself.'

'I can't imagine why. No one's been there for years – or at least, not from this side. The public access is from Woodlands Road, which, as you probably know, runs parallel to Belmont, but I don't know if anyone still uses it. Possibly courting couples; I know they used to.'

Kate stood up. 'Let's go and look, then.'

They collected their coats from the hall and set off down the garden. This time, the bolts, top and bottom, slid smoothly back and, at a brief push from Lewis, the old gate creaked open. 'God,' he said, 'I wonder when I was last here.'

Brambles and bushes clogged any footpath there might have been, and they all stood uncertainly, looking about them.

163

'Did you play anywhere in particular?' Rona asked.

'Yes, we'd made a tree house in one of the clearings.' He gave a brief smile. 'That's how I know about the courting couples. We had a good view.'

'Horrid little boys!' Kate said.

Rona, though, did not smile. A pulse had started to beat at the base of her throat. 'Can you remember whereabouts it was?'

'I think I could find it, though everywhere's so appallingly overgrown.'

He looked about him for a minute, then set off slightly to the right, holding back overhanging branches for the women following him. They pushed determinedly through the undergrowth, their clothes caught in brambles and their hands and faces scratched, but eventually the trees grew wider apart and they found themselves in a clearing.

'The house was up there.' Lewis gesticulated at a tree that stood slightly apart. 'My God!' he said wonderingly. 'It still is! See that rotting board in the fork up there? That would have been the platform. And look at this.' He bent forward. 'The remnants of the rope ladder are still here, too.'

Kate and Rona turned from the slanting board to the frayed rope in his hand. Rona said with an effort, 'Did Freya ever come here with you?'

'Freya? Good Lord, no. She was only a toddler. We were all ten years older, and didn't want her trailing after us.'

'Could she have followed you, without your knowing?'

Lewis stared at her, then moistened his lips. 'She certainly tried to tag along, but we'd never let her. It's *possible* she could have followed us, because, of course, while we were in the wood, the gate was left on the latch. When we came back, though, it was a strict rule that we should bolt it top and bottom. The bolts were a bit stiff even then, and the top one was too high for her to reach. God knows how it came to be unlocked that day.'

'You're thinking about the dream, aren't you?' Kate said in a strangled voice. 'Being high up?'

Rona nodded. 'Suppose, when Lewis was at school, she found the gate unbolted and decided to go to the tree house

164

by herself. I'd wondered about trees before, but it seemed unlikely so young a child could climb high enough to be hidden from below. But if there was a rope ladder, it would have been much easier.'

There was a silence, while the three of them looked from the rope in Lewis's hand to the decaying planks of the house, still wedged in a crevice of the branches above them. Then Lewis said, 'You're thinking she might have climbed up there, then someone came into the clearing and frightened her? Who, exactly?'

'I've no idea. Miss Gray thought it might have been a tramp.'

'They'd stopped coming by then. My father told me that when he was young, beggars, tramps and so on regularly went into the woods, principally to drink from the well, but often staying to doss down for the night. There was one of those iron cups on a chain, to scoop up the water. Can you *imagine* how unhygienic that was? But the spring that supplied it dried up during the war sometime, and the council boarded it up.'

'Where *is* the well?'

'A bit further along. So –' he finally let go the rope he'd been holding, and it fell back against the tree trunk – 'I don't think there's much more to see. Has it been any help?'

'It could have a bearing on the dream,' Rona said cautiously, 'but without knowing what, if anything, she saw while she was up there, we're not much further on.'

Slowly they retraced their steps to the garden, and Lewis bolted the gate behind them. Rona shivered. There was a cold breeze and she was glad to leave the confined silences of the woods.

'After-lunch coffee?' Kate suggested. 'A bit late, but it would warm us up.'

When they were seated round the fire, Lewis returned to the subject of the unbolted gate. 'I feel dreadful,' he said. 'Just a moment's carelessness, and the result was years of distress for Freya.'

'If Nanny hadn't fallen asleep,' Kate said sharply, 'no

harm would have been done. It was her fault, not yours.'

'How much do you remember of the day your mother left?' Rona asked him.

Lewis sipped his coffee thoughtfully. 'My clearest memories are of what came afterwards. I used to spend hours trying to recall exactly the last time I'd seen her, and exactly what her last words to me had been. And wondering if something I'd done had driven her away.'

Kate reached for his hand, and Rona said, 'You were at school, of course?'

'Yes. When I got home, I found a parcel on my bed, which turned out to be an engine I'd been wanting for my train set. There was a little card that said, "With love from Mummy."

'I ran downstairs to thank her for it, but of course she wasn't there. Dad came back from the shop, and we held back supper for a while, but Mum didn't come, so eventually we had it. When we'd finished, Dad went up to say goodnight to Freya. Then went into his bedroom and – found the note.'

Lewis stopped speaking and they sat in silence. 'He didn't tell me, mind you,' he continued at last. 'When he came back downstairs, he looked very pale and I asked if he was OK, and he just nodded. Then he wanted to know if I'd any homework, and when I sat down to do it, he went to the phone. I think he called Bruce and Jan, but I didn't hear what he said, and of course at that stage I wasn't really interested.' He paused, and added reflectively, 'I've always thought he didn't tell me for so long, because he kept hoping she'd change her mind and come back.'

'Will you tell Freya about the tree house?' Rona asked.

Lewis frowned. 'I'm not sure. I'll have a word with my father. We don't want to add to her stress, and we might be way off-beam.'

Rona nodded, but she didn't think so. She was relieved, though, they didn't want her to break the news.

Kate said thoughtfully, 'If courting couples went there, she could have seen a lovers' tiff.'

Lewis shook his head. 'It would have to have been pretty violent, to leave such an impression.'

'If they were making love, it could have *looked* violent to a young child.'

It seemed no one else had anything to offer. Rona picked up her handbag. 'I'd better be going,' she said. 'I've taken up enough of your Sunday.'

They didn't try to detain her. As she drove out of the gate, she saw them standing in the open doorway, Lewis's arm across Kate's shoulders, and felt a sharp pang of envy. Oh, God, she couldn't face going home to Max's stony silence.

She pulled in to the kerb, took out her mobile, and dialled Lindsey's number. It rang and rang, then the answerphone came on. She tried her mobile, but it was turned to voice-mail. Damn! Rona thought. Where are you, when I need you?

In desperation, she pressed the key for the Ridgeways, and was rewarded by the engaged tone. At least that meant they were home. Rona snapped her mobile shut and, emerging from Brindley Grove, turned in the direction of the town centre.

There were lights in the downstairs windows when she drew up outside the house in Barrington Road. She went up the path and rang the bell. It was Gavin who answered it.

'Rona! Hello! What a pleasant surprise!'

The sight of his familiar figure, and, behind him, the house that was like a second home to her, caught her off guard and her eyes filled with tears.

'Hey!' Gavin's smile faded and he reached for her. 'Come in, love. What's the matter?'

She shook her head blindly and felt his arm come round her as, minutes before, she'd seen Lewis's encircle Kate.

'Sorry,' she said. 'I'm all right. Really. Just . . .'

Magda's voice called, 'Who is it, darling?' and she appeared in the kitchen doorway.

'Rona!' Then, sharply, 'What's wrong? What's happened?'

Rona shook her head, and as Gavin released her, went forward into Magda's outstretched arms, feeling them tighten about her.

'Come into the kitchen,' Magda said, leading her through the open door.

167

'You sound like your mother!' Rona told her, with a shaky laugh. Paola King had been of the opinion that most ills could be cured by, depending on the hour of day, a plate of home-made pasta or a cup of cappuccino and the little pastries she called *copate*.

'Sit down.' Rona obediently did so, and Magda sat down opposite her, gazing at her intently. 'Right; now – what's happened?'

'I've had a row with Max,' Rona said.

Magda raised an eyebrow. 'Hardly the first, I imagine.'

'But the worst so far.'

'Do you want to tell me about it?'

Rona hesitated. 'That's why I came here,' she admitted, 'but now I'm not so sure.'

'When did this take place? Just now?'

'No, last night.'

Magda clicked her teeth. 'And you let the sun go down on it? That's not like you.'

'It had gone down before we started,' Rona said, with the ghost of a smile.

'So what have you been doing today? Avoiding each other?'

'Pretty well. I had to go and see someone this afternoon, and suddenly felt I couldn't go home. Which is why I turned up on your doorstep. Sorry.'

'Lindsey not being available?'

'No.'

'Then where else would you turn up?' Magda asked briskly. 'Would you like some coffee?'

'I've just had some, but it's made me thirsty. I'd love a cup of tea.'

'No problem.' Magda set about making it. 'Whoever did you have to see on a Sunday afternoon?'

'Kate and Lewis Tarlton.'

Magda turned in surprise. 'The jewellery people?'

'Yes.'

'Regarding your new series?'

Rona smiled. 'More regarding the "flighty wife", as Gavin called her.'

'The one who went off with her lover?'

'Yes; she left her daughter with a lasting trauma, and I'm not sure Lewis escaped unscathed.'

'Old Robert certainly didn't,' Magda said, putting mugs of tea on the table and sitting down again. 'So where do you come in?'

And, glad to have something other than Max to think about, Rona told her about Freya's dreams and that afternoon's visit to the wood.

'Spooky,' Magda said.

'It was, a bit.' Rona sipped the hot tea, and found it soothing.

'Do you think the tree house is significant?'

'Yes, but I'm not sure how.'

'If you told Freya what you've worked out, it might be enough to bring the rest of it back.'

'Yes, but I'm happy to leave that responsibility to her family.'

Magda stood up. 'Well, if you're sure you don't want to talk about Max, let's go and join Gavin. He'll be glad to see you.'

Dear Magda; unlike herself over Adele, she never betrayed the slightest hint of jealousy. Not that she'd any cause, though, in her present anti-Max mood, Gavin's arm round her had been very comforting. Perhaps it was as well Magda had appeared when she did.

They sat by the fire, chatting and listening to CDs, for a couple of hours before Rona reluctantly made a move. Gavin, possibly primed by his wife when Rona wasn't looking, had made no reference to Max, so there'd been no awkward moments.

'How are your parents?' Magda asked, as Rona slipped on her coat in the hall.

'On speaking terms, thank goodness. We'll be having Christmas lunch together after all. Max has booked a table at the Clarendon.'

'That's great.' She opened the front door on to winter darkness, and Rona's heart, buoyed up by her friends' company, plummeted again. Perhaps her expression betrayed her, because Magda gave her a quick hug and whispered in her ear, 'Good luck!'

Slowly, Rona drove home.

As she shut the front door, Gus came bounding to greet her, closely followed by Max.

'I was beginning to wonder where you were,' he said. 'Have you been at the Tarltons' all this time?'

'No, I went on to the Ridgeways.'

His eyes narrowed. 'And told them I'd been with another woman?'

'No,' she said tiredly, 'just that we'd had a row.'

After a minute he said, 'Thank you for that. Let's go into the sitting room.'

Obediently she did so, seating herself on the sofa facing the fire. He followed, and stood looking down at her. 'I was beginning to wonder if you were coming back at all.'

'If you'd checked, you'd have found I hadn't taken my toothbrush.'

'It's been a hell of a day.'

'I know.'

'At least you've had company all afternoon.'

He sat down next to her and reached for her hand. She made no effort to withdraw it.

'Are you prepared to let me explain now?'

'I suppose so.'

'The first thing I have to say, my love, is that you were right and I was wrong. Adele *was* making a bid for my interest. But I swear to you—'

'Just tell me what happened.'

Calmly and without embellishment, he did so. 'It came totally out of the blue,' he ended. 'I hadn't seen it coming, but with hindsight perhaps I should have done.'

'It was so humiliating,' Rona said softly, 'hearing that horrible man talking like that, and the rest of them sniggering.'

'I know, sweetheart. I wanted to knock his teeth down his throat, but it might have raised the odd eyebrow. However, when you left the room, I made myself crystal-clear. By the time I'd finished, no one was in any doubt that Adele was simply a student who – and here I admit I lied – had called in to collect some sketches she'd left behind. Charlie had the grace to apologize.' He sighed. 'I know I should have told you straight away, but you'd always been against her, and I knew the fur would fly.'

She said in a low voice, 'I wondered if that was why you made love to me on Friday. Because of a guilty conscience.'

He pulled her roughly into his arms. 'You little goose,' he said against her hair. 'I made love to you because you mean everything to me, and always have, and always will, and all the Adele Yarboroughs in the world can go to hell as far as I'm concerned. Does that satisfy you?'

'Almost,' she said, and turned her head to meet his mouth.

Gerald Fairfax locked the front door of his cottage and walked down the path to the gate, where he paused for a moment, looking up and down the road. In Dean's Crescent North, he thought with satisfaction, no two houses were the same. Some, like his, had a front path, while others, such as Farthings, where the artist lived, opened directly on to the street. Some were thatched, some steep-gabled, some of stone, some of brick. It was an interesting place to live, and he was glad to be a part of it, rather than lodging at the hotel. He spent enough time there as it was, and he needed his space.

Nevertheless, he thought with a smile, he was on his way there now, even though it was his evening off. True, he was anxious to see how Darren coped with the new duck recipe, but his main reason for going was to ask his brother's advice about a Christmas present for their father. Chris was closer to Stephen than he was, and had a clearer idea of what appealed to him.

He walked slowly to the corner of the Crescent, glancing into lighted windows as he went. He felt no guilt for his voyeurism – if the inhabitants wanted privacy, they should draw their curtains – and enjoyed these brief snapshots of other people's lives. Occasionally, he amused himself by imagining their daily routines, their places of work and their

171

interaction with each other. He wondered if life on the inside of those windows was as idyllic as it appeared to those on the outside, or whether there were secrets and infidelities, crises and deceits in even the most united-seeming families.

Turning into Guild Street, he considered his own. They'd be surprised how much he knew about them – things they considered private to themselves, but which he'd absorbed without conscious effort. He'd been aware, for instance, of Chris's affair with Coralie Davis, long before it became common knowledge. His grandmother's secret fear was that she was losing her sight, and he'd added it to his own worry list. His father drank more than anyone appreciated, and was given to bouts of what Gerald suspected was severe depression, though he managed to disguise them pretty well. Only his mother, he thought fondly, had no secrets as far as he was aware.

Since he intended to see Darren first and offer encouragement on the duck, Gerald opted for the rear entrance. He turned into the kitchen passage, and was passing the small room he used for breaks, when, remembering he'd left some papers there, he decided to collect them en route.

He pushed open the door, and had taken a couple of steps inside before registering that the light was on, and someone was already there. Though never put into words, it was tacitly agreed that the room was his private domain, which was why he'd left personal items there. Now, to his annoyance, he found himself confronting Ted, one of the waiters, who was staring at him in consternation, his face flooding with colour.

'Oh – Chef! I didn't know you were coming in this evening.'

'Obviously.'

'I'm sorry – I'd no right—'

'No, you hadn't,' Gerald agreed sharply, wondering how often his privacy had been violated, and by how many members of staff. 'Do you make a practice of coming here?'

'No, really, I just . . .' His voice tailed off miserably as Gerald frowningly looked about him.

'So what were you doing? Not relaxing, from the look of it.'

172

The man was, in fact, standing in front of the bookshelves, and a closer look revealed that one of the recipe books was slightly out of alignment.

Gerald moved towards it, and Ted said rapidly, 'I was just checking something – it's not important. Please – there's no need—'

Ignoring him, Gerald lifted out the protruding volume – a technical tome that could be of no interest – and, aware of the man's mounting unease, reached into the recess left by its removal. His fingers encountered something soft and silky, and he withdrew his hand to find himself holding a brilliantly coloured scarf. Even as he stared at it in bewilderment, something fell from its folds and rolled under his desk – a shining gold cylinder.

Slowly, Gerald raised his eyes and held the waiter's. Ted had now paled and was moistening his lips nervously.

'Well?' Gerald said.

'I know I done wrong,' the man said rapidly. 'I – was going to return them.'

At Gerald's patent disbelief, he went on miserably, 'I saw them when I was doing room service. It was a spur of the moment thing, I never—'

'*Two* spur of the moment things,' Gerald corrected. 'Which doesn't sound quite so feasible, does it?'

Ted's eyes fell. 'I'm sorry, Chef. Give me a break, will you? I'll never do it again, honest.'

'Honest isn't the word I'd have chosen.'

'Couldn't you just say you found them?'

'In my room? What are they doing here, anyway?'

'I thought they wouldn't be missed for a while, but when that notice went on the board, I panicked. I'd taken them home, like, but I brought them back, meaning to sneak them up to the rooms again. But before I could, the police came to question us. I had to get rid of them quickly, so I—'

'Hid them here.'

He nodded miserably. 'I know it was stupid, but it seemed the only place.' He paused. 'You're going to turn me in, aren't you?'

'I'll tell my parents, yes, but it's out of their hands now.

As you say, the police are involved, and until the culprit's named, everyone's under suspicion.'

'I didn't know they were so valuable,' Ted muttered.

'Stealing is stealing, whatever the object's worth.'

He nodded again, and, avoiding Gerald's eyes, turned and left the room. Gerald bent to retrieve the fountain pen from under his desk. It was a Mont Blanc – one of the world's most expensive. No wonder the owner had reported its loss.

The man was sure to be sacked, he reflected, and with Christmas coming up, too. But honesty was essential in hotel work, and they'd never be able to trust him again. Still, that was one thing, thank God, that was *not* his problem. Abandoning his intention of a word with his sous-chef, Gerald pushed open the door leading to the main part of the hotel.

Thirteen

It was late afternoon when the call came, and Rona, having finished work for the day, was making a cup of tea.

'Rona?'

For a moment, she didn't recognize the voice, but she was given no time to wonder.

'It's Kate. The most appalling thing has happened. Oh, God!' She broke off with a choked sob and Rona, suddenly alarmed, sat down heavily at the kitchen table.

'What is it, Kate?'

'I wish to God I'd never started this!' Kate was going on hysterically. 'Damn it, the dreams would have stopped in their own good time. They did before.'

'Kate, what's happened? What are you talking about?'

'The well,' Kate said in a whisper. 'The bloody well.' She drew a long, shuddering breath, and in the silence the kettle started whistling shrilly. Rona, who'd nearly leapt out of her skin, hurried to turn it off.

'Sorry,' she said into the phone. 'Go on.'

'After you'd left yesterday, Lewis decided to take a look at it. He'd been mulling over what we'd said about it earlier, and that *if* Freya had seen a lovers' tiff, it would have to have been a violent one, for her to remember it. So finally, to satisfy him, back we went, armed with a powerful torch and tools to prise off the cover.'

Her voice began to shake again. 'God, Rona, it was like a nightmare. Because when we got the top off and – peered down, even in the light of the torch we could see something at the bottom.'

Rona said in a croak, 'Some*thing* or some*one*?'

Kate didn't answer. 'We hurried back to the house and

phoned Robert, and he got in touch with Bruce and Jan, and we all went down. The well's not very deep – about fifteen feet, I should say, and of course it's been dry for decades.'

'What *was* it, Kate?'

She gave a kind of sob. 'We couldn't tell. So we phoned the police, and they said they'd be round first thing in the morning. It was dark by then, and they must have thought, since there was obviously no urgency, that they could work better in daylight.'

'And this morning,' Rona said clearly, 'they found a body.'

'A skeleton,' Kate corrected, 'with shreds of material clinging to it, and lying on top of it – oh, God! – was a mouldy, decaying suitcase.' She paused. 'You know what's coming, don't you?'

Rona nodded, realized Kate couldn't see her, and said in a whisper, 'Velma.'

'Almost certainly. And now,' Kate went on wildly, 'they've taken Robert away for questioning! Everyone's in a total state of shock. Oh Rona, what have we done?'

Rona said shakily, 'So Freya, up in the tree house . . .'

'I know. It doesn't bear thinking about, does it? And to add to everything, they've taken a blood sample from her, to compare the DNA.'

'Kate—' Rona broke off, cleared her throat and tried again. 'You do realize that if the dream progresses any further, she might see who it was?'

'I almost forgot – that's why I'm phoning. Lewis says we mustn't mention the dreams to *anyone*. If the killer's still around, and finds out about them, she could be in serious danger.'

'But he *can't* still be around, can he? Not after all this time? Surely it was her lover, whoever he was; they had a row, he killed her, threw her in the well, and then fled. After all, he disappeared at the same time.' So Gavin had told her.

Another thought struck her. 'If Freya's had to give a sample, does that mean she knows everything now? About being lost in the woods, I mean?'

'Yes; we couldn't keep it from her.'

'How is she?'

'Shocked, to find the dreams were based on memories, and terrified to go to sleep, in case she sees the murderer's face.' Kate paused. 'Though in fact,' she went on thoughtfully, 'the dreams were all about *sounds*, weren't they? Whistling, shouting, sobbing. She's never mentioned *seeing* anyone, or even the possibility of a woman being there.'

'Perhaps it was blotted out at some deeper level.'

'Perhaps. Still, to be on the safe side, don't tell anyone about them, will you?' Her voice sharpened. 'Or have you already?'

Oh God, Rona thought, yes, she had. Max, of course, and Magda, who'd probably passed it on to Gavin, and Nanny Gray . . .

'I might have just—'

'It's sure to ring a bell, when the story breaks. You must get on to them straight away, and tell them to keep quiet. *Promise* me you'll do that?'

'I promise,' Rona said aridly. Then, 'You'll be carrying on as normal, though? At the shop?'

'We've no option; if we don't, people will assume we've something to hide. It won't be easy, though; as soon as it gets into the press, they'll start to talk. In fact, it's probably already in this evening's paper, and we've had the first of the nationals round. We can only be thankful this blew up on a Monday, when at least the shop was closed and we could deal with it.'

'Was it definitely murder? She didn't commit suicide, or fall down the well accidentally?'

'There doesn't seem much doubt, but they need the forensic evidence to be sure. If there's any left to find.'

'It depends how she died. Blows on the head might show on the skull, and a stab wound could have nicked a bone—' Realizing what she was saying, she broke off, horrified, but Kate gave a choked laugh.

'I was forgetting you'd had several brushes with murder.'

'Kate, I'm really terribly sorry about all this. If I hadn't asked to see the woods—'

'Forget it. It was my fault, for involving you. I bet you wish to God I hadn't.'

*   *   *

177

As soon as she rang off, Rona called Max and told him the news.

'So you've flushed out another murderer,' he observed. 'I don't know how you do it.'

'Max! That's an awful thing to say! And I haven't, anyway. They're interviewing Robert Tarlton, who's obviously not guilty.'

'And exactly what basis have you for that opinion? His wife had been unfaithful for years, according to Gavin. Perhaps, when he found out she was leaving him, it was the last straw.'

Rona felt suddenly cold. That, no doubt, was the way the police were thinking. Were they right?

'The reason I'm ringing,' she went on after a minute, 'is to ask you to keep quiet about Freya's dreams.'

'Dreams?' he repeated blankly. 'What the hell are you talking about?'

Belatedly, she realized that although they had loomed large in her own thoughts, and Kate's, she'd barely mentioned the dreams to Max, who appeared already to have forgotten them.

'The girl who fainted. She – but if you don't remember, fine. Just don't mention her having nightmares.'

'I'm hardly likely to, am I? Now look, Rona, I want you to keep away from that family. The police will have to release Tarlton, on bail if nothing else, and if he thinks you're poking your nose in, he might well decide to stop you.'

'All right,' she said meekly. It was no use arguing with him, and she had, after all, done what had been asked of her: she'd found the cause of Freya's dreams.

'I have to go now, love. I'll phone later, as usual.'

Magda, to whom Rona had spoken about the Tarltons more recently and in considerably more detail, was consequently more shocked by her call.

'How awful for you!' she exclaimed. 'And that poor girl! Did she actually see her mother being killed?'

'It seems likely,' Rona said. 'But the point is the dreams, Maggie. If the killer—'

'My God, of course! She could be in real danger.'

'So the reason I'm ringing, apart from giving you advance notice of what's happened, is to ask you not to mention the dreams to *anyone*.'

'Of course I won't.'

'Did you tell Gavin about them?'

'I mentioned the gist of it, after you'd gone, but I'm not sure he was paying much attention. He was watching a sports programme.'

'Well, could you impress on him not to say anything, either? It really could be vital.'

'Don't worry about Gavin; I'll see he keeps quiet.'

Which left only Nanny. Rona lifted the phone again, then thoughtfully replaced it. For Violet Gray, the news would have considerable personal impact, and she was an old lady. There was no way Rona could break it to her over the phone, and the family would be too distraught to think of contacting her. There was no help for it; she'd have to go back to Stapleton House, and this evening, at that – hopefully before word of the day's discovery reached the residents.

She stood up. It was now almost six o'clock, and Chesham was a forty-minute drive away. She could only hope she'd make it in time. At worst, she could fill in details the media wouldn't have.

It seemed a longer than usual drive in the dark, and Rona was grateful for Gus's comforting bulk on the back seat. Out in the country, the roads were rimed with frost, and wreaths of mist shrouded the tops of the trees. It was a relief to see the lights of Chesham. Five minutes later, she was at the reception desk, asking for Miss Gray.

The woman who had answered the bell – Sylvia Marsh, according to her badge – looked at her reprovingly. 'We do ask visitors to try to avoid meal times,' she said.

'I'm so sorry; I realize it's inconvenient, but I have some news that I know Miss Gray will want to hear as soon as possible.'

The woman frowned. 'Is it likely to upset her?'

'It might well,' Rona admitted. 'But there's no way she can be spared from it.'

'I ask, because she's been feeling tired today, and in fact spent it in bed. Oh, she's not ill,' she added, seeing Rona's concern. 'She does have rest days from time to time, and spends them reading or knitting or listening to the radio.'

Rona could only hope she'd not listened to the radio this evening. She was led down the familiar corridor, and her guide paused to say, 'If she becomes distressed, you will ring the bell, won't you? It's hanging over her bed.'

They reached the door just as a woman came out bearing Miss Gray's supper tray. She smiled and stood aside for Rona to enter, and Sylvia Marsh, with a last worried glance towards the bed, nodded and turned away.

Miss Gray was propped up against a mound of pillows, a pale blue bed jacket fastened at her throat. A book, presumably discarded at the arrival of her meal, lay face down on the coverlet. It was a Mills & Boon romance.

The old lady was looking at her in surprise. 'I'm not due for my medication, dear,' she said. 'I've only just finished supper.'

'Yes, I know. I'm Rona Parish, Miss Gray. Do you remember, I came to see you last week, about Freya Tarlton?'

'Of course I remember,' the old lady said crossly. 'You were in the shadows, that's all; I couldn't see your face. What is it this time?'

She gestured at the chair beside the bed, and Rona obediently sat down.

'There have been some developments,' she began cautiously, and saw the veined hands tighten.

'Concerning Freya?'

'Indirectly. Miss Gray, there's no easy way to say this. Some – remains have been found. In the well in the woods.'

'Remains?' Miss Gray repeated sharply. 'A body, you mean?'

'Yes. The police believe it's that of Velma Tarlton.'

The old lady stared at her, her mouth working. 'Mrs Robert?'

'Yes.' Rona paused, and added, 'I'm so sorry.'

'So she didn't go off after all?'

'No, though I think she intended to. A – suitcase was also found.'

'And there I was, slating the poor lady for abandoning her family, and all the while . . .'

'I think she meant to go,' Rona repeated, hoping to lessen her guilt.

'Then who stopped her? That's the question, isn't it?'

Rona nodded.

'How's Mr Robert taking this?'

Rona fell back on a cliché. 'He's been – helping the police with their enquiries.'

Miss Gray was not deceived. 'They never think *he* did it?' Her voice rose indignantly. 'Stuff and nonsense! He wouldn't have harmed a hair of her head.'

'It seems likely whoever she was going away with changed his mind,' Rona said quickly.

'You can change your mind without killing someone.' Then, as Rona had fearfully known they must, her thoughts turned to her charge.

The old eyes suddenly dilated with horror. 'In the woods, you said. You think Freya *saw* something? While she was lost? Oh, my dear Lord!'

Rona leaned forward quickly and passed her a glass of water, thankful to see the emergency bell hanging close at hand.

'It's very important,' she went on, speaking more slowly and clearly, 'that no one knows she's been suffering these nightmares.'

Again, her tact was wasted. 'Because if the murderer hears of them, he'll think she saw him.'

'Yes,' Rona confirmed reluctantly.

'My poor lamb! What she's been going through all these years, and all because I was wicked enough to fall asleep when I should have been watching her!' She took another sip of water, then asked more calmly, 'When did all this come to light?'

'Only this morning. I wanted to tell you myself, before you heard about it.'

181

'That was good of you.' Her eyes strayed to the television set, but to Rona's relief, she didn't suggest switching it on. 'Poor Mr Robert,' she added softly. 'It will bring it all back, like losing her a second time.'

She, at least, entertained no doubt that he was innocent. But then, as his childhood nanny, she wouldn't. Other people might be less charitable. Perhaps it was the last straw, Max had said.

'What will happen now?' Miss Gray asked.

'I don't know,' Rona answered honestly. 'The events of that day will have to be gone over again, and everyone's movements checked.'

'And this time, it will come out that I failed in my duty. I can't keep quiet, now murder's involved.'

'I'm not so sure,' Rona said slowly. 'If Freya's nightmares are not to be made public, I think you'll have to.'

'You told the family, I presume?'

'Yes; if you remember, you gave me your permission.'

Miss Gray sighed with relief, and leaned back against her pillows. 'Then I needn't worry; they can decide whether or not the police should be informed.'

Her initial agitation had subsided, Rona was glad to see. 'I'm so sorry to have had to bring you this news.'

The old lady shook her head resignedly. 'Not everyone would have troubled to come all this way to tell me. I'm very grateful.'

'I'm sure the family will be in touch soon.'

'They've enough to think about at the moment,' said Violet Gray, 'but they'll contact me over Christmas. I used to spend it with them, but I've cried off the last two years. They always go to the Clarendon, and though it's very grand and that, not to mention very generous of them, I now find the noise and bustle too tiring. So they come here instead, on Boxing Day, and we have a quiet drink together.'

There seemed little more to say, and Rona rose to her feet. 'Would you like me to ask someone to sit with you for a while?'

'No, my dear, I shall be all right. I need a little time to go over things, then maybe I'll listen to the news later. At least it won't come as a shock now.'

*   *   *

182

It did, however, come as a shock to other people, among them Sophie Fairfax. She stared with horror at the pictures on the screen, of yellow police tape sealing off the entrance to Brindley Woods, and the reporter talking excitedly of a skeleton in the well. 'Identity has not been confirmed,' he was saying, 'but the discovery of a suitcase with the body points to it being that of Velma Tarlton, of the well-known jewellery family, who disappeared twenty-five years ago.'

'She didn't *disappear*,' Sophie contradicted forcefully. 'She ran off with her lover.'

'It seems not,' Chris said mildly.

'God, it will tear them apart, if it really is Velma. Oddly enough, I was talking about her with Freya, only the other day.'

She broke off and turned to her husband, her eyes widening. 'Oh, dear God, Chris! Freya's been having nightmares! Do you think she could be telepathic?'

'No, I don't,' Chris said roundly.

'But why, after all these years, should they suddenly look in the well?'

He remained silent, fighting the jealousy that engulfed him at any mention of the Tarltons. It was intensified a minute later, when Sophie went on, 'I must write to Lewis – tell him we're thinking of him. And Robert, of course. Oh, poor Robert! He kept hoping she'd come back.'

Chris nodded at the screen. 'Ten to one he's "the man" the police are interviewing at the moment.'

'But that's ridiculous! They can't think he had anything to do with it!'

'The husband's always the prime suspect, and if she'd been having a string of affairs, he might just have snapped.'

'Not Robert,' Sophie said decisively. 'You don't know him like I do.'

'I'm related to him, damn it!' Chris retorted, stung. 'I've known him all my life.'

'But not *well*! How often do you see him? Family weddings and funerals, and at Christmas, when they all lunch in the restaurant? Chris, he was my *father-in-law* for three years!'

'You don't have to remind me of that.' His voice was stiff

and she stared at him for a minute before understanding came. She perched on the arm of his chair, and pulled his resisting body towards her.

'You silly old duffer,' she said fondly. 'You *know* I've no feelings left for Lewis; they were long gone before we even divorced. But that doesn't stop me being sorry for him, when he's just found out his mother was murdered, and his father's being interviewed by the police. And I'm sorry if you don't like it, but I'm still very fond of Robert and Freya, both of whom must be going through hell at the moment. OK?'

She turned his head to face her, and as she bent to kiss him, he pulled her down into his arms.

'I wish I didn't love you quite so much,' he said.

As arranged, Robert asked the police car to drop him off at Brindley Lodge. They were all waiting for him – Kate and Lewis, Bruce and Jan, Nicholas and Susie and poor little Freya. His heart contracted when he saw her, and he held out a hand. She ran over and hugged him fiercely.

'Daddy, I'm so sorry,' she whispered. 'This is all my fault.'

'Nonsense, my darling. At last, after all these years, things are coming to a head. We can be thankful for that.'

Lewis passed his father a glass of whisky. 'Did they actually arrest you, Dad?'

'No, no, nothing so dramatic. They stressed all along that it was a voluntary interview, I was not under arrest, and free to leave at any time. They did, however, tape the whole thing, which was a bit unnerving.'

'You had Paul Singleton with you?'

'Yes, though as it turned out, only for moral support. Thankfully, he didn't have to do anything.'

'So what actually happened?'

They all seated themselves round the room, their eyes anxiously on him, and Robert took a sip of whisky.

'Well, they went over the day Velma left in detail. Where I'd been, if I'd left the shop during working hours, what time I got home, when I realized she'd gone.'

'And *had* you left the shop?' Nicholas asked.

'Fortunately, no. It was your father who'd skived off, to visit the dentist. Remember, Bruce?' His mouth twisted. 'They were very interested in the note, particularly since the only people I showed it to were Bruce and Jan. They asked, very circuitously, whether you were familiar with Velma's handwriting – the inference being that I could have written the thing myself.'

'But why would you—?' Kate began, and broke off, as she suddenly saw why.

'Exactly,' Robert said. 'I wouldn't have done so unless I'd already killed her.'

The stark words rang round the room. A log shifted in the fire, and they all jumped. After a minute, Robert continued. 'They also asked a lot of questions about her previous "visits to friends", and whether I knew whom she'd been with.'

'You did, in some cases,' Bruce put in.

'But she'd moved on since then. There was no point in naming the men she'd known previously, and ruining their marriages for them.'

'Unless an old affair was rekindled?' Nicholas suggested.

Robert wiped a hand over his face. 'God, I hate discussing her like this.'

'But you have to,' Jan said firmly, 'if it's a case of saving your own skin.'

'Had you any idea she was thinking of leaving you?' Susie asked, leaning forward with her glass between her hands

'None at all. She was given to spells of restlessness, during which she often looked elsewhere, and this time didn't seem any different. The affairs only lasted a week or two, and I was prepared to go on turning a blind eye. Fool that I was,' he added bitterly. 'If I'd shown more spirit, she might have stayed with me.'

'She did love you, you know, in her way,' Jan said awkwardly.

Robert went on as though she'd not spoken. 'The point was, she'd asked me not to look for her, so I didn't. In any event, I was too proud to run after her and beg her to come home; my main concern was Freya. She wouldn't talk or eat properly for weeks on end, and we couldn't fathom out what

185

was wrong with her. As you know, the specialists we took her to said it was a result of her mother's desertion – which struck me even then as an easy option. But – God – we never suspected the truth.'

He emptied his glass, and Lewis got up and refilled it.

'Consequently,' Robert continued, 'nothing was gone into at the time – whether Velma had received or made any significant phone calls, if she'd been seen with anyone.'

He paused, and added painfully, 'In the early days, we used to go into the woods to pick bluebells.'

'My friends and I often played there,' Lewis said, 'but we certainly never saw her.'

'She couldn't have walked boldly down the garden, carrying a suitcase,' Kate said suddenly. 'Freya was playing out there, and Nanny was supposed to be watching her. Come to that, if they were in the habit of meeting there, it would *always* have been too risky to go down the garden.'

'She must have used the alley,' Susie said. 'It leads to Woodlands Road, doesn't it, where there's public access to the woods.'

'Well, it's too late to look for evidence now,' Bruce said briskly. 'So why the boys in blue are still camped out there beats me.' He turned to his brother. 'Robert, you mustn't stay in the flat while all this is going on, and I'm not sure that here would be a good alternative, with the ongoing police activity. Jan and I discussed this, and we'd be very glad if you'd come to us till it all blows over. It's the most sensible solution all round, and we can drive to and from the shop together.'

Robert stared into his glass. 'I'm grateful,' he said. 'I admit I don't relish my own company at the moment.' He looked up, his eyes going from one of them to another. 'We've spent all this time cold-bloodedly discussing what could have happened and who might have killed her, but we've been forgetting the tragedy behind it all. She was a young and beautiful woman – only thirty-four, for God's sake – and however badly she behaved, she didn't deserve what happened to her.'

'And nor did you,' Jan said quietly, putting her hand

over his. 'Now, I think it's time we all went home and tried to get some sleep. Lord knows, it's been a long and traumatic day, and tomorrow's not likely to be much better. We'll stop at the flat, Robert, for you to collect some things.'

'How are you getting home, Freya?' Nicholas asked. 'Can we give you a lift?'

'It's all right, thanks; Matthew's waiting outside.'

'He's been there all the time?' Kate exclaimed. 'Why—?'

'He wouldn't come in,' Freya said quickly. 'He thought you wouldn't want anyone here who wasn't family.'

And Kate, knowing this was true, said simply, 'There's devotion for you!'

She and Lewis stood at the door while the others got into their cars and drove away.

'You told Rona Parish not to say anything?' Lewis asked her.

'Yes.'

'How's this going to end, Kate?'

She sighed. 'I don't know. I feel so guilty, for starting it all.'

He shook his head as they turned back into the house. 'Freya couldn't have gone on much longer. One way or another, it had to come into the open.'

'No matter what the consequences?' Kate asked fearfully.

'No matter what.'

Only partially reassured, she collected the glasses and took them through to the kitchen. As Jan had said, they had difficult days ahead, and for the life of her she couldn't imagine what the outcome would be.

Matthew Davenport surfaced from a deep sleep, to the awareness that his right side was cold. Automatically reaching for the duvet, his groping fingers touched the nubbly surface of Freya's dressing gown, and, struggling awake, he made out her silhouette on the edge of the bed, sitting forward with her head in her hands. The last strands of sleep fled and alarm rushed in.

'Freya? Are you OK, honey?' And then, fearfully, 'The dream hasn't progressed, has it?'

She didn't turn her head. 'I saw her,' she said expressionlessly. 'My mother. She was lying on the ground under the tree, staring straight up at me. Only she couldn't see me, because she was dead.'

Matthew closed his eyes in a spasm of horror. He slid swiftly over to her, putting his arms round her from behind and pressing his warm, living body against her cold back.

'Not that I knew she was,' she continued, in the same lifeless voice, 'but that long, unblinking stare frightened me.' She shuddered. 'I couldn't see the well from the tree house, but when I eventually came down – by the ladder; I didn't fall after all – she'd gone. And I was afraid to go home, in case she was still staring.'

Holding her tightly, he began to rock with her, saying nothing.

'I'd been aware of other things too, before that. The outline of a man, walking up and down, and whistling that tune. Next time, perhaps I'll see him clearly, too.' Her voice cracked. 'Wait for the next, nail-biting instalment.'

Gently, he pulled her back on the bed with him and lay down, holding her to him and stroking her hair. She lay rigid in his arms, and he knew her eyes were open and staring. He tried desperately to find the right words, but she forestalled him.

'It must have released some spring in my brain, what we learned today; something that had been battening down the things I'd seen. Now, they're slowly coming to the surface. It's – like watching a negative gradually develop. Matthew –' her voice sank to a whisper – 'suppose it's Daddy I see down there?'

Fourteen

It was the last week of classes before Christmas, and Max had, some years previously, begun the custom of serving wine and mince pies at the end of each one. Since Rona wasn't interested in baking – or cooking of any description – he made them himself, and had spent Sunday afternoon, while she was out at the Tarltons', enveloped in a spicy aroma producing this year's batch.

At least, he thought, as he set out glasses for his Wednesday class, he needn't worry about Adele turning up. She wasn't likely to show her face after their last encounter, and in view of the subsequent embarrassment with first Charlie and then Rona, he could only be thankful. He was therefore completely dumbfounded when, with a shy smile and a nod of the head, she emerged from the stairwell and took her accustomed place at her easel.

He cleared his throat and, avoiding her eye, addressed the class in general as he explained what he hoped they'd achieve from the display before them – predictably, an arrangement of poinsettia, holly and candles.

'It doesn't have to be an exact representation,' he told them. 'Use it as a basis for your imagination – what Christmas means to you personally, perhaps. Or you might like to adopt one of the styles we've been discussing this term – cubist or post-Impressionist, for example. If you need any help, let me know, otherwise I'll leave you to get on with it.'

He settled down at his own easel, glad of the screen it provided between himself and Adele. Thank heaven this was the last class of term; by January, she'd either have dropped out, or he'd have put the embarrassment behind him.

He sketched rapidly, his mind only half on what he was

189

doing. Rona seemed on edge about this Tarlton business, he mused. Too bad they'd been on the spot when that girl keeled over; it had made her feel involved. When he was home this evening, he'd try to talk some sense into her. He must give his father a ring, too. Perhaps arrange to fly up there again in the New Year; Cynthia had said there was a bed for him any time.

The studio clock struck three, and he hastily switched on the kettle for the half-time cup of tea. This was always a welcome break, and everyone took the chance to stand up and move about, often going to look at each other's work and pass judicial comments. Max took the opportunity to do the same. As usual, there was a wide divergence of form and structure. Some of them had followed up his suggestion of other styles, Dorcas Madden producing a very creditable attempt at surrealism. Adele's offering, however, was an almost photographic reproduction of his display.

'I didn't feel I could improve on your creation,' she said, with a flutter of lowered lashes, and Max felt an unworthy spurt of irritation. Her work was meticulous as always, each brush stroke with its own weight, adding to the overall picture.

'It's very good, Adele,' he said a little grudgingly, 'but I'd rather you'd attempted a more individual interpretation.'

'Why?' she challenged him. 'So you could get into my mind?'

He stared at her in surprise. This was the most she'd volunteered in class since she'd joined it the previous summer. He was aware, too, of turning heads.

'You flatter me,' he answered shortly. 'I'm a mere artist, not a psychologist.' And, mug in hand, he moved on to the next easel. He was, nevertheless, glad when it was time to resume their places. Damn it, he'd never before felt uncomfortable in one of his own classes, and he resolved not to lay himself open to the possibility again.

Since there was only half an hour between the end of this class and the beginning of the next, he ended it twenty minutes early, to allow time to partake of the wine and mince pies. There was a general atmosphere of bonhomie as people

190

discussed their plans for Christmas, and Max was presented with a bottle of whisky that the class had clubbed together to buy for him. Having thanked them all, he was completely taken aback when Adele produced a brightly coloured package and pressed it into his hand.

'Another little present for you,' she said. 'Happy Christmas, Max.'

There was a sudden silence as everyone turned to look at them. What *was* her game? he thought furiously.

'Thank you,' he said abruptly. 'I'll keep this one till Christmas Day.'

'Oh, but I want to make sure you like it,' she persisted. 'And I'm sure everyone wants to see it.'

She looked round at them, and there was a subdued murmur of agreement. Willing himself to keep his temper, Max fumbled with the ribbon and tore off the wrapping, to reveal a little blue sugar bowl.

'It's – very pretty,' he said after a minute. 'Thank you.'

'I noticed, when I came to tea those times, that you didn't seem to have one.'

Max stared at her, aware, now, that his face was flaming, though with rage rather than embarrassment, and that the whole class was gazing at them in amazement. Silent, timid Adele, and Mr Allerdyce? Well, still waters certainly ran deep!

'I hate to hurry you,' he said, 'but time's moving on, and I have to set up the next class. Happy Christmas, everyone, and I look forward to seeing you in the New Year.'

They hastily put down their glasses, crammed the last of their mince pies into their mouths, and collected their things together. Then, with a chorus of 'Happy Christmas', they clattered down the stairs and out of the house, Adele among them.

Max turned and looked at the sugar bowl, smug and shining on his desk. Then he picked it up and hurled it across the studio, where it crashed against a chair and shattered into fragments. If only the speculation it had caused could be disposed of so easily.

* * *

191

All that week, the local news bulletins carried the story of 'The Skeleton in the Well'. DNA tests on the bones had confirmed that it was indeed that of Velma Tarlton, who had disappeared in September 1980, telling her husband she was leaving him for good. That juxtaposition disturbed Rona; it did not seem to bode well for Robert. Though she longed for first-hand news of the investigation, she felt unable to contact Kate. At best, it would be intrusive; at worst, she could be taken for a journalist after a story. And how accurate would that have been? she wondered wryly.

Her downbeat mood was not helped by Max, who'd been monosyllabic on Wednesday evening, and whose phone calls since hadn't been much better. In response to her query as to what was wrong, he'd muttered something about the calendar not going well, and changed the subject.

Adding to her restlessness was the fact that she'd nothing to work on. Having wrapped up the parent series, she could scarcely begin interviewing the Tarltons at the moment, and the Fairfaxes, second on her list, would be far too busy, with the approach of Christmas, to grant her any time. There was nothing for it but to resign herself to putting everything on hold until the New Year.

The phone interrupted her musings, and at the sound of her sister's voice, Rona brightened. But Lindsey's first words rang a warning bell.

'Well, sister mine, what do you think of our very own local murder?'

Hurriedly, Rona tried to remember if she'd mentioned her proposed series to Lindsey, and realized with a sense of disbelief that she hadn't. Though they'd spoken on the phone a few times, it had been on other matters, and they'd not seen each other since Pops's retirement party.

This conclusion was confirmed by Lindsey's next comment. 'At least this is one you *haven't* had a finger in!'

She said obliquely, 'It seems a long time since I've seen you.'

'That's why I'm ringing. Are you free for lunch?'

'Oh, Lindsey, I am!'

Lindsey laughed. 'My, my! That sounded heartfelt!'

'Actually, I was feeling a bit down. Where shall we go? The Gallery or the Bacchus?'

'The Gallery, I think. I could do with a bit of old-fashioned gentility.'

One fifteen saw them settled at a table and studying the menu.

'So what have you been doing since I saw you?' Lindsey enquired idly.

'Finishing off that last series, among other things.'

'Any thoughts on the next project?'

'Max wants me to do another bio,' Rona said. True, if not the answer to the question.

'So you should. You're good at them, and something in hard cover must be more rewarding than articles that, once read, are thrown away.' She put the menu down. 'I'm going for the quiche. How about you?'

'I'll join you, with a salad on the side.'

The waitress brought their bottle of wine, and took their order.

'Heard from Pops lately?' Lindsey asked.

'I dropped in to see him last week, on the spur of the moment.'

Lindsey raised her eyebrows. 'A long drop, wasn't it?'

Rona smiled. 'Not really; I was up that way making a delivery.'

'How was he?'

'He seemed OK. He's hoping to invite us all to dinner soon.'

'With or without Her Ladyship?'

'Does it matter?'

Lindsey shrugged. 'Perhaps not. It's a fait accompli, after all. Incidentally, Hugh bumped into him the other day, at the pillar box in Talbot Road.'

'Did sparks fly?' Rona asked with amusement.

'No, there was a civil exchange, according to Hugh.'

Rona said flatly, 'You're seeing him, then?'

'Of course I'm seeing him. You saw us at Serendipity, didn't you?'

193

'I mean regularly?'

'You mean,' Lindsey corrected, 'am I sleeping with him?'

'And are you?'

'It's none of your business, but as it happens, no, not yet.'

Rona digested this rider. 'What about Jonathan?'

Lindsey flashed her a glance. 'I'm seeing him, too. And to save you the trouble of asking, yes, I *am* sleeping with him. Shocking, isn't it?'

'I hope you know what you're doing. It could all blow up in your face, you know.'

'A regular little prophet of doom, aren't you?'

Their food arrived, saving Rona from answering. Feeling that a change of subject might be wise, she asked, 'Are you going to the Grants' party tomorrow?'

Lindsey shook her head. 'I only know them through you and Max.'

It was odd, Rona reflected, that she and Lindsey moved for the most part in different social circles. Lindsey had a lot of legal friends, and was still on visiting terms with people she'd known during her marriage to Hugh. Only where old friends were concerned did the two of them attend the same parties.

'Have you spoken to Mum recently?' she asked, feeling a stab of guilt at her own dereliction.

'Yes, actually; she's full of beans, interviewing plumbers and builders for this conversion she's planning. And she's very chuffed to have received several party invitations for the next few weeks. She thought she'd be out on a limb without Pops, but not a bit of it, apparently.'

'That's great. I must give her a ring – I've been meaning to, but . . .'

'The road to hell?' Lindsey supplied.

'Exactly.'

'But you're doing the decent thing over Christmas. It was good of Max to grasp that nettle.'

'Yes; he booked the table weeks ago, without saying anything. He knew if he waited till we'd all made up our minds, the place would have been fully booked.' Rona hesitated. 'Like to come to us on Christmas Eve, and stay over?

We could open stockings together, like old times.'

'Oh, Ro, I'd have loved to, but I promised I'd go to Mum's. She'll be all alone for the first time.'

'Of course. It was just a thought.'

Her first New Year Resolution, Rona decided, would be to keep in regular touch with *both* her parents.

Tom Parish sat in front of his television, along, no doubt, with most Marsborough residents who were home at lunchtime, watching the latest reports on the gruesome findings. Velma Tarlton, that bubbly, laughing girl he remembered seeing about town all those years ago, murdered: he'd known her by sight before either he or she were married, and, truth to tell, had had the odd fantasy about her. Unbelievable that she should have met such a grisly end. The family must be going through hell, though apparently they were still open for business. Putting a brave face on it, he supposed.

Well, good for them. He hadn't intended looking there for Christmas presents, but he and Avril had patronized the firm all their married life, and they deserved a bit of loyalty. He'd go in this afternoon; see if he could find something for Catherine. Show a bit of support, if the chance arose. Heaven knew, there was little else he could do.

There were a lot of people Rona didn't know at the Grants' party. Simon, like Max, was an artist, and so, she gathered, were the majority of the guests. Max seemed to know quite a few of them, but their names jumbled up in her head, and she knew she'd never remember them. Glad to see familiar faces, she gravitated, as soon as politeness allowed, towards Georgia and Patrick Kingston. The woman they were talking to turned as she approached, and smiled at her.

'It's Miss Parish, isn't it? From Chase Mortimer?'

Rona smiled back. 'Right name, wrong sister. Lindsey's my twin.'

'Oh, I'm so sorry! I don't know her well, but you're terribly alike, aren't you?'

'So we've been told.'

195

'Allow me to remedy the situation,' Patrick put in smoothly. 'Rona Parish, meet Carol Hurst.'

By an effort of willpower, Rona held her smile in place. Jonathan's wife! Then he'd be here as well. How would he react to seeing her?

'It must be lovely to be a twin,' Carol was saying. 'I was an only child, and always felt I missed out. Are you a solicitor, too?'

'No,' Georgia answered for her, 'Rona's a writer.'

'Oh dear! Should I have heard of you?'

'Not unless you read biographies or *Chiltern Life*.'

'Neither, regretfully. I'm not much of a reader, I'm afraid; I never seem to have the time. I have two children, and since we live outside town, I'm always having to ferry them to after-school activities or friends' parties. When I *am* able to relax, I promptly fall asleep! My husband despairs of me!' She turned back to Rona. 'Whose biographies have you written?'

'Arthur Conan Doyle, Sarah Siddons and William Pitt the Elder,' Rona replied. 'A motley crew, aren't they?'

'Are the books in the library? I promise to take one out and educate myself.'

Rona laughed. 'I won't hold you to that.'

She liked her, she realized with a pang. This attractive, friendly woman believed she was happily married, and all the time—

'Ah, there you are, darling!'

The remembered voice. Rona turned, saw his eyes widen in shock. Perhaps he, too, had in that first instant mistaken her for Lindsey.

'Jon, this is Rona Parish. She's a writer, but I'm afraid I mistook her for her sister. My husband, Jonathan.'

Rona hesitated, but Jonathan acted swiftly, holding out his hand with a bland, unrecognizing smile. 'How do you do? Rona, is it? Is your sister here?'

Briefly, Rona considered teasing him, but thought better of it. 'No, she doesn't know the Grants very well.'

'They are alike, aren't they, Jon?' Carol said again.

'In appearance, certainly,' Jonathan agreed smoothly. 'It

196

must lead to a lot of misunderstandings.' A dig there. Before she could react, he had taken his wife's elbow. 'If these good folk will excuse us, there's someone I'd like you to meet,' he said, and, with a general smile of apology, led her away.

'Suave devil,' Patrick commented.

More than he realized. Though to be fair, Jonathan couldn't have admitted to knowing her; it would have involved telling his wife that they'd had dinner together, along with his mistress, that self-same twin. She must find Max and warn him not to give the game away.

'Another drink, Rona?' Patrick was saying.

'Oh.' She saw with surprise that her glass was empty. 'Thank you, yes.'

'Rona!'

Magda and Gavin were approaching, and Magda gave her a quick hug. She looked very exotic, with her dark hair pinned up and held in place by a red rose, complementing her chiffon dress.

'I must say, you're a good advertisement for your boutiques!' Georgia told her. 'I love the scalloped hemline.'

'Available in red or black,' Magda replied, 'and a bargain at the price!'

They all laughed, and under cover of it, Magda said in Rona's ear, 'I gather all's well with Max again?'

'Yes, thankfully, though he's been a bit grouchy this last week.'

'So has Gavin. It's the time of year. They see the joint bank account rapidly diminishing.'

The evening wore on, and Rona was introduced to a group of people from Woodbourne.

'What's all this about skeletons in wells?' one man asked jovially, helping himself to a canapé. 'Makes a change from closets, I suppose.'

'Yes, you've been hitting the headlines, haven't you?' a woman cut in. 'And I always thought Marsborough was such a quiet, respectable place!'

'She means dull!' said someone else.

'Do you know the people involved?' the first man asked curiously, and to Rona's relief, Max materialized at her side.

'They're the town's best jewellers,' he said. 'We've been in the shop countless times.'

'Reckon any of them could be a murderer?'

The woman laughed in embarrassment. 'Really, Pete! That's enough!'

'They're a very pleasant family,' Max said firmly. 'I'm sure none of them has anything to hide.'

The man called Pete shook his head. 'I shouldn't bet on it,' he said with owlish solemnity. 'It usually turns out to be the nearest and dearest.'

Across town, Tom and Catherine were also discussing the murder.

'You actually knew her, when you were all young?' Catherine asked with interest.

'Not knew, exactly, but I saw her around, and we were at some of the same parties.'

'What was she like?'

'To look at, gorgeous – no denying that. But she was the kind of girl who flirted with every man she met, and getting married didn't stop her.' He gave a short laugh. 'I even saw her try it on once with her brother-in-law. It must have been hard on her husband.'

'Some husbands like to think other men fancy their wives.'

'I doubt if that applied to Tarlton. When she was carrying on, he used to look as if he could murder her.' He broke off with an embarrassed laugh. 'Forget I said that.'

Catherine topped up his coffee. 'But do you think he could have done?' she asked calmly.

Tom stared at her for a minute. 'Good God,' he said slowly. 'You read about murders all the time, don't you, but you never expect them to happen to anyone you know, even vaguely. Nor do you expect to look at someone who's been around for years in the light of a potential killer.'

He drank his coffee. 'Is a *crime passionnel* a let-out in this country? I think perhaps it should be. It's possible, in certain circumstances, to be driven to extremes.'

'You didn't answer my question,' Catherine reminded him. '*Do* you think her husband could have killed her?'

198

'Let's just say I shouldn't like to be in the jury box,' Tom replied.

Lindsey said, 'I told Rona the other day that I wasn't sleeping with you.'

Hugh looked at her sharply. 'We could soon remedy that; though what the hell it has to do with your sister is beyond me. Don't be influenced by her,' he added, refilling her wine glass, 'she's never liked me.'

'I'm not influenced by anybody,' Lindsey said lazily.

He sat down on the couch opposite her. 'Can we stop playing games? You know how much I want you, and what's more, you want me, too.'

She shook her head.

'Then why break your own rule and come here this evening?'

'Because I've never seen your flat, and wondered if it was like Pops's. Not that I've seen his yet, either, but Rona says an invitation's imminent.' She glanced across at him. 'I'm sorry if you took my arrival as the green light.'

'What else was I to think? God knows, we've spent a fair bit of time together over the last month or two. It's a natural progression, surely?'

'Not with us. Remember what happened last time.'

'We've both grown up a bit since then.'

'But I enjoy things as they are, Hugh; dinner, goodnight kisses – fine, but I don't want things to get too heavy.'

'They needn't.'

'But they would, you know they would. With us, once the touchpaper's lit, it's a question of "retire immediately".'

'To bed?' he asked with a faint smile. 'That's what I'm suggesting.'

'You know what I mean; when we get together, we're dynamite. We've blown our lives apart once; let's not risk it again.'

'But it worked well, all those months I was in Guildford, and came up at weekends.'

'That's because it was finite. I knew you'd be going back on the Sunday.'

'Well, thanks very much!' He stared down into his glass. 'You're seeing someone else, aren't you?'

'I don't have to answer that.'

'Is it the chap I saw you with at the pub that time?'

'I haven't said there is anyone.'

'Oh, there is, all right. If there weren't, you'd be more amenable to my advances.'

She laughed lightly. 'You sound like something out of Jane Austen!'

'You're a heartless little devil, aren't you, Lindsey? You enjoy keeping me dangling – it suits your vanity. Well, I warn you – I'll only dangle for so long.'

She shrugged. 'You're a free agent.'

He stood up abruptly, seized both her wrists and pulled her to her feet. 'One of these days,' he said unevenly, 'you'll get more than you bargained for. That's what happens to teases.'

And as she stared at him, suddenly uneasy, he started to kiss her savagely. Immediately, as always happened with Hugh, her body responded and her passion rose to match his. *Just*, she thought incoherently, what she'd wanted to avoid.

With an immense effort of will, she tore herself free of him and they stood looking at each other, both of them breathing heavily.

'Thanks for the drinks, Hugh,' she said shakily. 'Don't worry; I shan't break the rules again.' She picked up her coat and let herself out of the flat, leaving him standing in the middle of the room, looking after her.

Sunday morning, and as usual they were still in their dressing gowns. Max had cooked a full English breakfast, including fried bread and sausages, and they were now reading the papers while they finished their coffee.

'I see our murder's made the Sundays,' he observed, 'albeit only a paragraph on an inside page.'

'Is there any hope of finding who did it, do you think, after all this time?'

'I doubt it, unless the murderer jumps out of the wood-work and confesses.'

'I'd love to know how the investigation's going.'

He looked up. 'Oh, no you don't!' he said firmly. 'It's in the police's hands, you keep well away.'

'I haven't much option, have I? But that doesn't stop me wondering.'

She returned to her portion of the paper, and Max glanced at her surreptitiously. Should he, he wondered, have told her about Adele's behaviour last Wednesday? He'd learned to his cost that it wasn't wise to keep such things from her; someone was bound to say something, and it would be much better coming from him. But how to explain why he'd not told her at once? She'd realized he had something on his mind.

He sighed. This awkwardness always arose when Adele's name was mentioned. Still, it would be as well to take the bull by the horns, and now was as good a time as any.

He cleared his throat, and as she looked up at him expectantly, the doorbell chimed.

He frowned. 'Who the hell can that be, at this time on a Sunday morning?' *Not, please God, Adele! He wouldn't put anything past her.*

'I'd better go,' Rona said. 'I'm marginally more respectable than you, and it might be Lindsey.'

She ran up the basement steps and opened the front door, surprised to see two uniformed policemen on the step, one of them Archie Duncan, a former student of Max's.

'Archie!' she exclaimed.

He did not return her smile. 'Good morning, Mrs Allerdyce. Is your husband at home?'

'Well, yes, but he's—'

'Could we have a word, do you think?'

'Yes, of course, but I'm afraid he's not dressed, either. We had a late night last night, and we're—'

'If you could just tell him we're here?'

Rona frowned, belatedly apprehensive. 'Is something wrong?' she asked sharply.

Neither man replied, and with a frustrated click of her tongue, she turned and went to the head of the stairs. 'Max,' she called, 'Archie Duncan's here to see you.'

201

A minute later Max came barefoot up the stairs. 'Archie! You've caught me déshabillé, I'm afraid. There's some coffee downstairs . . .' His voice trailed off as his eyes moved to the other policeman, silent at Archie's side.

'It's not a social call, sir.' Archie was unusually stiff, not meeting their eyes.

Max frowned. 'Then what the hell is it?'

'Mr Allerdyce, I'm arresting you on suspicion of assault on Mrs Adele Yarborough. You do not have to say anything, but it may harm your defence if you do not mention when questioned something you later rely on in court.'

'*What?*'

'I'd be grateful if you'd accompany us to the station for questioning. We'll wait in the car while you get dressed.'

And the two policemen turned in unison and went back down the steps. Max stepped forward and slammed the door behind them.

Rona was staring at him in shock. 'They can't do that, can they?'

'It seems they already have,' he said grimly. He started up the stairs, and she ran after him.

'I'll come with you.'

'No, you most definitely won't. God knows what garbled story they've got hold of, but I don't doubt we can sort it out. It might take time, though, and I don't want you hanging around the station all day.'

She stood helplessly in the bedroom, watching him dress.

'I don't see how they can possibly—'

'She must have fabricated something. She was behaving very oddly at the last class. I – meant to tell you.'

'But you didn't,' Rona accused, her apprehension deepening.

'Well, I'm telling you now.' He pulled on a sweater. 'She intimated to the whole class that we'd been meeting over cups of tea—'

'Which you had.'

'Not at my instigation. And then, if you please, she gave me a Christmas present.'

Rona stared at him. 'What did you do with it?'

He smiled grimly. 'When they'd all gone, I hurled it across the room and it shattered in pieces. It was a sugar basin.'

'A *sugar* basin?'

'She said she'd noticed I hadn't got one. God, Rona, I wish I'd listened to you in the first place. She's a manipulative little devil, all right. Lord knows what game she's up to now, but don't worry, darling. I'll be back soon.'

He gave her a swift kiss and went downstairs to the waiting policemen. In the silence of the bedroom, she heard the car drive away.

Fifteen

It was the longest Sunday of her life. Immediately after Max had left, Rona phoned Lindsey, who, blessedly, asked no questions but said simply, 'I'm on my way.'

She hurriedly showered and dressed, but the everyday routine did little to dispel her sense of shock. She'd always *known* that woman was trouble, from the very first mention of her name, but Max, whose protective instincts had been aroused by her seeming helplessness, had been too macho to see it. Even so, she'd thought flirtation was on her mind, not something altogether more dangerous.

The bell rang as she was brushing her hair. She dropped the brush and ran downstairs to open the door to her sister. Lindsey caught her in a fierce hug, and Gus, nosing his way between them, gave a soft whine.

'Thanks for coming,' Rona said unsteadily.

'What else could I do, when you tell me Max has been arrested? I just can't *believe* that woman would go so far.'

Rona's eyes filled with tears. 'Bless you, Linz. Bless you for not even considering there could be any truth in it.'

'Well, of course there isn't!' said Lindsey, who had wondered just that on her mad dash to town.

They turned into the sitting room and Rona, realizing the central heating had switched off, lit the gas fire. They both sat down, and Gus came and leaned heavily against her legs. She patted him absent-mindedly.

'So what was the build-up to this?' Lindsey prompted.

'You saw them together at the Gallery,' Rona began.

'I did indeed. And you said there was nothing in it.'

'Apparently she told him she was suffering from depression, and speaking to him made her feel better.'

204

Lindsey gave an unladylike snort.

'Well, a week ago she suddenly turned up at the studio, asking – literally – for tea and sympathy. Max was livid – he'd just mixed some paint and didn't want it to dry – but short of throwing her on to the street, there was not much he could do. So he went to make the tea, but in the kitchen she suddenly tried to kiss him.'

'Why doesn't that surprise me?' Lindsey asked rhetorically.

'He put her straight on a few things, and she rushed off.' Rona twisted her hands. 'The horrible thing is that someone saw her running from the cottage, and at the Dawsons' party the next night, he teased Max about having a bit on the side.'

'Oh, Ro!'

'Until then,' Rona continued steadily, 'he hadn't told me about it, presumably because he guessed how I'd react. We had a stormy session, a day of not speaking, and then it all came out. Anyway, after all that, he didn't think she'd turn up at class last week, but she did; and not only that, but in front of the whole class she gave him a sugar basin as a Christmas present, because when they had tea in the kitchen, she'd noticed he hadn't got one! It didn't seem to occur to her that neither Max nor I take sugar. The packet was only for cooking.'

'Then what?'

'Well, that's all really. She must have seen he was underwhelmed, but nothing specific was said. And the next we know, we have Archie Duncan and his chum on the doorstep, talking of assault.'

'No doubt she's shown them those bloody bruises,' Lindsey said darkly.

'No doubt. We always guessed they had their uses, didn't we?'

'So what happens next?'

'I've no idea. Presumably at some stage Max will come home. They're not likely to bang him up, are they? Not until they've got more to go on, anyway?'

'So what are you going to do?'

'Wait, I suppose.'

'Shall we drive out somewhere for lunch? It would help to pass the time.'

'Lindsey, I can't. Suppose he phones or comes back, and I'm not here? He'd think I was doubting him.'

Lindsey sighed. 'OK, we'll dig ourselves in for the duration. How about a cup of coffee, for starters?'

And Rona, glad of something to do, led the way down to the kitchen.

At the police station, Max was finding things were more serious than he'd assumed. He learned that Adele had phoned 999 in the early hours of Saturday morning, and told the emergency operator she'd taken an overdose of sleeping pills.

'Where the hell was her husband?' he interrupted.

The man who was interviewing him glanced at his companion, who nodded.

'We understand he's taken the children on a four-day trip to Lapland, to see Father Christmas. Mrs Yarborough was supposed to be going with them, but cried off at the last minute. So far, we've been unable to contact him, but her parents have come down from Ipswich and are with her now. When she regained consciousness, she made a statement alleging that you'd assaulted her on several occasions, because she refused to sleep with you.'

Max stared at him with incredulity. 'Did she say exactly when and where these fictitious assaults took place?'

'We can't divulge specifics, sir, but we understand you live apart from your wife during the week?'

'Meaning it was an ideal set-up? But if Adele wanted to keep me at arm's length, why come to the cottage? Wouldn't that have been asking for trouble?'

'We'll do the questioning, sir,' the inspector said mildly. 'Are you suggesting the interest was, in fact, on her side?'

Max sighed. 'It would seem so. My wife always warned me, though I couldn't see it. But to get the facts straight, Inspector, it was she who made overtures to me, a week or so ago at the cottage. I made it plain I wasn't interested, and I presume this is her revenge.'

'Mrs Yarborough has severe bruising to her arms, legs and

206

neck, sir, and we're informed there are also older bruises and evidence of previous fractures.'

'I'm not surprised,' Max said shortly.

The policeman's eyes narrowed. 'Would you care to explain that comment?'

'With pleasure. As you might know, I'm an art tutor, and Mrs Yarborough joined my class last May. During that very hot spell, I noticed she always wore either a cardigan, or a dress with long sleeves. One day, her sleeves rode up as she reached for something, and I saw her arms were covered in bruises.'

The two policemen exchanged glances.

'My wife will bear me out on this, because I mentioned them to her. Later, in view of Mrs Yarborough's pallor and general timidity, I became even more concerned. I asked my wife and her sister to invite her to tea, and let me know what they thought.'

'And what did they think, sir?' the inspector asked stolidly.

Max flushed. 'That the bruises had been caused by heaving furniture about during the Yarboroughs' recent move. But the other week, I saw more bruising. To be frank, I was convinced her husband was abusing her. Once, she even "fell" downstairs; it transpired that he'd been upstairs at the time, and what's more, my sister-in-law, who lives opposite, had more or less to force him to take her to hospital.'

He looked challengingly from one man to the other. They returned his gaze impassively.

'On reflection,' Max continued heavily, 'it figures, doesn't it? She suddenly finds she can't take any more, but she daren't say anything against her husband, either because she's frightened of him, or because it might split up the family. So, as soon as he's out of the way, she picks on me, thereby killing two birds with one stone, since it would pay me back for rejecting her.'

'An interesting theory, sir.'

'I think you'll find it's the right one,' Max said.

It was four o'clock when the police car brought him home. Rona rushed into the hall to meet him, Lindsey tactfully remained in the sitting room.

'What happened?' she demanded as she hugged him. 'Has it all been cleared up?'

'Not really, no. I'm released on police bail "pending further enquiries", and have had to undertake not to go within a hundred yards of Adele. As if I'm likely to.'

'Lindsey's been waiting with me,' Rona said, and led the way into the sitting room. Her sister came forward and kissed Max's cheek.

'Sorry you've been landed with this,' she said.

He smiled ruefully. 'It's not as if you didn't both warn me.'

'Did you contact Barry?'

'No, I didn't think it was warranted. They offered me a solicitor, but I declined.'

'That was unwise,' Lindsey, the solicitor, rebuked him.

'No doubt, but I don't think I did too badly in my own defence.'

Lindsey smiled. 'We can't have you doing us out of a job.'

He sat down, patting Gus who had come up wagging his tail. 'It was more serious than it seemed,' he told them soberly. 'She'd taken an overdose of sleeping pills.'

They looked at him in consternation. 'Is she all right?'

'Yes, they pumped her out, or whatever it is they do.'

'But – where was Philip?'

'That's what I wanted to know. He's taken the kids to Lapland, if you please, to see Father Christmas. Adele was going with them, but dropped out at the last minute.'

'So she was alone in the house?'

'Presumably. They've not been able to contact him; I suppose, going for only four days, it didn't seem worth adapting his mobile, especially as until the last minute he thought she'd be with him.'

'When's he due back?'

Max shrugged. 'Some time tomorrow, I suppose.'

'I wonder if they'll question him about the bruises.'

'Well, at least I got in my pennyworth. With luck, it might have sown the seeds of suspicion.'

* * *

208

The next two days brought no further news, but at lunchtime on the Wednesday, Max phoned.

'I've just had Archie Duncan round,' he announced. 'The allegations have been dropped.'

'Well, thank God for that. Was there any explanation?'

'No. I think Archie was jumping the gun, bless him; he'd been highly embarrassed about the whole thing. He just said that I'd be hearing officially, but he wanted me to know as soon as possible.'

'Has Philip been arrested?'

'Darling, I'm telling you all I know. At least someone's seen sense. Look, since there are no classes I've a free afternoon, so I'm pressing on with the calendar. But I'll be home earlier than usual – say sixish?'

'I'll have the champagne on ice,' she said.

'I didn't think you were serious about the bubbly,' Max commented, opening the bottle.

'Well, it's a celebration, isn't it? I didn't fancy being married to a jailbird!'

He poured it carefully into the glasses, and as they toasted each other, the doorbell rang.

'Somebody smelt it!' Rona said.

'Let's take it up, anyway, and savour it in comfort. You carry the bottle, and I'll bring the tray with the glasses.'

Rona led the way. Max rested the tray on the hall table before opening the door, and she went ahead into the sitting room, stiffening as she heard him exclaim, 'Yarborough!'

'Please don't shut the door,' Philip was saying quickly. 'I realize I must be the last person you want to see, but I have to speak to you.'

Max hesitated, and Rona came into the hall. 'Come in, Philip.'

'Thank you.'

Max reluctantly stepped aside, and Philip passed him and, at Rona's gesture, followed her into the sitting room. He looked wretched, she thought, with a stab of pity.

'First, on behalf of my wife, I owe you both the most enormous apology. I can't think what came over her.' His

209

eyes fell to the champagne bottle Rona had set down, and he produced another from behind his back. 'You've pre-empted me, but I hope this will come in useful over the New Year.'

Rona glanced at Max's face, which remained stony. 'Thank you,' she said.

'And the second thing I owe you,' Philip continued, 'is an explanation. Adele's ill – you must have guessed that, but perhaps you don't realize quite how ill.'

'She told me she suffers from depression,' Max said stiffly.

'Yes, but that's only a part of it. I'm well aware what you, and doubtless other people, have been thinking about me.' He glanced at Rona. 'And I know your sister blamed me for not taking her straight to A and E when she fell downstairs; but the simple fact is, I was embarrassed to do so. I could see she wasn't badly hurt, and we've been to every hospital in the area so many times, I couldn't face it again.'

'In which case,' Max said, 'I'm surprised the medical authorities didn't contact the police. They must be used to stories of walking into doors and so on—'

'—from battered wives?' Philip finished bitterly. 'Exactly. But the truth of the matter is, she's been harming herself.'

Rona and Max stared at him in disbelieving horror.

'It's a form of Munchausen's syndrome. No doubt you've heard of it?'

They both nodded.

'It's partly my fault it's got this bad. I was convinced it would pass, that with love and care she'd stop doing it. Sometimes she'd go for months without harming herself, and then something would start her off again. This last time, it must have been leaving Suffolk and her family, and coming here. She's steadfastly refused to have treatment in the past, despite her parents and I pleading with her, but this time I think she frightened herself. Incidentally,' he added, 'the sleeping pills weren't sufficient to do serious damage. They were just another symptom, a means of attracting attention and sympathy.'

'It must have been terrible for you,' Max said.

'Frankly, it's been hell. Obviously I'd have had no choice if it had involved the children, but it never did. She's devoted to them and they to her.'

Rona said awkwardly, 'Would you like a drink? I'll bring another glass.'

He shook his head. 'You'll understand if I don't feel like celebrating.'

'So what are you going to do?' Max asked.

'Well, since I can't look after her myself, because of work and everything, she'll be going back to Ipswich with her parents. They'll get her started on the treatment, and if she responds well, as we're all hoping, she'll soon be back with us. In the meantime, my sister's coming to keep house for me and look after the children. They're well settled at school, and it didn't seem right to uproot them again.'

'Is there anything we can do?' Rona asked.

'Thank you, but no. Adele's caused enough upheaval in your family.' He glanced at Max. 'I'm not entirely clear what happened, but she asked me particularly to thank you for your encouragement with her painting, and to say how sorry she was that things got out of hand.'

'Give her my best wishes,' Max said stiffly.

'Well, I must be going. I have to pack a case for her.'

'It's too bad it's happened so near Christmas,' Rona said.

'Yes, but the children and I will go up to my parents-in-law, and we'll all spend it together.' He moved towards the door. 'Again, I'm deeply sorry for all the trouble, especially this latest episode. If I'd been home, it would never have happened. I do hope, though, that when everything's settled a little, we can remain friends.'

'Of course,' Rona said, and after a minute, Max nodded.

They showed him out, and returned to the sitting room, their mood of relief tempered by the news they'd heard. The champagne seemed hardly appropriate.

'Perhaps we should toast Adele,' Rona suggested, 'and her speedy recovery?'

'I'll drink to that,' Max said.

* * *

211

It had been agreed that Max's arrest and the events leading up to it should remain between Lindsey and themselves. There was no point in going over it with Tom and Avril, and the sooner the whole thing could be forgotten, the better. But over the next day or so, the shadow cast by it overlay the preparations for Christmas, and decorating the tree and hanging up the cards didn't generate the usual pleasant anticipation.

'I'm glad we're going to the Trents' tomorrow,' Rona said, on the Friday evening. 'It might lift our spirits a bit. Though goodness knows, the Tarltons have more need of spirit-lifting than we have. What with all the business with Adele, I've hardly thought of them this week.'

'There hasn't been anything new, anyway,' Max said. 'Quite honestly, I don't see how there can be.'

'In which case, they'll have to spend the rest of their lives wondering who killed Velma. What a ghastly prospect.'

'Especially if they start suspecting each other,' Max said.

For Avril, too, it was a lacklustre run-up to Christmas. The cards falling on her mat in undiminished numbers were, of course, addressed to both herself and Tom, and she hadn't the heart to put them up. Instead, she read the messages they contained, ticked them off in her record book, and laid them aside to pass on to him when she saw him on Christmas Day.

In a moment of defiance, though, she had bought a small artificial tree and set it up on a table, decorating it with tinsel and silver balls, and laying the parcels she had wrapped around it. She was glad they'd all be together for Christmas lunch. By next year, she'd have had time to get used to her changed status.

The phone rang, and Lindsey's voice said, 'Hello, Mum. I wondered if you'd like to come to the flicks this evening? They're showing that new film everyone's talking about. It doesn't start till eight, so we could have a bite to eat first.'

'That would be lovely, darling,' Avril said gratefully.

*   *   *

As always, Rona felt herself relax as they drove through the Trents' gateway. The trees in the comfortably overgrown garden had been decked with coloured lights, and there was a large holly wreath on the door.

She'd brought an armful of presents for everyone, including the three cats, and amid profuse thanks, they were placed on the pile under the tree.

'Yours are here, too,' Dinah told them. 'Remember to take them when you go. And, of course, there's also something for Gus.'

Gus, always sure of his welcome here, looked up at her with lolling tongue, before trotting over and lying down in front of the fire. Two of the cats, already in position, opened an eye to see who'd arrived, and closed it again. A non-aggression pact existed between them.

Rona hadn't seen Mitch, Melissa's husband, since their wedding, and she'd forgotten how tall and broad he was. With his tanned, open face and crew-cut hair, he was un-mistakeably American.

'How much longer will you be out in the Gulf?' Max asked him.

'I'm halfway through; it was a six-month assignment.'

'And how are you liking it?'

'It's OK, though I miss the family, of course. Luckily I've avoided the worst of the heat, but it was still pretty fierce when I arrived.' He smiled at his mother-in-law. 'Dinah's turned up trumps and volunteered to look after the kids for a week in February, so Mel can fly out and join me.'

'That should be lovely!' Rona exclaimed, turning to his wife. 'No doubt you'll make for the gold souks?'

'My first port of call,' Melissa confirmed.

Rona accepted the glass of hot punch Barnie handed her and sat back in her chair, her eyes going contentedly round the familiar room, now dominated by the enormous tree whose twinkling lights lent it an air of magic. As always, she wished she could feel as relaxed with her own family as she did here. And thinking of her family, she realized that Barnie and Dinah didn't know of the split. She was wondering how best to bring it up, when Dinah did it for her.

'I suppose by now your father will have retired?' she asked, perching on the pouffe beside Rona's chair.

'Yes, at the end of last month. Actually . . .' She waited until she had everyone's attention. 'I'm sorry to say, he and my mother have separated.'

'Oh, my dear!' Dinah exclaimed. 'I'm so very sorry.'

'They were making each other unhappy, so it seemed the best thing.'

'What's happening to the family home?' Barnie asked.

'Mum's staying on there. She's decided to take in lodgers, for company.'

'And your father?'

'He's renting a flat in Talbot Road.' She'd no intention of mentioning Catherine and hurried on, 'However, after initial hiccups things are more amicable now, and we're all having Christmas lunch together.'

'Well, I suppose that's something,' Dinah said doubtfully. 'Do you think there's any chance of their coming back together?'

Rona shook her head. 'None,' she said.

Melissa, sensing the air of embarrassment, said quickly, 'Isn't it exciting, having a murder in the town? We've been telling Mitch about it. Pity you're not on the *Gazette*, Rona; you'd be au fait with developments!'

Rona shot Max a warning glance. 'I feel very sorry for them all,' she said.

'You were thinking of researching the family, weren't you?' Barnie remembered. 'Better put that on hold for the moment.'

'Oh, I don't know,' Mitch put in. 'It'd be an even better story now.'

'It depends on the outcome,' Max said.

Everyone turned to him.

'Do you think the husband did it?' Melissa asked. 'That's how it usually turns out.'

'I know no more than the rest of you, but Robert Tarlton doesn't strike me as a killer.'

'Under sufficient provocation, anyone could be,' Barnie said darkly.

214

Dinah jumped to her feet. 'Dinner's almost ready; I'll go and put the finishing touches to it. Mel, you could bring in the first course for me, if you would.'

The meal was as sumptuous as always: melon with prawns, roast goose with all the trimmings, and an iced Christmas bomb for dessert.

'I didn't want to pre-empt the turkey,' Dinah said, 'but it had to be Christmassy!'

As they were finishing, a group of carol singers came to the door. Barnie went to open it, and they sat in silence, listening as the familiar tunes reached them.

'There are some mince pies in the kitchen, Barnie,' Dinah called, when they came to an end.

'Beautifully stage-managed, Dinah!' Max said. 'All we need now is some snow, and it will be really Dickensian.'

'It's quite cold enough for me, thanks!' Mitch protested. 'The temperature's already some twenty degrees lower than I'm used to.'

They returned to the fireside for coffee, but Max and Rona declined the offer of liqueurs. 'We have to drive home,' Max said regretfully. By now, talk was desultory, and when a cry from upstairs summoned Mel, it seemed time to make a move. Dinah searched out their presents from under the tree and Mel, having resettled her daughter, came down in time to say goodbye. The whole family gathered in the doorway to see them off, and they drove away to a chorus of 'Happy Christmas'.

'I do hope it will be,' Rona said. 'For everyone.'

Sixteen

Freya said, 'I do wish we were spending Christmas together.'
Matthew nodded. 'Me, too. Trouble is, up to now we've both spent it with our families, and since we're not engaged or anything, it's what they still expect. In fairness, I've not seen my lot for a month or two; I feel I owe it to them.'

'And I couldn't desert mine, especially this Christmas. Dad looks like a ghost, while everyone else is going round with false smiles plastered on their faces. And it's all my fault.'

Matthew reached for her hand. 'No, *it isn't*. You couldn't help having those nightmares. It's a wonder you've kept so sane all these years, after what you went through.'

'It's Christmas lunch I'm most dreading. We've always gone to the Clarendon, the whole family, including Nanny until a few years ago. I was sure they'd cancel it, but they seem determined not to. So we'll be sitting there in the middle of the restaurant like a prize exhibit, with everyone staring at us.'

Her voice wobbled, and Matthew squeezed her hand. 'I'm sure it won't be like that. You said business has been good these last weeks, with everyone offering support.'

'Or coming to see for themselves how we're coping.' She gave a little shudder. 'I still can't believe Mummy's been there all this time, so *close* to us all. It's – macabre.'

'Have the police any leads?'

'No. They keep questioning me. I'm sure they think I'm keeping something back, that having actually *been* there, I must know who killed her.'

'But you don't,' Matthew said stoutly. 'If you did, you'd have remembered by now.'

216

Freya turned her white face towards him. 'Matt, I *must* have seen him! He was walking about immediately beneath me.'

'Then it's obvious you didn't know him, isn't it? Which is why you can't remember his face.'

'That's what I keep telling myself. But suppose my subconscious is blocking it because I *did* know him? Very well?'

She pulled her hands from his and covered her face with them, while Matthew, whose thoughts had been along the same lines, could only watch in helpless despair.

Stephen said, 'Are you quite sure you've ordered enough? It's not as though there's a choice of main course on Christmas Day – apart from vegetarians, everyone will be having turkey.'

Gerald gritted his teeth. 'Dad, this will be my sixth Christmas in charge. I do know what I'm doing.'

'And the desserts? Not everyone will want the pudding, you know.'

'We've already discussed this; there's also a choice of chestnut soufflé, iced cranberry ring or mincemeat flan. And, of course, the usual selection of cheeses.'

Stephen nodded distractedly. 'How many are booked in the Grill Room?' At Christmas, the smaller and more intimate restaurant was, paradoxically, reserved for parties of a dozen or more.

'Ten tables. Capacity. And before you ask, they're catered for.'

'As long as you're sure. Remember that for most people, this is the most important meal of the year.'

'No pressure, then,' returned Gerald drily.

But Stephen was not the only member of the family with misgivings.

'I've been expecting the Tarltons to cancel every day,' Dorothy remarked to Ruth, as they checked the list of bookings. 'I hope they don't cast a pall on the rest of the diners, poor souls.'

'I think they're being very brave, not pulling out,' Ruth said.

'Oh, I agree; but bravery doesn't make for a festive atmosphere. People will either pointedly ignore them, or stare unashamedly.'

Ruth gave a protesting laugh. 'Dorothy, it's our clients we're talking about, not a bunch of yobbos!'

'But they'll be drinking more than usual, and that weakens inhibitions. If that poor girl had to be found, why couldn't it have been at the height of summer? Then everything would have died down by now.'

'She was a member of the family, don't forget.'

Ruth's voice was mild, but her mother-in-law flushed. Then she smiled, and patted her hand. 'You're quite right, my dear; I'm a self-centred old woman, I admit it. It's just that everyone works so hard in the run-up to Christmas, it would be too bad if events beyond our control spoiled it in any way.'

'Then we'll have to make sure they don't,' Ruth replied placidly, and returned to her checking.

The days passed in a round of last-minute shopping, present-wrapping and card-hanging.

'I think we should gather here first,' Max said on the Thursday evening. 'We can exchange presents over a bottle of champagne, then go on to the Clarendon together.'

'Good idea. Lindsey can bring Mum; she's going over there on Christmas Eve, so Mum won't wake up alone on Christmas morning.'

'Your father will,' Max reminded her.

Rona looked worried. 'Do you think we should invite him here?'

'It's not really feasible, is it, with no spare room? We can't expect him to camp out on the sofa. The only alternative would be for us to move out of our room, and the sofa wouldn't hold us both.'

'At least he won't be in a house that used to be filled with people.'

'He'll be fine,' Max assured her.

Three days later, Tom was telling himself the same thing. It was odd to be lying alone on Christmas morning, listening to church bells pealing across the town. No aroma of slow-cooking turkey reached his nostrils; there were no excited voices on the landing. Oh, there *were* people in the building – of course there were – below him, above him, alongside him, but they weren't his people. There might even be small girls clutching stockings and creeping into their parents' room ahead of time, but they weren't his small girls.

He moved impatiently. Why did Christmas always evoke the past, and the distant past, at that? It was the future that concerned him now, the future and, especially today, the present. He hoped to God the lunch would go off all right. It was good of Rona and Max to have arranged it, and to fix for them all to meet at their house.

What was Catherine doing now? he wondered. Probably still asleep, since she'd told him they went to Midnight Communion, a tradition that had never featured in the Parish Christmases. He couldn't even picture her, since she was in surroundings he didn't know, but they'd arranged to speak on the phone before he went out. He hoped she'd like the sapphire and diamond brooch he'd so extravagantly bought her – partly because he couldn't resist it, and partly as a gesture of support to the Tarltons. They wouldn't have much to celebrate this year, poor devils.

Thinking of the brooch reminded him of the package she'd given him the day before, gaily wrapped in red and gold. It was on the table beside him, and he reached for it eagerly, tearing away the paper to reveal an oblong box. Inside, shining against the velvet, lay a magnificent gold watch. Almost reverently, he lifted it out, admiring its clean, modern lines, and as he turned it over, he saw there was an inscription etched on the back. *Tom. All love, always. Catherine.*

He sat staring at it for a long time, wondering if he'd any right to be so happy.

The Tarltons had also arranged to gather beforehand, and the chosen venue was Brindley Lodge. Lewis and Kate had put up the usual tree, and as always there were presents piled beneath it, but it was increasingly hard to act as though this were a normal Christmas.

Kate watched them all as they opened their presents – Bruce and Jan; Nicholas, Susie and little Amy; Lewis, Robert and Freya – and was struck, as always, by their individuality. How could one hope to draw such disparate personalities into one homogenous whole to make 'a family'? They all had their secrets, ambitions and worries that were hidden from the rest of them. Even the biggest worry of all, which they were trying so hard not to think about, must, although shared, strike different responses in each of them. There were, for example, those who had known Velma, and those such as herself, Susie and Amy, who had not. *Did* one of those others – Bruce or Robert or Jan – even Freya – know more about what happened on that far-off day than he or she had admitted?

Kate shivered, and Lewis came over and put an arm round her. 'All right, love?'

She smiled resolutely up at him. 'Of course.'

'It's time we were making a move. The table's booked for one.'

Kate's stomach lurched, but she immediately got to her feet. This was harder for Lewis than for her, and she owed it to him to be strong. 'I'll organize the coats,' she said.

The Dickensian snow had not arrived, but the morning was cold and sunny, with the remnants of an overnight frost lingering in the shadows. Tom and Lindsey had both found spaces for their cars, and it was decided to leave them where they were and walk to the hotel.

So far, so good, Rona thought, as she set off with her mother and sister, Max and Tom following behind. The initial slight awkwardness had thawed under the influence of the champagne – which, she'd noted, had been the bottle Philip Yarborough had brought. Fleetingly, she thought of him and Adele and wondered how their Christmas, sure to be equally strained, was progressing. As for themselves, the present-exchange had gone well, everyone seeming delighted with their gifts, though part of her still regretted the little musical box she'd intended for Lindsey. *Auprès de ma blonde . . .*

She wrenched her thoughts away. The watch Max had given her had been much admired, but her father had not referred to the one he himself was wearing, which she'd not seen before. A retirement present? Or one from Catherine? The latter, she suspected.

Fullers Walk was almost deserted, but, unhampered today by parking restrictions, cars lined both sides of Dean's Crescent, proof that Dino's was enjoying its fair share of clientele.

They emerged on to Guild Street, and there, across the road, was the imposing bulk of the Clarendon, festooned with lights and with a giant holly bush on either side of the swing doors.

'The bar will be like a madhouse,' Max commented, 'I suggest we go straight to the table.'

In the foyer, arriving guests were being swiftly and efficiently directed to bar, Grill Room or restaurant, keeping the entrance clear for new arrivals.

'Table for Allerdyce,' Max told the young man at the door to the restaurant. He glanced at the sheet in his hand, made a tick in the margin, and summoned a waiter to show them to their table. Tom took Avril's elbow, and, looking up at him with a smile, she allowed him to escort her across the crowded room. Behind them, Rona and Lindsey exchanged a glance of relief.

Sophie was in the foyer when the Tarlton party arrived, and caught her breath at Robert's changed appearance. His eyes, circled with dark shadows, seemed to have sunk into their sockets, and he was walking with a stoop she'd never seen before.

She went swiftly up to him and kissed him on both cheeks. 'Happy Christmas, Robert,' she said softly, then turned to kiss Freya at his side and shake hands with the rest of the party. Freya was as white as a sheet, she noted anxiously, and Lewis also looked tired and drawn.

'Your usual table's ready for you,' she said brightly.

'I thought you might have tucked us away in a corner,' Bruce said, with a half smile.

221

'Why should we do that? You're family, and entitled to a prime position.'

At the door to the restaurant, Robert squeezed her arm. 'Bless you, Sophie,' he said, and, having handed them over to a waiter, she turned quickly away to hide sudden tears. It wasn't fair, she thought passionately. They shouldn't have to go through this. But the fact remained that one of their number had been murdered, and her killer still not brought to justice.

The meal had been delicious. After an hors d'oeuvre of smoked salmon and dill, the turkey and all its accompaniments – stuffing, bacon rolls, sausages, potatoes, sprouts and red cabbage – were cooked to perfection.

The earlier, twelve thirty, sitting had now left, and there were empty tables dotted about the restaurant. Those who remained were wearing paper hats, and the sound of crackers being pulled punctuated the conversation. It occurred to Rona that this was the first Christmas lunch she'd had away from Maple Drive – another indication of the end of an era. Because this would surely be their last all together; next year, her father would be with Catherine.

She glanced across at her parents, intent now on their desserts, and wondered if the same thoughts had occurred to them. Mum was looking like her old self again – better, in fact, because her hair and clothes were more stylish than they had ever been, and she'd caught the flash of admiration in her father's eyes. Why, Rona thought despairingly, hadn't she pulled herself together earlier? Then all this might have been avoided.

But it wasn't only Mum's appearance that had deteriorated over the last year or two, she reminded herself; she'd been bitter and discontented, carping at them all and generally making life miserable, particularly for Pops. Had her attitude changed as well? Rona admitted, to her shame, that she'd not seen her mother often enough since the split to find out.

* * *

Sophie said urgently, 'Chris, I have to speak to you.'

He turned in surprise from the group of guests he was chatting to in the bar.

'Not at the moment, Sophie. We're in the middle of—'

'Please! It's important.'

'Sophie, I'm with guests. Can't it wait?'

She knew she was breaking one of the first rules of hotel-keeping, but she *had* to speak to him, and straight away.

'No, I'm afraid it can't.'

She could tell he was embarrassed at her persistence, furious with her for putting him in this position. 'I'm afraid it'll have to,' he said curtly. 'I'll be with you shortly.' And he turned back to his guests.

For a moment longer she stared at his unyielding back, panic rising inside her. Then she turned and walked blindly out of the bar. What could she do? *What could she do?*

Rona had just finished her coffee when she saw Sophie Fairfax in the doorway. She looked strained, Rona thought, and her eyes went automatically to the Tarltons who, like themselves, were now lingering over coffee. Perhaps she was still worried about Freya – and with reason. Rona had glanced at the girl from time to time during the meal, and as far as she could tell, she'd scarcely eaten anything.

To her surprise, however, it was to their own table that Sophie came.

'Rona, I'm sorry to disturb you, but I wonder if I could have a word?'

'Of course,' Rona replied, bewildered. 'Now?'

'If you wouldn't mind.'

Rona sent a small, apologetic glance round the table, and, rising, followed Sophie out of the room, across the foyer, and into a small office behind the reception desk.

'Is something wrong?' she asked. Close up, it was clear Sophie was struggling for control.

'Yes, I think there is,' she replied jerkily. 'I'm sorry to drag you into this. I tried to speak to Chris, but he was tied up with guests and I couldn't extract him.'

'What's happened, Sophie?' Rona asked gently.

Sophie's hands clenched at her side and she drew a shuddering breath. 'When Freya told me about her dream,' she began raggedly, 'she talked about hearing the whistling, and she hummed the tune for me – the tune from the musical box, that had made her faint.'

Rona stood immobile, her eyes fixed on the young woman's face. 'Go on.'

'I didn't recognize its name, but I knew I'd heard it somewhere.'

'Sophie . . .'

Sophie put trembling hands to her face. 'Oh, my God!' she whispered.

'*Sophie, what is it?*'

'I've – just heard it again.'

Rona stared at her, scarcely breathing.

'It was Stephen,' Sophie said in a rush. 'When he's concentrating on something, he often whistles under his breath. And he was doing it just now, down in the buttery, and – and it was that tune.'

Stephen Fairfax? Rona's head was spinning. 'It doesn't necessarily mean anything,' she said slowly, trying, as she spoke, to marshal the thoughts that were crowding into her head. 'I mean, it's a folk song, and quite well known.'

'Yes, but – I gave a little gasp – I couldn't help myself – and he turned and saw me, and – and stupidly, I just turned and ran. At best, he must be wondering what on earth's wrong with me.'

'Did he know Velma?' Rona asked.

'He must have done; Robert's his second cousin, or whatever. Rona, what should I *do*? He's my father-in-law, for God's sake, but then so was Robert, and if there's anything in this, I can't let him go on suffering. I'm very fond of him, and he was so kind to me when everything went wrong with Lewis. He never blamed me for it.'

'You'll have to go to the police,' Rona said, and broke off as the door suddenly opened and Stephen Fairfax stood looking at them.

'There you are, Sophie,' he said, his eyes going from one

of them to the other. 'And – Mrs Allerdyce, isn't it? Did I hear you mention the police?'

For a moment, neither of them spoke. Then Sophie, her control finally snapping, started to cry. 'I'm so sorry, Stephen,' she sobbed.

Stephen stiffened, and as Rona watched, the colour seeped out of his face, leaving only two red patches on his cheeks, like a Dutch doll.

'Sorry about what?' he asked softly.

Since Sophie seemed incapable of answering, Rona did so. 'Velma,' she said.

Stephen let out his breath in a long sigh. Then he straightened his shoulders.

'Pull yourself together, Sophie,' he said, his voice surprisingly normal. 'Dry your eyes, and go and ask the Tarlton party if they'll join us for liqueurs up in our apartment. I'll root out Chris and Gerald. Mother and Ruth, I know, have already gone up.' He glanced at Rona. 'In the circumstances, I think you'd better come, too,' he added.

The next few minutes were surreal. Rona waited in the foyer as instructed while Sophie went to collect the Tarltons. Max turned and saw her in the doorway, and she raised her shoulders in a gesture of helplessness. She saw him frown, but before he could get up, Sophie had shepherded the Tarltons out of the restaurant.

Robert was saying, 'This is very kind of Stephen. We certainly didn't expect VIP treatment.'

Sophie smiled stiffly and did not reply.

'Rona!' Kate was smiling at her. 'Are you joining the party?'

'It seems so,' Rona said, and saw her friend's puzzled frown. Then Stephen reappeared with his sons, said briskly, 'Good to see you all,' and pressed the lift buttons. Two adjacent sets of doors opened, they all piled in and rose in unison to the top floor of the hotel.

Stephen went ahead and flung open the door to his apartment with a flourish. Over his shoulder, Rona caught a glimpse of his wife and mother, who turned in surprise as he motioned the group ahead of him into the sitting room.

'A family reunion,' he announced, still in that brisk, staccato voice.

Dorothy Fairfax swayed suddenly. 'Stephen, no!' she said sharply. '*No!*'

Ruth looked quickly at her husband, and something she saw in his face made her take her mother-in-law's arm and lower her gently into her chair. Then she turned to face the crowd who had so unexpectedly invaded her privacy.

'How nice to see everyone,' she said, 'do please sit down. Chris, there are more chairs in the other room.'

'And Gerald, will you see to the drinks?' his father directed.

Sophie, who didn't seem able to stop shaking, saw Chris glance at her, his face a mixture of guilt and bewilderment. Yes, she told him silently, things might have happened differently if you'd come when I asked you. Though the eventual outcome would doubtless have been the same.

Dorothy was lying back in her chair with a hand across her forehead and Ruth, once everyone else was seated, had taken her place beside her, and was holding her free hand. When they'd all been given a glass, Stephen raised his, said, 'Happy Families!' and laughed.

Everyone looked at him, uncertain of his mood, but they dutifully repeated, 'Happy Families.'

'Only they're not, always, are they?' Stephen went on. He was standing by the fireplace, one arm resting along the mantelpiece. 'Even weddings hold hidden dangers. They certainly have in our family; Lewis and Sophie fell in love at one of them, which caused a lot of heartache, though fortunately it's since been remedied. However, a previous occasion proved considerably more lethal.'

He took a drink from the glass in his hand, and his eyes went over them. Amy, drowsy after her meal, had fallen asleep on her father's lap, but the adults were attentive and now faintly apprehensive.

'You see,' he continued deliberately, 'at a wedding many years before that, I fell for Velma Tarlton, and she for me.'

There was total silence, broken at last by a low moan from Dorothy. Ruth sat frozen beside her, her face a pale mask.

226

Robert cleared his throat. 'I don't understand. You're surely not saying—?'

'I'm afraid, old man, that's exactly what I'm saying.' His eyes flickered to Ruth. 'Forgive me, my darling. If you remember, we were going through a bad patch around that time.'

He paused, but if expecting a reply, he was disappointed. Her expression remained blank.

'So I repeat, weddings can be a dangerous time. Too much champagne is drunk, love is in the air – often, it's said, one wedding leads to another. In our case, I regret to say, it led to an affair. I'd met her before, of course, but only casually, and – forgive me, Robert – I'd heard rumours about her. She was beautiful, she was a little drunk and so was I. We found an empty room at the reception, and . . . made love.'

He took another drink. 'To be honest, I thought that was it. A bit of foolishness, best forgotten. But the next week, she rang up and asked me to meet her. Stupidly, I did so, and after that things became a lot more serious. We were besotted with each other, but our main problem was finding somewhere to go where we wouldn't be recognized. Then Velma had the idea of meeting in the woods behind her house. I'd drive along Woodlands Road, park the car out of sight under low-hanging bushes, and make my way into the woods from that end. If Nanny and Freya were out, Velma came through the garden. Otherwise, she'd cut down the alley. It went on all summer, sometimes we managed to meet two or three times a week, at others, ten days or more would pass without seeing each other. God knows how long it would have lasted, but one day she startled me by suggesting we went away together.'

At the beginning of this account, Lewis had gone to stand behind his father's chair. Now, he laid a hand on his shoulder, and Robert, moving like an automaton, reached up to pat it.

'Admittedly, life was a little dull at the time,' Stephen continued. 'The hotel was in the doldrums, Ruth and I were having problems, and there were two children to support. Now, suddenly, I had the chance to leave it all behind and

227

fly off to romantic places with a glamorous blonde. I told myself I'd be a fool not to go, but something held me back.'

He sighed. 'If I'd had any sense, I'd have told Velma my doubts, but I didn't want to burst her bubble. So, like an idiot, I kept quiet, and the next thing I knew, she'd settled on a date and was planning to leave Robert a note, telling him not to try to find her, because this time she'd gone for good. I immediately panicked and started back-pedalling, but she laughed it off as cold feet. It was arranged that she'd bring her suitcase to the clearing, and we'd drive to Heathrow and start a new life together.'

Stephen went over to the drinks cabinet and refilled his glass. He held the bottle up enquiringly, but nobody moved and he set it down again and returned to his position by the fireplace.

'I knew by now I didn't want to go, but still hadn't the courage – or honesty – to tell her. Then, the evening before we were due to leave, I found Ruth in our room in tears. We had a long talk, reaching far into the night, and the long and the short of it was that I realized she was the one I wanted, and always had been. I also saw that I'd been criminally weak and cowardly in not being honest with Velma, and at this stage, there was no way to avoid hurting her. All I could do was turn up as arranged, and try to break the news as gently as possible.'

There was a long silence, while he stared down at the floor. 'I was the first to arrive,' he said at last. 'I paced up and down waiting for her, and as time went by, I began to hope something had gone wrong, and she wasn't coming after all. I was on the point of leaving when she turned up with her suitcase, all excited and eager to go.'

He broke off. 'God, I wish I still smoked!' he said.

Dorothy sat up in her chair. 'Stop there, Stephen,' she ordered. 'We've heard quite enough.'

Stephen looked at her, his eyes full of pity. 'You knew, didn't you?' he said softly. 'I never realized till just now, when we all came in.'

'I knew you were having an affair, and with whom. Of course I did. I'm not blind, and you're my son. Then, when

228

you became so withdrawn and I heard she'd gone off with someone, I assumed she'd dumped you. That *is* what happened, isn't it?'

'I wish it were,' he said. 'I told her as gently as I could, but she became hysterical, crying and screaming, and clawing at me. I just couldn't reason with her. She was clinging to me like a wild thing and I began to lose patience. Finally, when she just wouldn't let go of me, I gave her a push. She stumbled backwards, tripped, and fell, cracking her head against a stone.'

There was another long silence. When he continued, it was as though he was speaking to himself. 'I waited for her to get up, and when she didn't, told her not to be so stupid, or words to that effect. Then I got hold of her arm and tried to pull her to her feet, but she just fell back again. And then . . .' For the first time, his voice faltered. 'I saw the blood, on the stone under her, and still pouring from her head. I couldn't believe what was happening. I gave her the kiss of life, tried artificial respiration, everything, but I couldn't revive her.'

There was total silence in the room, as everyone pictured the scene.

'After about twenty minutes,' Stephen went on heavily, 'I had to accept that she was dead. And then the panic set in. I couldn't *tell* anyone she was there, because how would I have known? Nor could I leave her for some kid to come across while playing. I thought wildly of carrying her to the car and disposing of her somewhere, but I'd read about traces of blood and hair being impossible to remove however hard you tried. I was sobbing uncontrollably by this time, from fear and regret and general helplessness. And then I remembered the well. Velma had told me about it, and once, in the early days, we'd prised off the top and looked inside. She dropped in a coin and made a wish that we'd always be together.' He wiped a hand across his face as the irony of this struck him for the first time.

'So I stumbled back to the car, found some tools in the boot, and prised the lid off again. Then I had to drag her through the undergrowth. It was horrible – her dress kept catching on brambles and I found myself apologizing to her. It was quite a struggle to heave her up and over the side, and there was a sickening thud as she landed at the bottom. No splash, though; the well had been dry for years. I replaced the lid, then remembered the suitcase, went back for it and dropped it in after her.'

He raised his ravaged face and stared almost defiantly at his stunned audience.

'Of *course* I should have reported her death, and that's the main thing that will go against me now. But whichever course of action I took, it wouldn't have brought Velma back, and I reasoned with myself that it was in the general interest to keep quiet. If I told anyone what had happened, quite apart from the consequences to me personally, two families would be destroyed. As it stood, Mother and Ruth would know nothing, and Robert would believe she was living happily with someone else – she'd told me she hadn't mentioned my name. What's more, no one would even look for her, because she'd asked them not to.

'So there you have it.' His eyes rested on Robert. 'I hope you believe I wouldn't have let you be charged with her murder,' he said. 'I wronged you once, badly, all those years ago. I wouldn't have done it again.'

Robert briefly inclined his head.

Stephen turned to Sophie. 'Now all that remains is to hear how you found me out. Because you did, didn't you?'

She nodded.

'Well?'

'It was the whistling,' she said.

'*Whistling?*'

'"Auprès de ma blonde".'

He stared at her. 'What the hell—?'

'The same tune,' Freya broke in, speaking for the first time and startling them all, 'that you were whistling just before you killed my mother.'

Stephen's face was white. 'I don't understand.'

Robert turned quickly to his daughter, but she shook off his restraining hand and addressed Stephen directly. 'All my life I've had periodic nightmares about someone whistling

230

that tune,' she said. 'But it's only in the last week or two that I learned why.'

She took a deep breath. 'Lewis and his friends had a tree house in that clearing, but they wouldn't let me play up there. That day, when Nanny was asleep, I went into the woods by myself and climbed up the rope ladder. I was there when you arrived.'

'My God!' Stephen breathed.

'I saw you pacing up and down, and then you sat on a log just underneath me, and started whistling that tune.'

'How old were you?' Stephen's voice cracked.

'Three,' she replied.

'My God!' he said again.

'I only remembered flashes, but the last one was of Mummy lying directly below me. Her eyes were open, and she seemed to be staring straight up at me.'

Stephen put his hand across his own eyes. 'You didn't recognize me?' he asked in a low voice.

'No. I don't suppose I knew you well, if at all. But a few weeks ago a musical box in the shop played that tune and I – I fainted. Sophie wanted to know what was wrong, and I told her. Today, she must have recognized it.'

Stephen drew a deep breath. 'Well, it's come out at last. I've hurt all of you – Ruth and Robert in particular, even little Freya, in a freakish, unimaginable way. All I can say in mitigation is that I never meant to kill her – even to hurt her. In my own way, I loved her, and what happened that day has haunted me ever since.'

Chris cleared his throat. 'So what happens now?'

'I go to the police.'

'Will anyone be there, on Christmas Day?'

'Christmas Day!' Stephen gave a hollow laugh. 'So it is. Believe it or not, I'd forgotten.'

'There'll be a skeleton staff,' Bruce said. 'It might be better to wait until tomorrow.'

Rona stirred. 'I should go; my family will be wondering where I am.'

Stephen turned to her. 'I'm still not sure of your part in all this.'

231

'She went to see Nanny Gray,' Kate said, 'who admitted falling asleep when she was supposed to be watching Freya, and later finding her in a shocked state in the woods. Everything fell into place after that. Except who you were, of course.'

'And my whistling gave me away. I didn't even know I was doing it.' He glanced almost fearfully at Ruth, then went over and, kneeling beside her chair, gathered her into his arms.

'Can you ever forgive me?' he asked.

'What will happen to you?' she whispered.

'Well, by asking casual questions here and there, it seems likely I'll be charged with manslaughter and sentenced to ten years, reduced to five. Which is probably better than I deserve.'

Rona, who'd become increasingly uncomfortable during the last few minutes, rose to her feet. 'I must go,' she said again. 'This is a family matter. I – hope everything goes as well as possible.'

'Thanks for your help, Rona,' Kate said quietly, and Sophie nodded. Across the room her eyes briefly met Stephen's. There would be no thanks from him, she thought ruefully. Dorothy, as undeniable head of the family, spoke for them all.

'I hope we haven't spoiled your Christmas, Mrs Allerdyce. Enjoy what's left of it.'

There was no answer to this. Rona simply nodded and left the room, closing the door behind her. Her ears still ringing with Stephen's confession, she paused for a minute in the carpeted corridor and drew a deep breath, thankful to be out of the miasma of guilt, anger, embarrassment and grief in the room behind her. It had, after all, been she who had brought them to this point, who had coaxed the truth out of Nanny Gray.

If Kate hadn't asked her to look into Freya's dreams, Velma would have remained buried in the well, Stephen would continue to bear his secret guilt, and the Tarltons would have remained ignorant of the truth. And Freya would probably have outgrown her nightmares. But Kate *had* asked her, and she *had* found out these things, and she didn't know whether to be glad or sorry.

Behind the closed door, the subdued murmur of voices had resumed. If they came out and found her here, they'd think she'd been eavesdropping. But they'd be wrong; she'd already heard more than she wanted.

She walked quickly back to the lift and pressed the button. The doors opened at once – it must have remained there since they came up – and she stepped into it. Enjoy the rest of your Christmas, Dorothy Fairfax had said. Whether or not that was possible, she wasn't sure. What she urgently needed now was her own family about her. She pressed the button, and with a sigh of relief, went down to rejoin them.